Praise for
Dancing on Rocks

"...a book that manages the rare feat of being a page turner as well as a satisfying exploration of the human heart. A book that, like the river that runs though Chimney Rock, is swift and deep."
—*Tommy Hays, Author,*
What I Came to Tell You and The Pleasure Was Mine

"...maybe it is inevitable that a story set in the shadows of one of the most famous crags in America would be a cliffhanger. And *Dancing on Rocks* is certainly that. But it is also a telling study of individuals, families and local history."
—*Fred Chappell, North Carolina Poet Laureate*
and Author, Ancestors and Others and Look Back All the Green Valley

"...Senehi weaves a multi-layered tale of emotional power and redemptive transformation. Simply put, the tale is a love story of rich complexity—love of land, love of family, love of what has been, and the longing love of what might have been. Senehi pulls you into her characters' lives and makes you care about all of it."
—*Mark deCastrique, Author, A Murder in Passing,*
A Sam Blackman Mystery

"Few locally set novels involve their settings as faithfully as *Dancing on Rocks* captures various aspects of Chimney Rock. Senehi does this by contrasting the history and the contemporary reality of the up-and-down tourist town. The dialogue is natural; the theme, 'we will survive.' Deftly, Senehi folds in mystery, romance, environmentalism, and oh!—a great character in the person of the heroine's spunky mom."
—*Rob Neufeld, Book Reviewer,*
Asheville Citizen-Times; Web Editor, "The Read on WNC"

"Senehi succeeds in portraying a pastoral backdrop where familial pains lurk beneath."
—*Kirkus Review*

ALSO BY ROSE SENEHI

RENDER UNTO THE VALLEY

THE WIND IN THE WOODS

IN THE SHADOWS OF CHIMNEY ROCK

PELICAN WATCH

WINDFALL

SHADOWS IN THE GRASS

Dancing on Rocks

Rose Senehi

K.I.M. Publishing, LLC
Chimney Rock, NC

Published by

K.I.M. PUBLISHING, LLC
Post Office Box 132
Chimney Rock, NC 28720-0132

Cover design by Debra Long Hampton

Published in the United States of America.

PUBLISHER'S NOTE

This is a work of fiction. Though there are numerous elements of historical and geographical accuracy in this portrait of Chimney Rock, NC, and its environs, the names, places, characters and incidents either are the product of the author's imagination or are used fictitiously, and any resemblance to actual persons, living or dead, is entirely coincidental.

PUBLISHER'S CATALOGING-IN-PUBLICATION DATA

Senehi, Rose.
      Dancing on rocks : a novel / Rose Senehi
          p. cm.
      ISBN-13: 978-0-615-89505-5 (trade pbk. : alk.paper)
      ISBN-10: 0-615-89505-0
      1. Chimney Rock—North Carolina—Hickory Nut
        Gorge—Fiction.
      2. Blue Ridge Mountains—Fiction.
      3. Appalachian Region, Southern—Fiction.
      4. Nature and environment—Fiction. I. Title.
        PS3619.E659C526 2014

Library of Congress Control Number: 2013919561

First Printing: May 2014

For all the people, past and present,
who have kept the Village of Chimney Rock alive

CHAPTER ONE

GEORGIE HAYDOCK WAS WELL AWARE of the capriciousness of the torrent tumbling beneath her as she paused on the bridge. She watched the muddy water race over and around the massive boulders like a raging beast ramming its way down the gorge. Two days of rain had made the river angry.

Her body swayed to the pounding of her heart as she gazed stonily into the distance. No matter how hard she tried, she kept seeing the thin little hand slip away, teaching her all over again what forever meant. She closed her eyes and took a slow, long breath. Stop it, she warned herself. You better watch out or you won't make it till September.

She took a moment to watch the veils of morning mist float across the granite cliffs above, and the shadow of cynicism that had tarnished her youth started to get its grip on her again. She knew the beauty of this North Carolina mountain gorge didn't come cheap. Those who lived there understood that sometimes it had to be paid for by hurt, or more torturous yet, by the fear of hurt.

Her ponytail felt like it was coming loose, so she took hold of it with one hand and pulled off the rubber band with the other, and this time, wound it tighter around the hank of long blonde hair. She swiped the back of her hand across her forehead, already sweaty from the humidity that hung thick in the air. She wondered how her patient, old Nannie Rae, was doing back in

Deep Gap, and hoped she wasn't going to regret asking for this four-month leave of absence to take care of her mother.

She kicked a pebble off the bridge with the tip of her running shoe and continued across to Main Street with the easy kind of stride that long-legged people fall into. Already nine-thirty and not one person in sight. By now, as a home care nurse, she would have been well on her way to seeing a patient, but she'd be willing to bet that half the shop owners were still snoring in their beds. That was how it was, running a store in this tourist town. It wasn't as if you rose up every morning driven to accomplish something. It was more like you got up resigned to deal with whatever life tossed your way.

That attitude had always bothered Georgie. It seemed Chimney Rock's store owners were always victims of fate as they kept busy stocking or dusting shelves, waiting for the tourists to appear. Oddly, even though she'd been away from this routine for thirteen years, it only took her a couple of days behind the counter of her mother's store to slip into the shopkeeper's habit of hypothesizing about the reason for another slow day. It was either too hot or too cold, gas too expensive for a day trip, or so cheap you could drive a lot farther than this little town.

Nursing was different. Instead of waiting around for something to happen, you did your darnedest to keep it *from* happening. Four months and she'd say goodbye to this place for the second time in her life and be back caring for the folks who lived in the coves and hollows of Watauga County.

She strode along the jumble of store porches that served as a disjointed walkway through the village, a mere two rows of mostly slapped-together buildings running haphazardly for a couple of blocks. Nothing more than a hodgepodge of mom-and-pop operations with rustic facades, yet the place never failed to excite a tourist's imagination when they caught a glimpse of it. The whole town managed to tap into people's underlying yearning to magically escape into an earlier time.

The postmistress emerged from the lonesome cinderblock building that housed the town's post office. Holding a watering can, Carrie Owenby used her foot to nudge a hefty stone she kept next to her flower pots to prop the door open. Georgie threw her a wave before scampering up the staircase squeezed between two stores. The noise from a kiddy show sounded as she opened the door to the upstairs apartment where she'd been raised. Her sister Ali's two boys were up and watching television in the front room, their cereal bowls on the floor in front of them.

"Grandma up yet?" she asked.

Without tearing his eyes from the action on the screen, Isaac answered, "Yeah. Mom's getting her dressed."

She made her way down the long narrow hallway her nephews used as a speedway for their miniature car races, careful not to step on any abandoned cars. Her mother's room was at the very end. She found her in her black leather recliner, her injured foot propped up on a colorful folded granny square blanket. That foot was what had brought Georgie back to town.

"Hi, Dynamite," Georgie said.

She bent down and gave her mother a kiss. She knew it would perk her up to hear the nickname she'd earned at seventeen. A handsome stranger had come into the sandwich shop in town where her mother was working one summer, and in front of a couple of locals, asked her what her name was. "Dinah," she had told him. "But they call me Dy...na...mite." She had raised an eyebrow and added, "That's because Dinah might, or Dinah might not." That remark was discussed at every dinner table in town that night and she never lived it down. In fact, the big stir it caused pushed her into finally unleashing who she really was.

But since then, Dinah's short, small-boned frame had arrived at the inevitable destination of a lot of women pushing sixty— twenty pounds too much of softening flesh. Her face had sunk into a somewhat pudgy mass, but she had hung on to her bright smile and energetic disposition.

"Georgie, I wish you wouldn't call Mom that in front of the kids." Ali was making a half-hearted attempt at putting their mother's bed in order. "It's bad enough explaining why she named you Georgia, and me Alabama. Heck, they've got no idea of what 'conceived' means."

Dinah laughed. "Thank your lucky stars I didn't do like old

Louisa Freeman and go and name you something like Aurora Borealis. The poor devil went through life as A.B."

Ali reached over and picked up the pile of scrapbooks and photo albums strewn over her mother's bed while Georgie got out her blood pressure paraphernalia and fastened the cuff around her mother's arm. She pumped it up and read the gauge.

"Mom, your pressure's up to 160 over 98 this morning."

Ali, who was about to go downstairs and open the store, waved an empty potato chip bag as she floated out of the room, telling Georgie all she needed to know.

"And, I'm gonna tell those boys, if they run out and get you any more of that kind of junk, they won't be hitting golf balls over at Fibber Magee's again till they're fifteen."

She reached for one of the pillows under her mother's elbow.

"Let me fluff everything up for you, Mom."

Noticing her mother's fisted hand slipping something furtively under the book in her lap, Georgie put out her hand for the suspected candy bar.

"Okay, Mom. Let me have it."

She studied the plaintive expression on her mother's face, and something told her she should just let this one go, but the trained nurse in her wouldn't let her. She picked up the book and froze. Staring out at her was a photograph of a little girl with short blond hair parted neatly to the side. Georgie remembered being six years old and clipping on the pink plastic barrette, shaped like a ribbon, to hold her sister's hair in place just before her fourth birthday party.

Georgie eased it out of her mother's hand. "Let's put it on the dresser, Mom."

Ever since Georgie got back home she had braced herself for coming face to face with the hurt that was always hiding under everyone's skin and waiting around every corner.

Her mother's words resounded like a slammed hammer.

"Shelby's not dead."

Georgie put the frame back in its place on the dresser and stared ahead, not seeing anything—just the scene that had played itself out hundreds of times before. When she was a kid, she and

Ali would lie silently in their beds listening to the commotion in the hall. Shadows would flicker in the light coming from under their door as her father struggled to get her mother back in their bedroom. The pillow over her head couldn't block out her mother's tormented pleas.

"Why? Why didn't I lock the kitchen door? Please, God, please bring my baby home."

When her dad was alive, he had always been the one to deal with it. Now, if she didn't succeed in keeping her mother's mind off her four-year-old daughter who went missing in the middle of the night some twenty-five years before, it would be her turn. Georgie couldn't help thinking it would be poetic justice.

The phone rang, startling her. It was Ali telling her they needed singles in the front cash register. She looked over at her mother. She was lying peacefully in her recliner, yet there was something in her eyes that made Georgie wary.

"I've got to go downstairs, Mom. Please, don't dwell on Shelby. It won't do you any good." She went over and kissed her tenderly on the forehead and brushed her graying hair away from her face. "Be a good girl and just concentrate on getting better. Okay? I'll be up later to take a look at your foot and change the dressing."

Georgie reluctantly left the room, then retrieved a bundle of ones from the lock box in her mother's office and started down the winding back staircase to the store. She knew every slanted worn step, every gouge on the heavily fingerprinted walls, but mostly the moldy smell that drifted up from the shop, almost as if it were an intrinsic part of the old-timey character of the place. She reached the storeroom and wove her way through the narrow path between the stacks of boxes that had made their way to the airy mountains of North Carolina from the stifling sweatshops of China.

She couldn't believe she had come back to the same place, with the same wound she couldn't heal. It was bad enough when she came for a few days. She always found the town exactly the way she had left it, except all the faces now wore masks. She shoved aside a feeling of impending doom. Something she was having to do more and more often. The passage from *Isaiah* that her father had read to them one Sunday afternoon and was etched in her memory kept sneaking into her thoughts: "...and what will ye do the day your sins shall be visited upon you?"

She entered the store and started to make her way past the tables of trinkets and toys one probably couldn't find all together in one place anywhere else but in this tiny mountain hamlet—rubber snakes, rustic slingshots fashioned from thick twigs, moccasins, toy cars, and unique old fashioned doodads of every description—all designed to suck people into the past.

Her sister was standing at the front cash register.

"Ali, why don't you go on up and get the kids rolling for the day. Just plan on coming down after lunch and helping me put up the new stock."

Ali registered relief at the prospect of getting back to her boys. As she started to leave, Georgie put her hand on her sister's arm.

"Keep an eye on Mom. She had Shelby's picture in her lap."

Ali's face melted in dread. "I'll get the boys to distract her."

Georgie opened the cash drawer and put some singles under the clip and the rest in the back of the drawer, then slid onto the smooth surface of the stool with its familiar green paint worn off the edges. With her elbow on the counter, she rested her chin on her fist and stared out the door she had propped open to let in the fresh morning air.

The doorway framed the view of the Chimney Rock on the mountain with the flag waving in the breeze wafting down through the gorge. Why was it that every time she saw it she hoped things were different? She'd always wanted to belong to this town, but the sight of this iconic image only filled her with regret.

Georgie's focus was suddenly jarred by the slight figure of an elderly woman entering the store. Her thick cloud of snow-white hair was pinned back in a loose bun. Her sky-blue dress sprinkled with forget-me-nots and her easy smile made a light-hearted impression. She leaned on her cane with every step, and a pained wince kept flickering on her smile as she made her way over. She hung the cane on her bony wrist and leaned against the counter, looking like she was proud of herself for having made it. She fingered a beaded bracelet hanging on a jewelry rack and seemed to want to say something as she eyed Georgie up and down.

"I've been comin' to this here town with my Joe every spring for just over forty years now," she finally offered. "Joe's not with us anymore, but I feel like I still gotta come. It's sort of a tradition."

She looked around as if she were searching for someone. "Where's the lady who owns this place? She's always sittin' on that there stool and I always make a point out of sayin' hello and passin' the time of day with her."

"Oh, that's my mother. She's not feeling well. She's upstairs."

A grin of triumph suddenly surfaced on the woman's face. The corner of her eyes wrinkled into a squint and she pointed a crooked finger at Georgie.

"I know you. I know who you are. Heck, when you were still in diapers, your ma used to set you right up on this here counter while she waited on me."

Georgie broke into a smile. This had to be the millionth time someone had recalled knowing her as a kid. Even though she'd been home for a couple of weeks now, she hadn't been able to shake a gnawing feeling of estrangement. But suddenly she felt irrevocably connected to the endless chain of people who over the generations had trudged from store to store in that old-timey niche in the mountains, searching for a taste of the past.

The old woman's eyebrow raised and a slight hint of a sneer washed over her face.

"I'm surprised to see you're still here. I remember when you were, heck no more than six or seven, and you told me kinda *uppity like,* that when you grew up you were gonna get outta here and be a nurse."

Georgie stared into the distance and mulled over the woman's comment for a moment.

"You're right," she finally said. "I was gonna get outta here."

CHAPTER TWO

D INAH HAYDOCK TOOK AFTER the flamboyant, yet illustrious, Flack side of the family that dated back to 1838 when the town was nothing but a dirt road running through the Hickory Nut Gap between Rutherfordton and Asheville. The patriarch of the family, James Mills Flack, had scooped up 100 acres on both sides of the Rocky Broad and carved out the town. He was one of the adventuresome entrepreneurs who poured into the North Carolina mountains during the 1800s to find their fortunes in its Wild West atmosphere.

Convinced that the towering Chimney Rock, jutting out from the mountain at the head of the gorge, would bring folks from far and wide, he was going to get in on the ground floor. Not only did he develop the town, he built a bank, a 41-room hotel that looked out at the monolith, and a power plant on the river, charging those who tied into it, twenty-five cents a month.

From the time she was a small child, the fact that her mother was a Flack went straight to Dinah Haydock's head and she grew up feeling she was descended from royalty. And in those days and in that little speck of a place, she pretty much was. But that was a long time ago. In the fifty-six years of her life, most of the stores and businesses had turned over two or three times and the legend of the Flacks had faded like hickory smoke on a soft mountain breeze.

Georgie, on the other hand, was tall and slender like her father, and of his practical sensibility. And on this morning, she was in her mother's bedroom systematically preparing to change the dressing on her wound.

"Ali, can you get me some coffee?" she asked.

"You could have poured yourself a cup as you came in."

"Yeah...but then I wouldn't have an excuse to get rid of you, now would I?"

"Ha, ha."

"Mom and I have to talk business and you've got to open the store."

Georgie went into the bathroom down the hall and washed her hands. She laid a clean pad under her mother's foot, then put a wound kit on a roll-away table she bought to use exclusively for this procedure.

"I'm going to have to open the bandage and take a look this morning. Hopefully, I won't have to debride it."

Her mother looked exasperated. "Girl, you can drop all that highfalutin' medical talk. We all know you're a certified wound nurse."

Georgie opened the wound kit. She carefully arranged everything on the table before sitting down, putting on a pair of gloves and unwrapping the ankle. She shook her head gravely.

"I'm afraid it's going to have to be amputated."

Her mother shot up. "Good God!"

Georgie nudged her with her elbow. "Just joking, Mom. Just joking. That's what you get for messin' with my highfalutin' medical talk. It took me four years to learn it and I've got a right to throw it around every chance I get."

She put on a new pair of sterile gloves and spread on antibiotic cream and redressed the wound.

"The swelling seems to be going down a bit. Maybe we can start you on your walker tomorrow."

The old bandages were discarded into a bag she had hung on the side of the table, then she peeled off the gloves and dropped them in, tying the bag before placing it in the waste bin. She went back into the bathroom, and as she washed her hands, yelled down the hall, "Where's the coffee?"

"Down the street at Coffee on the Rocks," came back at her.

Georgie waited at the doorway with her hand on her hip until Ali appeared with a cup.

"Thanks… now you better get down and open the store."

"Yessum, right away," said Ali with a sarcastic curtsy, making Georgie roll her eyes.

Georgie came back into the bedroom, made some space for her cup on the cluttered table next to her mother and sat down. Three weeks ago, when she got word of her mother's motorcycle accident, she started to worry. Her mother always took risks when she felt cornered. Like the time she threw the whole family into turmoil by running off for two days after her husband put his foot down about the lake house she wanted to buy.

Last night, as Georgie studied the four credit card accounts, it was evident her mother was meeting her monthly minimums with cash advances. It was equally evident she couldn't do this much longer.

"Mom, I finally got the books all straightened out. Daddy would turn over in his grave if he knew how you've been keeping them." Georgie looked into her mother's eyes long enough for that to sink in.

"The store's doing well enough for you to keep on making a decent living. That is, once we get all those damn credit cards paid off. They're killing you. Are you aware that they're almost hitting fifty thousand?"

Georgie was trying to gauge her mother's emotional state. She had to be careful not to push her too hard. But the years of listening to shoppers spout volatile opinions on everything from politics to religion had made her mother an expert at concealment.

Dinah blew out a gusty breath. "Is that all? I figure I'm good for a lot more than fifty thousand."

"Well, you won't be for very long if we don't clean them up." Georgie remembered how proud her father had always been of his good credit and she started to get angry. "How could you have speculated on land with nothin' but a fistful of plastic?" She pulled a list of the balances she had made the night before from her pocket and tossed it on the table for effect.

"Mom, you're going to have to let those Harleys go."

"You're just itching to sell them, aren't you?"

"You bet I am! Why you went for a ride through the gorge with sandals on, I'll never know. It's a miracle you didn't tear that foot clear off. If you did, then where would you be?"

Georgie bit her lip. She needed to hold her tongue. Her mother had no idea how close she came to severing the limb. Before Georgie left Boone, she was caring for a boy who had skidded on his motorcycle and ripped an arm off on a guard rail.

More than putting the finances in order, more than getting her mother back on her feet and the house and store back on a routine, in the next few months she had to deal with what was making her mother take so many risks. She suspected it was something she'd seen before: a woman loses her life's partner and either reinvents herself as a single person and gets on with it, or she chases a gamut of escapes, refusing to come to terms with the heart-breaking reality. Her mother was only fifty-six and had been in good shape when her father was alive. How could six months of mourning have played such havoc?

Her mother slowly shook her head and solemnly muttered, "There are so many memories... your dad and me on those bikes...." She threw her head back and clasped her hands. "There's nothing like feelin' the wind through your hair...all your senses come alive. When you roll down those roads, you can feel the lay of the land. It's like you're part of this good earth."

She took Georgie's hand and squeezed, her eyes glazed over. "Every time I think of that bike, I see your dad grinnin' at me with that handsome mountain man look he had...and Jack sayin', 'Fire up, gal, and let's ride.'" She shrugged. "I don't think I can ever sell them, I... I just can't."

"You've got no choice, Mom. They're gonna get you out of a whole lotta trouble. They'll take care of at least half of those credit cards. And if the summer goes all right, I bet we can finish the other half off before I leave."

"Why can't we just sell the rental house... or the two lots

that got me in this fix in the first place?"

Georgie could see her mother was getting agitated. She tried to speak more soothingly. "I'm living in the rental house, Mom. Remember? Besides, I don't think you could dump those lots no matter how much you lowered the price. The bikes are going to be the easiest to unload. Just think how many people have already tried to buy them from you?"

Tears began pooling in her mother's eyes as if she were beginning to face the seriousness of her situation. Georgie rose and went to the window determined not to cave in. She pushed aside the lace curtain and looked out on the street below with its two narrow lanes, barely wide enough for cars to park. Nothing much had changed since she was a teen—as usual, the back end of a huge SUV was sticking out beyond its space, Peter O'Leary was rolling out a couple of sale racks and Barry Gurley was packing his truck with cakes from his bakery to be delivered all over five states. Georgie stood twisting her ponytail and thinking, barely listening to her mother trying to justify her gamble.

"Boy, I've made a mess of things. We were sitting pretty when your dad was alive. It's just that everyone was making so much money flipping property that I thought I'd get in on it. Heck! That's how these mountains were developed in the first place. The minute the Revolutionary War was over, land speculators started streaming into this gorge and buying up the place at fifty shillings a hundred acres."

The remark snapped Georgie out of her reverie.

"Come on, Mom. That was two hundred and fifty years ago, for Pete's sake."

"The point I'm trying to make is that human nature hasn't changed all that much. Gamblin's in our blood."

Georgie threw a quick glance over her shoulder, "With your sugar problem, you're gonna have more than gambling in your blood, if you don't watch out."

Dinah disregarded the warning. "I should have grabbed that offer from those Florida folks, but I thought if I held out *just* a little longer... then... bam... that big stock firm in New York went bankrupt and spooked the hell out of 'em."

The two women were silent for a while, with Georgie gazing out the window at the giant monolith on the mountain in front of her and her mother absentmindedly flicking pages of a book with her thumb.

Finally, Dinah broke the silence. "Ali was telling me Ron Elliott has been hired by the park to lead a bunch of nature hikes again this summer."

Georgie came away from the window and started putting her medical supplies neatly into a bureau drawer.

"Mom, I don't want to be hearing 'Ron this' and 'Ron that' all summer. I've got a good life in Boone... a lot of friends..." She closed the drawer and reached for a towel and a crumpled tee shirt at the foot of her mother's bed. "...and, believe it or not, Watauga County has no shortage of men."

She didn't dare bring up the doctor who had come with her to visit once. She'd been dating him for over a year, but when he pressured her to get married, she had decided to let their relationship cool during the four months she'd be in Chimney Rock. She needed to think things over carefully. After one failed marriage, she couldn't afford another mistake.

Her mother slapped her leg. "Attagirl. I knew you had some Flack in ya." Her voice softened. "Do you ever hear from Butch?"

Georgie dropped the clothes into a wicker hamper that had lost its top years before, then, as she spoke, continued moving around the room, picking up toys the boys had left behind.

"Not really. Just what his mother tells me when I run into her at the hospital. But, if he ever shows up, I'd like to think we could have a beer together. Maybe a few laughs."

She straightened the throw rug lying on the brick patterned linoleum with her foot. Nearing her mother's chair, her tone hardened. "But that's about it."

She stood hugging an armful of stuffed toys. "How does that song go? You've been too gone too long."

Her mother grabbed hold of Georgie's arm and squeezed. There had always been a discernible distance between them. Georgie's taking off the day after she graduated from high school had left a sad thread woven into every cranny of their relationship; yet, Dinah looked into Georgie's eyes and comforted her in the age-old unspoken language of a mother to her daughter.

"You're a good girl, Georgie. You really deserve better than what you've gotten out of life."

"Don't worry about it, Mom. I'm happy enough."

"I want you to know how much I appreciate your coming back to help. With your dad gone six months now, I guess you're the only one...." Her voice trailed off. "Your sister's got a good heart, but with the kids, and Cal in Afghanistan..."

Georgie patted her mother on the shoulder. "Mom, I would have come whether you asked or not."

The stuffed animals got tossed into a big wooden box that her grandfather had made for her mother when she was a child. The room grew quiet except for the muffled sound of the TV coming from the living room and the thunder of a truck barreling down Main Street.

"Mom, are you going to be all right about the bikes?"

"No, but go ahead. Sell 'em anyway."

Georgie had hoped this was how the conversation would end. As much of a dreamer as her mother was, she could always be made to face reality in the end.

"If I get a chance, I'll go over and post a notice in Heavenly Hoggs this afternoon."

Dinah considered the remark for a moment, then said, "No, you don't have to bother. Let me put 'em on eBay. It'll give me something to do besides rotting in this room."

CHAPTER THREE

T HE MAN ROLLED OUT OF THE VAN and stepped out into the forest, still glistening from the early morning rain. Billowy pink clouds reflected the glow of the sun rising beyond the tree tops, and the sweet smell of balsam lingered in the air. Suddenly a Carolina wren in search of a mate broke out in song. It was moments like this that convinced Ron Elliott he had found his niche on the planet.

He opened the van's passenger door, slid onto the cold front seat and reached for his laptop. A few last-minute details he'd thought of as he was drifting off last night were added to his management report. He'd email it to the land trust he worked for once he got near a wi-fi location. Nowadays, that meant almost anywhere you could grab a cup of coffee.

Satisfied with the report, he got out and went over to a pail next to the van's side door. He splashed some water on his face, then reached in and got a razor from a plastic tub next to his bed. Massaging the five-day-old bristle on his jaw, he decided he better use some soap if he wanted a clean shave for the nature hike he would be leading that day in Chimney Rock.

He dug a bar from the pail and lathered up, then stooped at the side view mirror. Tranquil light blue eyes peered back at him, contradicting the weather-hardened face he'd earned from years of trekking in the wild.

A red-tailed hawk flapped over the spruce fir forest and

caught his eye. That was the third one he'd seen in the past five days at the preserve. Their young were still in the nest and they were probably on the hunt to feed the fledglings.

Ron was the land manager of a three-thousand acre preserve on the southern rim of the Smoky Mountains. He worked for a land trust out of Pennsylvania and was in the initial stages of figuring out what the property needed. Since fall, he had walked over most of it and mapped the existing roads and trails. The next step was inventorying all the flora and fauna.

He checked his watch. Almost eight. He'd better get started if he wanted to arrive for the hike on time. His trail shoes showed the scars from tramping through hundreds of miles of rugged terrain and rocky streams, and the field pants he had picked up at Goodwill were pretty worn; but they'd do. In his line of work, it didn't make sense to buy anything new. He still remembered the down Patagonia vest his wife had bought him. The first time he wore it, he slipped on a rock, and a thorn from one of the hawthorns he was examining ripped it from one end to the other. He still felt a pang of self-reproach, remembering the blank stare on his wife's face when he came home with duct tape across it.

Every vehicle he owned had to meet the same criteria as his clothes—tough but dispensable. His red beat-up four-wheel drive pick-up was parked between the van and his Subaru Outback. The three mud splattered vehicles looked like a line-up in a road construction fleet.

The truck was bought used, and he had racked up another hard-driven two hundred thousand miles on it. The old workhorse had seen him through everything from the Big Thicket swamps in Texas to the steep rocky terrain of the Southern Blue Ridge. The cargo van was the only vehicle he had ever bought new, but once Ford decided to stop producing their powerful E-150 with five-speed overdrive transmission, he snapped one up.

Finished shaving, he peeled off his tee shirt, splashed some water under his arms and dried himself off. He pulled out a cardboard box from underneath his bed, fished around for a shirt with the Chimney Rock Park's logo and put it on. Between his job at the preserve and the book he was writing about hawthorns, leading a hike wasn't Ron's idea of the most productive way to spend his time, but his relationship with the park was special. He'd been their naturalist and nursery curator for seven years before striking out into the land management field. Over the years, they had counted on him to lead three or four of what they billed as "Off the Beaten Track" hikes, and he was happy to do them.

Two and a half hours later, his green Subaru was crawling behind the bumper-to-bumper traffic making its way through the village of Chimney Rock. He swung onto the park entrance bridge that crossed the Rocky Broad River. Just a ways up, he glanced at the house they used as an office and scanned the lot for the park naturalist's car, but it wasn't there.

He continued up the steep winding mountain road through dense forest, dark from the thick canopy of hickory, oak and ash towering a hundred feet overhead. One mile later, he emerged onto an expansive sunny plateau. There were three cars lined up at the toll booth ahead of him, and being a Saturday, both ticket windows were operating.

He recognized one of his favorite volunteers as he pulled up to one of the toll booths. She was somewhere in her late fifties. Years before, he'd bonded with her the minute she opened her mouth and the familiar sound of a southern mountain twang floated out.

"Hey there, Molly. How's life treatin' ya?"

He took off his well-worn trail hat with the rim curled up on both sides, ran his fingers through his dark brown hair, and slowly slid the hat on again.

"You back again this year?" she asked. "Thought they ran you off for good."

A shy smile slowly surfaced. "They ran me off all right, but not for good."

She left the window for a moment, came back with a park walkie-talkie and handed it to him.

"You git on ahead... and don't leave anyone on the trail."

"That's one thing I've never done." He gave her a wink and grinned. "But if I ever do, it won't be by accident."

He continued up the road that twisted through the rugged boulder-strewn forest to the parking lot where the hikers were supposed to be waiting. The final hairpin turn revealed a cluster of people milling around the tunnel entrance up ahead. It led to an elevator that would take them up to the base of the chimney.

He pulled into a parking space next to a family clambering out of a van. The kids were casting about in wonderment with the mother yelling for everyone to get their backpacks on, while the father wrestled a toddler from the back seat.

Ron attached the walkie-talkie to his backpack and got out. The sun was high in the stark blue sky and the damp chill from the morning had burnt off. He put on the backpack that contained everything he needed: several bottles of water, field glasses, a rain parka and a first-aid kit. Everyone who signed up for the hike was told to bring water and lunch. He'd grab something at the concession stand when they got off the elevator.

He glanced ahead at the expansive eastern view of the valley and Lake Lure, and could see why the Indians called this region The Land of the Sky. Ron gave himself a moment to take it in and thought if he ever became blind, he would still know when he was on this mountain. If the eighteen turns on the three-mile climb didn't tell him where he was being taken, once he got there, the rope hardware clanking on the flagpole would. The pole sat at the top of the chimney, and the eternal breeze coming down the ten-mile gorge guaranteed you heard it the minute you stepped out onto the parking lot below.

He neared the cluster assembled at the tunnel entrance and couldn't help noticing the anticipation on everyone's faces. Good. He'd evidently met their expectations of what a botanist should look like. He counted eight in the senior citizen category, a set of parents with a teenage daughter who was busy texting someone, and a couple with a young child being toted in a backpack. Only fourteen. He'd been told there'd be two more. He ran through the description of the hike and said he'd meet them upstairs in the plaza outside the gift shop. He added a warning that this would be their last chance to find a public bathroom or get a snack for the trail.

They streamed down the dark, dank 198-foot long cavern drilled out of solid rock to the elevator. Ron gathered that the fellow operating the lift knew who he was by the way he acknowledged him with a nod. The young man announced the elevator would zoom up the 26-story channel chiseled from rock in 35 seconds, then he delivered a commendable pitch for the gift shop and deli. Or at least, one a lot better than Ron had come up with the first summer he'd worked at that job just before starting college. After two days, the park manager had switched him to trail walking. Answering questions about the plants and trees along the trails came a lot easier than reeling off a litany of merchandise available in the shop.

He bought a sandwich at the food concession, stuffed it in his backpack and went out on the plaza that was no more than a large platform anchored onto the side of a massive granite outcrop. The flag on the top of the chimney snapped crisply in the breeze.

A bridge traversed the craggy precipice below and led to the staircase going up to the 315-foot tall chimney jutting out from the mountain like a thumb. Across from it, another staircase scaled the bald face of Chimney Rock Mountain.

The group soon clustered around him and he counted heads again. Still only fourteen. He explained their next destination would be the promontory called Exclamation Point. It was the peak of the bald mass of rock that traversed the face of the mountain for almost a mile.

They were climbing the series of flights that would get them to the trail above when he heard someone calling out, "Yoo-hoo… trail person… we're here."

Two women were scrambling up the steps, one waving wildly with outstretched arms. They had to be the two missing hikers. They were three flights down, so he told the group to wait for him at the top.

He smiled to himself as the two neared. They were decked out from head to toe in the latest hiking gear. He figured they must have been a godsend to some outfitting store. The trekking poles and wrap-around Polaroid sunglasses alone must have set one of the women back at least a couple hundred dollars. He couldn't help observing that even though she was shapely enough to get away with the shorts she was wearing, they were too brief for a trek in the deep woods.

He guessed they were single professionals in their forties, out for a new adventure. In the nearly ten years he'd been leading hikes, he'd met a lot like them, and it always surprised him how some ended up as halfway decent amateur botanists.

He shepherded them to the top of the staircase and they all started on the climb to the summit. The hike up the mountain was strenuous, so he kept stopping to point out something of interest while he waited for the rear to catch up. It being spring, he had no problem finding wildflowers all along the trail.

"Is that a bloodroot?" the mother of the teenager asked. "I think I've read about it. Doesn't it have a liquidy red root that the Indians used for dye?"

He told her yes, and a glimmer of pride crossed her face. The father nudged their daughter in approval.

Ron had seen the typical hiker change over the years. At the beginning of his career, he found that most of them were satisfied to simply learn the common names of a few trees and wildflowers native to the area. Today, they were generally more informed. It had to be the plethora of nature programs and an overall awareness of the environment. But mostly, he figured the world was getting smaller and the consequences of ignoring the threats to nature were starting to hit home.

He stopped to point out a colony of yellow lady slippers, and the woman with the wrap-around sunglasses managed to get close enough for him to smell her perfume. He wondered if the park had forgotten to ask the hikers not to put any on. No, they wouldn't have forgotten, he told himself. But this lady wasn't going to step one foot outside her door unless she had doused herself with a scent with a name like "Temptation," no matter what anyone told her.

"We are now in an old growth section," he explained. "Old growth is a forest made up of trees 100 years or older, though this is a definition people get into arguments about."

The woman raised an eyebrow. "You don't have to worry about *me* giving you an argument," she said with a little too much innuendo.

"Thank you, ma'am," he said, and then continued. "The term old growth doesn't deal with the size of a tree, it's the age that matters. The oldest known tree here in the park is more than 350 years old."

"You know so much about this place. It's *sooooo* amazing," she gushed.

"Oh, brother," someone moaned.

The hike continued along a wider path, with the woman struggling to stick close to him. He paused at a colorful hedge to give her a chance to catch her breath.

"Here's a fine example of Carolina Rhododendron," he announced. "It starts blooming down in the valley in early April, but we don't see it this high up till later in the month." He pointed to a plant with a whorl of three mottled leaves and large maroon petals reaching upward. "That's a trillium commonly called Little Sweet Betsy. It's at the end of its blooming cycle."

"That's me. Little Sweet Betsy," the woman piped up.

"Talk about being at the end of its blooming cycle," one of the seniors quipped.

Ron could see Betsy was hurt by the comment, and he wished it hadn't been said, but maybe it would settle her down.

Once they reached the Exclamation Point, he let everyone take a moment to enjoy the west view of the gorge and the town below, before leading them off the trail onto an old logging road on the backside of the mountain. They hiked single file at a vigorous pace through woods, going diagonally across the contours of the mountain.

By now, everyone had worked up a sweat and the breezes wafting through the gorge were a welcomed relief. When Betsy bemoaned having to walk through a couple of stream beds in her new trail shoes, someone asked in exasperation, "What in the heck did she buy 'em for? To wear to the mall?"

They reached a small clearing where there had been a big blowdown of an old hickory. Ron decided this was a good place to tell them about the various tree communities. Near a sweet birch, he snapped off a twig and handed it to a hiker. "Bite into that," he said.

The man took the twig and bit. "It tastes like wintergreen."

Several broke off twigs and tasted. Ron pulled off a few leaves from a nearby basswood tree and passed them around.

"This time of year these leaves are very highly veined and delicate... they don't have any tannin so you can eat them raw. You can even use them on a sandwich like lettuce."

"Cool," said the teenager.

He gave everyone a chance to taste, then started up again.

By this time, Betsy had abandoned her friend and was sticking to his side whenever the trail would allow. She struggled to keep up, and he had to keep finding an excuse to stop so she could catch her breath. He smiled inwardly. She sure was persistent. He was ashamed to admit it to himself, but he was warming up to her.

"You certainly do know a lot about nature," she said as they walked along.

He nodded, figuring next she was going to come up with some kind of invitation.

"Do you ever give personal tours?"

"No, ma'am."

There'd been a time years ago before he'd married Mary when he might have taken her up on it, but not anymore. His wife moving to New Mexico with his eleven-year-old daughter, had left too big of a hole in his heart to hold anyone else; and he was in no mood for a casual affair. Those things always ended badly with one partner's expectations usually far exceeding the other's. Right now, he was concentrating on keeping close tabs on Mary, and calling little Jennifer every day. They were coming for two weeks in August. He knew it was only to gather up what belongings they had left behind; but it was something to look forward to.

The mountain laurel thicket ahead signaled they were nearing their destination. They made a sharp turn, and a massive rock surface with a spectacular view lay in front of them.

"Don't go out too far," he warned. "This outcrop rounds off and you could fall several hundred feet if you don't watch out."

He studied the group and could see they were all pretty much white-knuckled and staying close to the top of the rock. The man toting the infant gripped a tree. The broad-winged hawks soaring below on the warm drafts rising from the valley intensified the aura of danger.

"We'll stay here and enjoy the view and our lunch for twenty minutes or so, then start back."

Taking sixteen people out on a massive outcrop with no guard rail was a big responsibility. Yet, in spite of having to concentrate on keeping a close eye on everyone and having to be prepared to respond to any kind of emergency, this was his favorite part of the trek. Even the most apathetic soul would be awed by the huge expanse of open space and endless skies.

He had a captive audience with their senses stimulated by the sheer force of the beauty in front of them. He relished telling them about the Henderson Gneiss rock they were sitting on that was thousands of years old and the haircap spike moss mats that prospered on this windswept ledge. He pointed out the unusual yellow honeysuckle that grew there, and told how lightning-strike fires helped plants like the corydalis. All of this was important to him. Even though at different times he had worked as a naturalist, a biologist, and a nurseryman, at heart he was a botanist.

Things quieted down and everyone concentrated on eating and enjoying the view. The teenager was jotting down notes on her iPad, and Betsy was nursing a scratch on her leg from a blackberry bramble. He went over to her, got out his first-aid kit and squatted down. "Let me put somethin' on that, Ma'am."

She smiled faintly as he doused a cotton pad with peroxide and swiped the scratch that ran from her thigh to where blood had trickled down to the pink pompoms on her socks, then he offered her a tube of ointment to spread on the wound.

"Can you do it?" she asked.

Just as he gave her a look, one of the older women snatched the tube from his hand and got busy spreading it on.

He struggled to keep from smiling as Betsy glared at the lady. The strenuous trek had pretty much done her in. Her glasses dangled from a strap across her chest and her face and neck were flushed. Errant strands of hair that had escaped from her ponytail were either stuck to her face or flying in the breeze. The UNC emblem on her pink tee shirt had turned maroon from sweat as had large patches under her arms. He could see she'd already gone through two bottles of water and her friend was urging her to drink more.

Ron noticed they didn't seem to have any food. "Didn't you gals bring a lunch?" he asked.

Her friend seemed embarrassed. "We're on a diet."

He started to fish around in his backpack for an energy bar when the mother of the teenager doled one out to each of them. Someone came forth with apples, and another with two sandwiches.

The return trip went at a good pace, being generally downhill. Betsy had given up on keeping up with him and straggled at the rear. They made their way into the old growth forest again, and Ron thought this would be a good opportunity to give everyone a chance to rest.

"You can see that the crown of the trees up there have had a chance to broaden out. This forms a canopy, and the understory—the stuff that needs light to survive—begins to thin out. In a young forest, the crowns of the trees are narrow because they're in competition to grow. Other signs of an old growth forest are uneven trees, fungi, fallen logs, decay, hollow trees, dense…"

A shrill scream startled everyone. Ron's eyes darted toward the cry. Betsy was sitting on a log with her hands over her face. The group rushed to her side. Ron crouched down in front of her, peeled away her hands and spotted a wasp sting that had already started to form a red blister on her cheek.

"Does anybody have a cigarette?" Ron said as looked at the faces of the concerned crowd.

One of the women elbowed her husband and said, "Arty does. Go on, Arty. Give him a cigarette."

Her husband pulled a pack out of his pocket and offered one.

Ron took it, snapped it in half and dumped the tobacco into the palm of his hand. He emptied it in his mouth and chewed, then spit a dark paste into his hand and spread it over Betsy's cheek.

"Is that one of those Indian remedies you've heard about?" asked the man.

"No, just what we used to do on the farm on Shumont Mountain when we got stung," said Ron.

Concerned about whether Betsy might get an allergic reaction, he asked her if she'd ever been stung before. The last thing they needed was for her to go into anaphylaxis. He relaxed once she said she had and had been okay. If he wanted to smile at her before, he now wanted to give her a hug. He radioed ahead to give the office a heads up that he had someone with a wasp sting, but added he had it under control.

By the time they reached the Exclamation Point and headed back down the mountain, the swelling on Betsy's face was beginning to subside. Most of the tobacco had fallen off, but enough remained to make her self-conscious about having anyone look at her. Several of the seniors had taken her under their wing and were helping her make the descent. When they reached the gift shop, she quickly disappeared into the women's room.

Ron was anxious to get over to the office to see if Angie, the park's naturalist, was still there and to make out an accident report on the wasp sting, yet he hung around the crowded gift shop. He felt bad about the way things turned out for Betsy. She and her friend had started out in such high spirits. Just a couple of gals out looking for a good time. He wouldn't be surprised if Betsy was in the same boat as he—recently dumped and looking for some reassurance.

Suddenly Betsy emerged from between two tee-shirt racks with her friend. She'd combed her hair, fixed her face and put on a new top.

"Are you gonna be all right, ma'am?" he asked.

She nodded.

Just then, the elevator opened and he stepped in. He turned and saw her looking at him as if she'd been deserted. He touched his hat, slowly smiled and said, "Bye, Little Sweet Betsy."

CHAPTER FOUR

"**Y**OU BOYS, PICK UP everything in the hall. It's hard enough gettin' around with that walker without havin' to dodge them cars of yours."

Dinah was sitting in her recliner with her foot propped up. Her laptop lay on the rollaway table that Georgie had left strict instructions was only to be used for her medical procedures. She adjusted the table so her computer could be positioned at a comfortable level, while Isaac obediently picked up the cars and carefully placed them in a plastic box. Michael, who, at six, was four years younger than his brother, draped himself on the arm of the recliner.

"Grandma, are you really gonna sell Grandpa's bike?" he asked.

She squinted at her screen for a moment, then reached for her glasses and put them on.

"Are you, Grandma?"

She booted up her "Flack" file and started skimming through the latest deeds she had Ali scan at the county courthouse.

Michael kept pestering. "Mama told us Aunt Georgie is making you sell both of 'em."

Her eyes shot over to him. "We'll see about that."

A slightly conspiratorial grin lit the boy's face.

"You know your Grandma, don't ya, boy." She put her arm around him and squeezed. "Don't worry, son. Grandma's not gonna sell Grandpa's bike. I'm fixin' to give it to your daddy when he comes home 'cause he's a hero. Just don't you be tellin' anyone."

Finished with the cars, Isaac came into the room and slid onto the recliner's other arm.

"You reading your deeds?" he asked.

'Yep."

"Grandma, I was thinking. I bet that wolf den on the cliff is somewhere on Roundtop Mountain. Don't you think your great-grandpa would have hidden his gold on land he owned?"

"Yeah, I do. Trouble is he owned land on both sides of this gorge. From up behind us on Round Top, to across the river and up to the chimney."

Michael was now sitting on the recliner's arm, his bare feet pulled up and his arms hugging his legs.

"Tell us about the wolf den, Grandma."

"You've already heard it a hundred times."

"I know. I just love the way you say it."

Isaac put his arm around her shoulder and leaned around so he was nose to nose with her. "Once more isn't gonna hurt."

"Okay," she said as she sank back in her chair, folded her hands across her belly and spoke in a slow story-telling cadence.

"It was one of those cold... windy... winter days with nothin' to do but listen to what the Indians called the *long winds.* I went over to that there window and watched the trees twist and writhe like they were havin' a fit, and listened to that never-ending eerie sound like a train goin' straight through town."

"How old were you, Grandma?" asked Michael.

"All of sixteen."

"Don't keep interrupting her," Isaac demanded as he reached over and pushed Michael, almost knocking him off the chair.

"There was nothin' to do, so I went over to that very book-case and got out my great-grandfather's Bible. As I was leafing through it, an old, yellowed piece of paper fell out."

Michael clasped his hands. "I love this part."

"There in his elaborate longhand were six words: *The wolf den on the cliff.*" An eyebrow lifted as she raised a finger in the air.

"The more I studied it, the more I became convinced it was a clue to the gold folks around here said my great-granddaddy hid in 1930." She glanced at each of the boys, "...'cause he was afraid all the bank failures would bring about lawlessness."

"Now tell us about the Englishman," Michael squealed.

"She hasn't finished telling us about the wolf den!" Isaac gasped in frustration.

"Okay, Mike. But then you guys are gonna have to let me get some work done." She straightened her housedress across her stomach and rested her hands on her belly once more.

"That wasn't the only gold that's supposed to be hidden on Round Top. Two hundred years ago a small band of adventurers out of England stumbled onto a gold mine in the hills to the north. They sacked all the gold they could carry and headed for Charleston, but just as they reached the end of the gorge, a band of Cherokee fell upon them."

Michael started punching the air as if he were in a fight and almost fell off the chair again. Dinah instinctively grabbed Isaac's hand as he reached over to smack him.

"Do you kids want to hear this story or not?"

They both straightened right up.

She continued with the story. "The Englishmen climbed to safety among the rocky heights of Round Top where they stumbled onto a deep, dark cave... but that night the Indians crept up and killed all but one who escaped and made his way back to England."

Ali suddenly appeared at the doorway and they all looked up. "Kids, I want you to go out and play. But don't be takin' off down the alley on your bikes. I'll have lunch ready soon."

"But Grandma was tellin' us about all the gold," mourned Michael.

"You've heard it a hundred times. Now git!"

The boys scooted out and Ali lingered, looking as if she had something on her mind.

"Have you found anything in the new deeds I got for you?" she finally asked.

"Heck, with all these dad-burned interruptions I haven't had a chance to read nothin'."

"I don't know how you read them at all, Mom. I look them over before I scan 'em with that gadget you got me, but I can barely make them out." She bent down, and with a grunt, swiped up a sock lying on the floor, stretching open the pockets on her shorts. "I'm making tuna fish sandwiches for lunch. Is that gonna be all right with you?"

"Whatever."

Ali crossed her arms and sank against the door jamb.

"Georgie said she's making you sell the bikes. Is it true?"

Dinah kept studying the screen.

"What Georgie says for me *to* do and what I *do* do aren't necessarily the same thing."

"Did you let her know you promised the boys you'd give Dad's to Cal when he got home from Afghanistan?"

"We ain't got to that stage of the argument yet." She looked up over the rim of her glasses. "That's my ace in the hole. I don't intend to use it till I've got my back to the wall."

Ali shook her head as she shoved away from the door jamb and started to leave.

"Well, don't look now, but that wall's about six inches from your butt. She's just like Dad."

The comment brought back Dinah's painful memory of the lake house Jack wouldn't let her buy. She'd had to forfeit the five thousand dollars she'd put down on it once he refused to go through with the sale.

"Close the door," she snapped. "I'm gonna need some peace and quiet if I'm gonna read this deed."

Years ago, everyone had chalked her theory of the wolf den up to a teenager's fanciful imaginings. Why would her great-grandfather who lived until 1949 leave gold in a wolf den once the depression was over? Surely if he had, he would have told his son, her grandfather, where it was. But no matter how much the idea was pooh-poohed, Dinah couldn't let it go.

She had grown up sitting around campfires listening to the lore of all the expeditions to recover the Englishman's gold. Once back in England, the one remaining adventurer lost his eyesight and could only dictate a map of where the precious metal was hidden. But an expedition failed to find it. For over two hundred years, people had searched that mountain with picks and shovels and with men and mules to no avail. A Confederate general even searched vainly for it with fifty of his slaves.

Dinah's stubborn belief that her great-grandfather's gold was sitting in an abandoned wolf den had led to her becoming a card-carrying member of the National Speleological Society when she was still a teen. She explored all the known caves on both sides of the gorge, the largest extending nearly 300 feet into the granite of Bald Mountain, which abutted the east side of Round Top and curved around to face Lake Lure. But mostly, she and Jack, after they were married, hiked all over Round Top and Shumont, its northern neighbor, searching for the elusive wolf den.

Dinah squinted at the screen and made out "on the Main Broad River." This deed was definitely worth studying, so she enlarged the view, but the deed had no mention of a den. Tired, she leaned back in her chair and looked up at the map on the wall. Every tear, every wrinkle, every grease stain meant something to her. Jack got it from the county courthouse in Ruther-fordton. Plat 223 they called it. She and Jack had used it to chart their treks and had marked all the caves and dens they discovered with an "X."

They would sometimes run across folks whose families had lived on those mountains for generations. They'd sit and neighborly listen to stories of deserters who hid out in caves during the Civil War; sometimes they were offered home-made corn liquor the mountain folks called "Knock 'em Stiff," or just "Shine."

They had searched on and off for fifteen years, only interrupted by the three agonizing years they'd spent trying to find their four-year-old who had disappeared during the night after they'd tucked her into bed.

Dinah knew Jack never believed these expeditions would lead to gold. He had told Georgie he just liked to watch how ideas lit her imagination and made her glow. "Your mother secretly believes there isn't any gold. She's using these searches as a relief valve," he had told Georgie.

That had been true to a certain extent. During the dark days after Shelby's disappearance, these hikes were one of the only things that took Dinah's mind off the gut-wrenching agony of not knowing.

Suddenly, Ali opened the door and startled her. "I'm going downstairs to help put up the new shipment. Do you need anything before I go?"

Dinah looked over her shoulder and pointed to a picture on the wall next to the map.

"Bring me the picture of your dad and me on the mountain."

Ali crossed the room and took the framed photo off the wall. She used a corner of her blouse to dust it off, handed it to her mother and sank down onto the arm of the chair. They both gazed at it in silence.

"Those were good days. Weren't they, Mom?"

"Yep. They sure were."

In the picture, Dinah was wearing shorts and sitting on a huge rock. Jack was in jeans and standing next to her with an arm around Ali. A turkey track that had been carved in the stone could barely be made out.

"This was the last time we were all up there together, wasn't it?"

Dinah nodded.

"Boy, did you go wild over finding that carving on that rock. Heck, you nearly killed us makin' us dig and scratch around there all summer." They both sank back in thought for a moment. "You looked dang good in those days, Mom. How old were you there?"

"Forty."

Dinah had stared at that picture and calculated hundreds of times that Georgie had taken it eleven years after Shelby's disappearance; but those sad accountings she kept to herself.

In an attempt to change her thoughts, Dinah said, "Isaac told me you gave him the needle made from bone you found in that Indian cave."

"Ever since you started looking through these deeds for the

wolf den, he's gotten real interested in our family history and stuff."

Ali got up and hung the picture back on the wall. Then she patted her mother on the shoulder, said goodbye and slipped out of the room.

Years ago, when the carving of the turkey track didn't lead anywhere, the disappointment put an end to Dinah's search for the wolf den. That was up until Jack's passing six months ago. One evening she was rifling through some old family papers and ran across a deed. Written with the old metes and bounds formula, it listed all the monuments on the parcel of land—everything from a large rock, to a cliff, and from a chestnut oak with three trunks, to a branch of a creek. Surely they would have mentioned a wolf den on the cliff if there were one, she reasoned.

That logic rekindled the obsession that had lain dormant for years. It was a long time and quite a few pounds since the days when she and Jack scavenged around those mountains, but she wasn't altogether done yet. If she had to, she was going to read every old deed in the county courthouse until she found a mention of a wolf den. Once she did, she'd know where the gold was hidden.

The sound of the boys playing in the sandbox drifted in through the open window facing the alley. The sandbox sat on the huge deck Jack had built above the stockroom. Half of the deck was covered with a roof, and for a good part of the year, the family spent evening hours there grilling, eating and lounging.

Dinah moved on to the next deed and skimmed it over. By now she knew enough to skip the "...grant, bargain, covenant and agreed..." part and go straight to the metes and bounds that started with "Beginning at a..." But this deed was different. The property they were talking about was a slave called Liz and her girl child. Curious, Dinah looked for what they cost. Four hundred dollars. She flipped back to the previous deed. It was for an eighty-acre parcel that went for $2 an acre. If a woman and her child in 1805 had the same worth as 200 acres of land, their master sure intended to get a lot of labor out of them.

Dinah imagined the fear the woman must have had of some

day losing her child. She was probably a toddler, or they would have sold her off separately. Dinah couldn't help thinking that the woman known simply as Liz had to be haunted by the realization that her cherished little girl would one day be taken away from her, only to suffer the same humiliation she had endured.

The pain Dinah wore like an old housecoat suddenly hurt as if it were from a fresh wound. Of all the agonizing thoughts she had of Shelby, the one that plagued her the most was that her little girl might be misused. "Where are you Shelby? Please God," she pleaded, "watch over her."

Determined to get up, she pushed the cart holding her laptop aside, then reached for the recliner's controls and slowly lowered the leg rest. Blood rushed to her injured foot and made it throb. She scooted forward and wrestled her walker so it was in front of her. Holding on tight and using her good foot, she thrust herself forward and upward, then took a moment to steady herself before taking the three painful steps to the bureau.

She reached for the tarnished frame Georgie had hidden behind Jack's picture, and her eyes melted on the image. The dimples were still embedded in the porcelain cheeks. The hair, parted at the cowlick, still looked like spun gold. Dinah closed her eyes and pictured Shelby as clearly as if she were right there in front of her. Then she let the small frame slip into her housedress pocket before wrangling the walker around and slowly making her way back to the recliner.

Seated again, she swiped away a tear, readjusted her glasses and clicked to the next deed. Jack had made her stop looking for Shelby once the law and the newspapers were no longer interested, but nobody was going to stop her from looking for the wolf den on the cliff.

CHAPTER FIVE

T HERE WASN'T A SINGLE sales counter or cabinet in the
store that matched, and the ceiling was a patchwork
quilt of tin and acoustic tiles. One rectangular section must have
been where a chimney had once stood. Right after she and Jack
were married, Dinah's Aunt Myrtle had let them stay in the
apartment upstairs with the understanding that Dinah would one
day take over the business below. She worked hard in the store
and Jack at his job at the mill, and by the time they hit forty they
were the proud owners of this 80 by 100 foot chunk of commercial real estate called The Olde Mountain Emporium.

Georgie was busy sticking tags on a stack of kites with the
pricing gun when the three women drifted in. They moved together in a line as if they were a caterpillar. One of them picked
up a tee shirt and draped it across her chest. What looked like
hand-painted letters boasted, "You mess with me... you mess
with the whole trailer park!"

They all laughed. "Nancy, that's you all right."

Georgie smiled at the women as they passed and then offered
any assistance the ladies might need. They moved along, examining items that caught their fancy. One of the women picked up
an old-fashioned cast-iron frying pan. She turned it over and
tapped her manicured nail on the label. "Look. Can you believe
it? Even these are made in China now."

"Oh, heck," said one of her friends. "Remember when we

were kids? Back then, everything was made in Japan. So what's the diff?"

After a leisurely stroll down memory lane, one of the women bought a dish decorated with a rooster decal that had compartments for holding deviled eggs. Another woman bought two coffee mugs with her grandchildren's names. They streamed out, anxious to get to the next store, and Georgie continued pricing.

Finished with the kites, she started on some red and blue feathered Indian headdresses. Georgie wondered what the people working in the Chinese sweatshop must have thought as they tacked on the phony raccoon tails. Or when they plastered images of John Wayne and James Dean all over the trays and lunchboxes.

And what in the devil had they thought of the decals of Betty Boop they had to slap on all those purses, compacts and spoon holders? The vast disparity in cultures between this purely commercial strain of U.S. memorabilia that her mother was peddling and that of the Chinese laborers must have baffled them; but then again, she thought, they probably got all kinds of Americana thrown at them every day in so many ways they simply were in the habit of letting it bounce off.

Alone in the store, a feeling of déjà vu crept up on her. The goal of getting out of that little hamlet had possessed her through her entire childhood, and now here she was—thirty-one, still single, and selling plastic tomahawks in Chimney Rock.

From the time Georgie could count change, she'd been earning it. Either in her mother's store, or babysitting, or lawn mowing... anything that would earn money. Not many kids hailing from a small town in the North Carolina mountains would have squirreled away more than five thousand dollars by age eighteen.

The most lucrative endeavor had been cleaning rental cottages that were wedged into the mountains on both sides of the river. During the summer, when most of the local kids were tubing in the river or splashing in the lake, she was sweating it out in shorts and a gritty tee shirt getting some cottage cleaned between renters.

It had been a bone of contention at the house, since they

could have used her to work in the store, but the minimum wages her mother paid couldn't compete with the twenty dollars she got for every place she cleaned.

By the time she was sixteen, any time someone needed some messy business done, they'd say, "Call that Haydock kid. She'll do it if you pay her enough." By her senior year she had already mopped up after one murder and a suicide.

The phone rang and she put the tagging gun down. It was Carrie from the post office wanting to meet her for lunch. Georgie phoned upstairs and told Ali to come down and cover for her at noon. Georgie didn't like springing last-minute changes on her sister, especially since everyone was trying to get the house back onto a normal routine, but she and Carrie had been friends since first grade and she knew she wouldn't be wanting to go to lunch unless she had something to say.

Ali put up a feeble resistance, going on about how she would be feeding Mom and the boys late. Georgie made her happy with a promise that afterward she could take the rest of the day off.

A BACKHOE ROARED as it tried to unearth a huge rock, filling the air with blue exhaust. Ron yelled above the noise.

"You're gonna want to put something tall like red buckeye in the back. Use nothing but native plants."

When he met with the park's naturalist after his trek the week before, Ron had agreed to consult the park on the replanting of their entrance, and he now found himself on Main Street with Joey Dykes, the grounds supervisor.

He moved close enough to the backhoe operator to be heard. "Get all those rocks in a cluster over there," he shouted, pointing to an area in the rear. He looked over at Joey, "You can toe-nail them in with small deciduous shrubs." He bent down, picked up a flat rock that might have been too heavy for most men to carry and toted it to a pile of large boulders. He pointed to the front of the cluster. "You can throw in grasses right along here for color and texture in the winter."

All morning the men and machines moved, dug and coaxed rocks around the large chunks of land on either side of the park's main entrance.

Joey finally shouted, "Let's call it a morning, guys."

The sudden silence made Ron's ears ring for a moment before the noise was replaced by the roar of a huge truck rolling down Main Street, loaded with giant hardwood logs. There goes another denuded slope, Ron said to himself. He noticed Joey watching it go by and figured he was thinking the same thing. How much of these mountains had they seen carried away over the years, and how much of the resulting barren earth had they watched wash into the river?

Ron finished a drawing in his notepad, then tore off four sheets and handed them to Joey.

"Here's a list and where it all goes."

Joey studied the sketches, flicked the sheets with the back of his hand and chuckled.

"Hell, that's what I call thorough. You even put in the Latin names." He nodded toward the cafe next to the park entrance. "Let's get some grub."

The Olde Rock Café belonged to the park, so Joey and Ron were greeted with a good dose of camaraderie as they gave their order. They went out on the deck and sat down. The large platform was snuggled up against the town's Riverwalk and overlooked the Rocky Broad. The muffled roar of water crashing on boulders created a background of white noise.

"You sure got a lot of azaleas," Joey said, studying the list.

Ron leaned back in his chair and gripped his drink, "Don't worry. You're gonna find there's enough difference in the varieties to give you prolonged bursts of color."

Someone coming through the door caught Joey's eye. He lowered his head and scrunched forward.

"Don't look now, but you won't believe who the cat just dragged in."

Joey's sudden uneasiness caused Ron to wait a moment before slowly glancing over his shoulder. Two women were making their way over to a table at the far end of the deck and starting to pull out chairs, their backs to him. Carrie Owenby looked to Ron like she could use a rest after toting herself from the post office, but the other woman had strolled across the deck like she owned the place.

Tall, with a willowy frame, the black, skin-tight Capri pants made her legs look even longer and the running shoes, her feet even bigger. It was Georgie Haydock, all right. Her curves were just enough more pronounced since the last time he laid eyes on them to tell him she had turned into a woman, and it made him ache. Her frilly top hung down lopsided on one side. Yep, it was her all right. There wasn't anyone else in town with that quirky sense of style.

He turned around and the look on Joey's face embarrassed him. His friend had to know what he was thinking.

"How long has it been?" asked Joey.

Ron put his elbows on the table and rested his chin on his clenched fist and thought.

"It's got to be a good thirteen years."

"She blew into town about a month ago. I was gonna call you but figured sooner or later you'd run into her."

"What's she doing here?"

"Her mom's had an accident. Georgie's some kind of nurse. She's just gonna stick around till Dinah's on her feet again."

Ron noticed his heart rate had quickened. He'd thought he was over Georgie. Scanning the street for her whenever he drove through Chimney Rock was just a habit.

Joey seemed to be making an effort at keeping the conversation on a comfortable tract.

"Gossip's not as bad as when we were kids," he said. "Heck, if I did something wrong at school or walked on someone's lawn, my mother would know about it and smack me on the side of the head the minute I walked in the door. Someone would've already called her. Couldn't hide nothin' from nobody."

The door opened and a waitress came out with their order and then went back in.

"Yep. Things have really changed," Joey continued. "The last time I counted, there were only five kids in this town. And, heck, three of them belong to the O'Leary's."

Once it became apparent to Joey that Ron wasn't listening,

he leaned over and whispered, "In case you want to know, she's not married."

Ron gave him the kind of glance that said it was an important piece of information. At the same time he wondered if Georgie knew about him and Mary.

Glancing over at Georgie, Joey added, "She still looks good. In fact, she looks damn good."

Not getting a response from Ron, he changed the subject again.

"Things were different when we were kids. When you lived in this town, summers you either worked for the park or for one of the shops downtown."

Ron took a bite of his Reuben sandwich, grateful for Joey's ramblings; it gave him time to gather his thoughts and process the fact that the enigma that had lingered in his thoughts for half his existence was sitting just a few feet away. At every junction of his life, he had re-analyzed Georgie's taking off the way she did, and finally added it up to one big miscalculation. He was two years older, and had never touched her other than the heated kind of petting that had made each of them familiar with every tantalizing curve in the other's body.

She had begged him to make love to her, but he'd held back, even though it almost killed him. He'd believed they were sinning enough with what they were doing. The pastor at the Chimney Rock Baptist Church had already given him the stern eye at church services. Plus, even though he hadn't known much about women in those days, he knew about love. Not the kind he'd had for his mother, but the kind that he would die without; and he had wanted everything to be perfect. Since then, he had second-guessed himself hundreds of times. Maybe, if he had gone ahead with it like he did with Mary, Georgie never would have left.

Joey was looking over Ron's shoulder acknowledging someone with a smile. Evidently Carrie and Georgie had noticed him. Ron was grateful they were to his back.

"Well, are you gonna go over and say hello?" asked Joey.

No, he thought. He needed more time. So he glanced up and let out a tsk.

The meal ended and the two men got up to leave, when a couple of park rangers walked out onto the deck. They came over to talk, causing just enough commotion to attract Georgie and Carrie's attention. Ron tried to steal a glance over their way and his eyes locked onto Georgie's.

There was no getting out of it now. He took a deep breath, grabbed his hat and went over. He said hello to Carrie first, then his eyes consumed Georgie. Her hair was still thick and blond, but she had lost what little baby fat she had ever had, making her chiseled features even stronger.

"I heard about your mom. I hope she's doin' better," he said.

"She's got a ways to go, but she'll be okay," answered Georgie. "I'll tell her you asked."

Georgie's precise enunciation bothered Ron, and it also bothered him that after all these years the only thing warm about their greeting was the sweat oozing from his pores; but mostly it bothered him that she was so self-possessed. That was the way she'd always been with everyone. Except him.

He kept folding and refolding his field hat, glancing out at the river, searching for something to say and wishing she would come up with one of those smart-alecky remarks of hers. Finally, he looked back down at her and forced himself to smile.

"Well, I've got to get along. Be sure to give your mom my regards."

He felt like a fool, but couldn't leave without some word that reached back into the deepest friendship he had ever known.

"It was good seeing you," he told her.

He looked over at Carrie, tossed his head slightly and said, "See ya at the post office."

On his way off the deck, he gave Joey a pat on the back, and then as he walked through the restaurant, threw a wave to the girls at the counter. He barely felt the sidewalk beneath him as he made his way to the Subaru. Ever since he was a kid, he had kept a running tab on all the creatures on God's earth he wanted to know, and he hated to admit it to himself, but Georgie was still at the top of the list.

CHAPTER SIX

C ARRIE HAD ALWAYS WONDERED what would happen if
Ron and Georgie ever faced each other again, and she'd
just had a front row seat for what most folks in town would rate
as a spectacle.

She picked up her drink and held on to the straw with her
pinky curled in the air as she took a sip. She placed the clear plastic glass back down, raised an eyebrow and said in her coquettish
manner, "I thought running into Ron would rattle you a bit more
than it did."

"Why should it?" snapped Georgie. "We're grown-ups."

"Weren't you the one who was going to marry him from the
time we were in the eighth grade?"

Recalling Georgie's quick temper, Carrie thought it unwise
to add that the whole town knew they were fooling around in the
cottages she cleaned.

"You're starting to sound like my mother," said Georgie,
tossing her napkin on the table. "Ever since Ali brought back the
cheerful bit of news that his wife ran out on him, she manages to
bring him up at least once a day."

Carrie always had to think things through carefully before
she spoke. As the postmistress, she probably knew what was going on around town better than anyone else and never wanted to
accidentally reveal anything she could only have picked up in her
position at the post office. It wasn't just a company rule; it was a

47

matter of public trust. So, as much as she wanted to mention the postal box Ron's wife rented, she kept it to herself.

There was only one reason Mary would need to get mail two towns over when the Black Mountain post office already delivered directly to their mailbox on Shumont Mountain. Carrie never laid eyes on her afterward, and she guessed she came in after the post office closed to pick up the letters that Carrie carefully noted always had the same New Mexico return address.

"So, what exactly has your sister told you about Mary?" Carrie asked as she pulled off a sheet of paper towel from a holder on the table and wiped her pudgy fingers.

"I don't listen to any of it."

Noticing an edge on Georgie's voice, Carrie thought it a good idea to let up on trying to get her to talk about Ron. Anyway, it didn't matter if Georgie listened to all the gossip or not. She had to know Mary had nearly driven Ron crazy ever since she wound up pregnant the summer after they graduated. And now there was her drinking problem everyone knew about.

When Ron had done the right thing and married her, it was a letdown for the whole town. He had been the golden boy from the time he came as a strapping thirteen-year-old to live with his Aunt Lucy over her store after his mother died. And when he started up with Georgie, whose parents owned the business across the street, everyone expected he would marry her some day—not the nobody who moved into town in the middle of her senior year and lived with her father in a rundown rental. The old timers still resented Georgie for taking off and spoiling what they felt was the natural order of things.

Carrie moved her empty paper plate to the side and reached for the piece of apple pie she had left on the tray. Georgie had finished her salad and was now fiddling with her fork while she waited for Carrie to tell her what this meeting was all about.

"Well, are you going to tell me or aren't you?" asked Georgie.

"You know I don't like to eat and talk at the same time."

Georgie rolled her eyes, then stared out at the river as they both fell silent.

Scraping up the last of the pie, Carrie could see Georgie was deep in thought and she decided to give it one more try.

"Ron didn't take this little chance meeting as well as you. It kinda surprised me."

The way Georgie's eyes were glistening when she pulled her gaze from the river made Carrie sorry she brought the subject up again, and she decided it was best to let it drop. Besides, she had come on another mission. She wiped her fingers and mouth, then stacked her dishes in an orderly fashion on the tray. It was time to put the intriguing afternoon drama behind her and attend to the business at hand. She twisted a ring on her finger and thought for a moment before she spoke.

"You have to promise you won't tell anyone where this information I'm going to give you is coming from."

Georgie rolled her eyes. "Good God, Carrie. You'd think you were working for the C.I.A."

"No, really. I could get in trouble if they found out I had anything to do with this."

"Okay, I won't breathe a word."

"The reason I phoned you this morning, was that I got a call from the postmistress in Brevard. Her supervisor told her the postal service is getting ready to close hundreds of offices, and Chimney Rock is on the list. Your mom was the only person I could come up with who might be able to stop this from happening."

"This'll rile her all right. She eats, sleeps and breathes this town. I bet she can rattle off the names of every postmaster this place has had since the 1800s."

"That's exactly what I mean," said Carrie as she took a card out of her wallet and pushed it toward Georgie. "I've written down two websites your mom can go to. One tells about the proposal the postmaster general is supporting, and the other is for a website that a community in Iowa has set up. They tell how they fought the closing of their post office last summer during the first round of cutbacks and got it reversed."

Georgie took the card, promised to give it to her mother and the two started back.

By the time Carrie got to the post office, there were two tourists waiting in the outer lobby that was no more than a narrow hall with a wall of postal boxes on one side and a small counter filled with postal forms on the other. The only thing of interest was the bulletin board at one end plastered with the obligatory postal notifications and posters displaying photos of wanted criminals ironically tacked up next to flyers promoting church pancake breakfasts and covered dish dinners. Carrie checked her watch as she unlocked the door at the other end that opened to the post office. No problem. She still had one minute left on her lunch hour.

It didn't take long to sell the visitors from Canada a couple of stamps for the post cards of the chimney they had purchased in one of the stores and engage in some friendly conversation. When they asked her about restaurants, she reached under the counter and came up with brochures from every eatery in town. Carrie took it upon herself to dispense a dose of public relations on behalf of the postal service whenever she could. The grateful visitors looked over the different menus, decided on one and left. The brochures were then carefully refolded and returned to their hiding place under the counter.

The postal service required every resident to pick up their mail from a box the service provided free, so Carrie knew each and every one of the one hundred and twelve permanent residents, personally. It amazed her how, during peak weekends, this small cadre of shopkeepers and park employees could cater to more than ten thousand tourists.

If they closed the post office, Carrie fretted, she'd be transferred to some other town that wouldn't mean one whit to her. Didn't the fat cats in Washington know this little post office was an institution that held the town together? Didn't it mean anything that it was the only place where the collective story of the town could unfold on a daily basis? Whatever happened to ... *Neither snow nor rain nor heat nor gloom of night stays these couriers from the swift completion of their appointed rounds?* She knew this was nothing more than a 2,500 year old quote from a Greek historian about Persian mounted postal carriers that was engraved on New York City's General Post Office, but surely the United States Postal Service had to be more than just a bottom line.

A steady stream of people drifted in for stamps and to mail packages, until eventually the post office became deserted. Carrie used the lull to fill her watering can and go outside and give the marigolds and zinnias a drink.

She took a moment to look out at the activity on the street she loved. A current of people ducked in and out of stores and restaurants like a school of colorful fish investigating a coral reef. The town had a quality that got under people's skin. Maybe it was because they didn't look down into the gorge from a remote highway above, but upward from deep within its bowels. There was nothing in sight beyond the rugged rocky ridges except open sky with a few hawks soaring on the updrafts. No horizon east or west, just a ribbon of road disappearing into the plush green womb of the mountain.

Scores of tourists had told her that when they drove around the curve and spilled into the town, the mountains caressed them like a close friend. But Carrie was aware there were some who lived in the village who felt trapped instead, and she suspected Georgie had been one of them.

All through their growing up, Carrie felt she knew Georgie. That was up until she took off right after graduation without a word to any of her friends. No one had any idea of what she was up to until she phoned her mother two years later to say she was in nursing school, leading Carrie to conclude no one ever really knew Georgie. This summer, her old school chum was going to be in town for at least a couple more months, and Carrie was determined to get to the bottom of it.

She finished watering the flowers and smiled, pleased with herself. All in all it had been a successful afternoon. If Georgie gave those addresses to her mother like she promised, Dinah was sure to cause a ruckus. Then, recalling the scene with Georgie and Ron in the restaurant, she chuckled to herself. If a picture was worth a thousand words, the body language between those two had been worth a million.

CHAPTER SEVEN

THE NEWS ABOUT THE POST OFFICE hit Dinah hard. There'd been a post office in town ever since 1843 when Dr. John Washington Harris canceled the mail by hand on the bar of his tavern on the old Hickory Nut Gap Road. In fact, the whole history of Chimney Rock could be traced with the trail of postal operations that had hopscotched up and down Main Street for the past one hundred and seventy years, landing everywhere from the Esmeralda Inn's reception desk to the counter next to the two slot machines at Dalton's sandwich shop.

Dinah sat in her chair fingering the card Georgie had given her. She had always pictured the village as a heroic woman who had fought off one onslaught after another with a resiliency that kept saving her from death. Now it was eating away at her that the town was facing this new threat.

Other little mountain towns had slowly dried up and died, but somehow this one had survived. Mostly because it had two things going for it—the first being the incredible beauty of the gorge. Just like a beautiful woman, it was loved and remembered for that fortunate accident of nature alone. Then, how many towns sat at the foot of one of the Southeast's biggest wonders that dumped thousands of visitors in their lap?

To Dinah's recollection, the town had been fighting for its life as a community on and off since its heyday in the 1920s. Like Hot Springs, Runion, Stackhouse, Marshall and dozens of other western North Carolina towns, Chimney Rock never quite recovered from the crash of 1929. Too many things happened all at once—but mostly it was the automobile that started altering the rhythm of life in the '40s.

It was paradoxical, since the automobile was the very thing that brought about all the prosperity in the first place. The phenomenon of nearly every family owning a car, made a visit to Chimney Rock more accessible, but it also made it easier for the people who lived there to seek out better paying jobs elsewhere and do their shopping out of town where there were bigger stores with larger selections and lower prices.

Dinah had watched with dismay as Chimney Rock reached the tipping point, and in twenty years, went from a thriving family-based community with three gas stations, a movie theater, bank, bowling alley, grocery, hardware store, and bus station with service three times a day in both directions, to nothing but a couple dozen souvenir shops and a handful of motels and eateries. The few permanent residents left in town were mainly store owners who lived above their establishments.

By the time the '60s rolled around, Chimney Rock had gone from a charming village in which to live and work, to solely a tourist destination with a smattering of summer cottages. But even in that state, Dinah was grateful the town was still alive. This hardscrabble place had always counted on the true grit of a cadre of folks determined to keep the town going, and she thought of herself as a depository of that history.

She figured she was born for the task. Her two sisters who grew up wanting to be nurses had married and moved away, but she knew from as far back as she could remember, that her destiny was to stay in this place and gather and harbor its story. She was a bridge between the past and the abyss that lay ahead.

Dinah sat stewing about the post office. She'd seen enough consequences of hard-boiled politics to know it would probably go the way of the local school that was no longer nearby. She studied the websites Carrie had given her and was relieved to see the town could still have a post office operating from one of the stores as in years before. The afternoon progressed with her coming to the conclusion that this was probably the way it would end. However, she wasn't going to let it happen without kicking up some kind of a fuss. Those Washington bureaucrats weren't going to get away with this without even hearing a whimper out of them.

She copied the petition from the Iowa website and used it as a guide. She wrote that the petition was not only speaking for the current residents of the town, but for all the loyal postmasters, long since gone, who believed the hometown post office was a sacred institution and who faithfully saw to it that the United States' mail was expediently and dutifully processed and delivered. She typed in their names: Dr. Harris, Mary Logan, Lillian Logan, Sam Hunsinger, Col. Thomas Turner, Vernal Freeman, Debbie Meliski, the Washburns, J.J. Meliski, D.C. Keller—every last one of them. At the very least, this slate of loyal federal workers spanning more than a century would make somebody in Washington ashamed of themselves.

Dinah shouted for Ali, and when she peeked into the room, demanded, "Go downstairs and send your sister up here. She's got to go around town and get this petition signed."

"COME ON, MOM, I want you outside getting some fresh air," said Georgie as she brought her the walker.

"How many signatures have you gotten so far?" asked Dinah as she grabbed the bar and started to lift herself.

"I'm not starting till tomorrow. I'll get to everybody in the morning before traffic picks up." What she really meant was she planned to get there while they were too busy opening their stores to want to stand around asking questions.

Ali and the boys were already on the back deck getting the cookout started, and a hint of smoke from the grill had drifted in through the screen door. When Georgie helped her mother up from her chair she could see the back of her wrinkled housedress had crept up enough to expose the folds of flesh that overlapped the crease behind her knees.

"Wait, Mom. Let's put on a fresh dress."

Georgie reached for one off the stack on the dresser.

"No. That's too old fashioned," said Dinah. "Hand me the one hanging in my closet."

"Mother, does it really matter? There's no one out there but family."

"You never know, gal. George Clooney could show up."

"Sure, Mom." Georgie got the dress and helped her get it on.

"That's not out of the question, gal. My mother never forgot the day Robert Mitchum walked into Ford's sandwich shop when they were filming *Thunder Road* here in '58."

Finished dressing, Dinah slipped her phone into her pocket, grabbed hold of her walker and started down the hall. She stopped and gave Georgie a wistful smile.

"I was only an infant back then, but my Mom always talked about what a tall, handsome man he was. She said he was right mannerly too, and went out of his way to be friendly and polite to Shirley Ford when he paid for the aspirin."

When they reached the kitchen, Isaac was just coming in.

"Hi, Grandma. We got everything ready for you."

He bowed and gallantly swished his hand past the screen door he was holding open.

A tall wooden fence at the edge of the deck blocked the view of the alley that ran behind the stores on Main Street. Called Terrace Drive, it climbed up and then traversed the side of the mountain dotted with dozens of summer cabins and a few permanent residences. Dinah struggled to make her way to a cushioned armchair that Ali and the boys had brought out. Isaac pushed an ottoman under her feet while Georgie poured her a glass of her favorite wine.

It was still light out, but the deck was mostly in the shadows of their building as the sun began its descent behind Chimney Rock Mountain. A mockingbird landed on a small tree to catch the last of the dappled light on the other side of the fence, and two chirping cardinals flitted around the treetops looming beyond their neighbor's wall. The scent of the Carolina jasmine blooming nearby mingled with the aroma of the sizzling steaks.

Clinking of dishes sounded as the boys helped Georgie set the table. They heard the sound of a car roll by the alley and stop. Then the slamming of a door.

"I wonder who that is," said Dinah.

"Oh, probably George Clooney," said Georgie, who was filling up a plate for her mother.

When they heard their neighbor's gate squeak open, Georgie shrugged her shoulders and made a disappointed face.

"Go on and laugh," said Dinah, "But Chimney Rock's not finished as a movie location just yet."

Georgie brought over a tray and placed it in her mother's lap.

"There. Start on your salad," she said.

"Boy, did Ali have a crush on that Patrick Swayze," chided Dinah as she speared a cucumber slice like she wanted to kill it.

Ali was standing next to the table with a platter of steaks.

"Geez, Mom, I was only five when they were filming *Dirty Dancing*. You're the one who's seen it a thousand times."

"Your dad thought they were crazy when they hired a bunch of men from town to spray-paint all the fall leaves green. Patrick and that Jennifer Grey almost froze to death in that lake, pretending it was summer in the middle of November."

"Grandma, is it true what Isaac said? Were you really in the *Last of the Mohicans?*" asked Michael.

"Yep. So was Georgie, 'cept they had to slap on a lot of makeup and put a wig on her. We were supposed to be Indians in a village they set up right on that mountain behind us."

"Your Aunt Georgie was only eleven, but did she have a crush on Daniel Day-Lewis," said Ali.

Everyone's eyes landed on Georgie.

"Curr...rush?" Georgie stretched the word into two extended syllables while looking at the boys. "I was out-and-out in *looove* with that *haaandsome* dog."

The boys laughed, obviously enjoying her playfulness.

"Were you, Aunt Georgie?" asked Isaac, obviously wanting the mood to last.

Georgie raised an eyebrow, twirled her fork in the air and feigned a dreamy look.

"The very next day after that shoot, there I was... innocently walkin' down Main Street..." She eyed the boys. "... without my makeup and wig, of course."

Isaac laughed.

"I was just mindin' my own business, when all of a sudden he bumped into me." She winked at Michael. "He was wearing a tee shirt with a big Mickey Mouse on it."

Michael clapped his hands and grinned.

"He looked me square in the eye for a long moment... and he was so handsome... I just wanted to hug him." She flicked her hand, "But then he went and spoiled it all by apologizing all over the place. I watched as he walked away, and nearly died when he turned and looked back at me and smiled."

"That was the year Ron came to live with his Aunt Lucy. Wasn't it?" queried Dinah.

The mention of Ron dampened Georgie's spirits. She reached across the table for the pitcher of iced tea as if she hadn't heard the question. The boys felt the change in her mood and slumped back in their chairs and continued eating.

Suddenly two phones rang, one in her mother's pocket and one on the kitchen counter.

"I'll get it," said Dinah. "Hello."

She listened a moment, then in great excitement started waving wildly to Georgie.

"Thank you for asking, Ron. I'm getting better every day with the way Georgie is nursing me along."

Georgie buried her face in her hands.

"Yes. She's right here. Ever since we heard about Mary goin' out west, we've all been waitin' for you to call."

Georgie's mouth fell open and she stared ahead in disbelief.

"In fact, Ron, we were all just talkin' about you."

Georgie threw her head back and let out a pained groan.

"Here, I'll let you speak to her." Dinah buried the phone in her bosom. "Georgie! Quick! Get on the phone in the kitchen."

Her tone sweetened. "She'll be right with you, son."

Georgie rose, glared at her mother through narrowed eyes and threw a threatening enough glance at Ali to make her stop laughing. Georgie stomped off the deck and closed the kitchen door. Instead of picking up the phone, she stood there thumping her forehead against the wall until she heard her mother call out.

"Are you getting that, darling? Ron's waiting."

She gritted her teeth. God only knew what her mother was telling him. He had to be amused at the warm reception his call was getting. And she was sure he was aware of how embarrassed she was.

She took a deep breath and switched on the phone.

"Ron, why in the hell are you calling?"

There was silence on the other end. She pictured him leaning back in a chair with his feet up, waiting for her to cool down, and it made her even angrier.

"Did you hear me, Ron?"

"I just wanted to ask you if you wanted to go on a hike."

A remote voice echoed from the phone.

"She'll be delighted to go."

"Just a moment, Ron. I'll be right with you," said Georgie.

She put the phone on mute, stomped back out onto the deck and threw open her outstretched hand.

"Give it to me, Mom."

Dinah quickly shoved the phone in her pocket, and when Georgie reached for it, she struggled to push her aside until it was finally wrestled away. Georgie took a moment to catch her breath, then turned the phone off.

"Mother, I mean this. You are not to say another word. I'm going back in the kitchen and I'm going to deal with this myself." She bent down and looked Dinah in the eye. "I mean this, Mother. Do you understand?"

Dinah threw up her hands, shrugged her shoulders and contorted her face into an exaggerated look of innocence, making the boys giggle. Georgie gave her a meaningful smirk, then took a moment to glare at the boys.

Back in the solitude of the kitchen, she found it hard to believe her mother could get so out of hand so quickly. She took several deep breaths and switched on her phone.

"Thank you, Ron. But I'm only going to be in town for a few more months, so there's no point in our seeing each other."

"Whoa, girl. I'm just asking if you want to go on a hike is all.

One of my clients thinks he's got a champion magnolia tree on his property and wants me to measure and verify it. It's located in a wilderness track, and he's only seen it from the air. I remember how much you liked to go hiking with a compass and finding your way out, and thought you might like to come along."

"Ron, if you're looking for an explanation why I took off the way I did, there isn't one."

"You don't have to explain anything to me, Georgie."

The sincerity of his tone touched her. Wasn't that just like Ron, she thought. Just a nice, decent guy who deserved better than she had given. A hike would give her plenty of time to clear the air. At least this would be one mess she had made that she could clean up.

"All right. When and what time."

"How about Monday?"

"Monday won't work. We're going to be too busy with the Memorial weekend crowd. Wednesday's better."

"Okay, I'll pick you up at six."

"I'll pack a lunch. I'm staying in our rental on Southside. You know, the one that's up on the cliff."

Georgie closed her eyes and winced, remembering the last time she was there with Ron.

CHAPTER EIGHT

THE FRIDAY of Memorial Day weekend, there was more bustle than usual on Main Street. A Boar's Head truck was unloading in front of the Riverwatch Bar and Grill. The driver, dressed in shorts, tee shirt and laced-up work boots, was at the rear stacking a handcart with cartons of hot dogs and meats for the deli. A dog was barking somewhere in the distance and the drone of Bob Mendenhall's blower hummed as he chased the debris from the sidewalk around Pam's Place, his wife's shop.

Suicide, the town's stray dog, was at the entrance to the Riverwalk chewing on some morsel he'd pilfered from someone's garbage. The little terrier had been around for nearly ten years, and in all that time, no one had been able to get near him. He slept in a lean-to behind a house on Terrace Drive and the owners put food out for him; but even they couldn't touch him.

The mangy cur had earned his name from his frequent walks down the middle of Main Street. The fact that he had never been run over, made the town tacitly beholden to the hundreds of kindly drivers who had patiently waited for him to cross in front of them as he went about his endless search for the master who had abandoned him.

Georgie came out of the store and stepped onto the street. She was surprised to see such a buzz of activity so early in the morning. The village seemed alive with expectation as she hurried with the petition to Laura's House before the Gurleys took off for Asheville with their cakes.

THE MORNING ROLLED ON in the small village, and by noon, a procession of pick-ups, SUVs and cars flowed through it like a string of colorful beads. Mostly folks getting a jump on the holiday weekend. Already, a lot of the parking spaces in front of the stores were filling up and vehicles were starting to trickle into the town lot.

The muffled resonance of six motorcycles became louder as they rolled down Main Street in a "V" formation. Decked out in black leather, with colorful do-rags wrapped around their heads, the riders appeared determined to get to their day's destination. A pick-up with an elderly couple in front and two Dobermans in the bed trailed behind them. The dogs gripped the side with their claws, straining from their chains at everyone they passed.

The Chevy Silverado pick-up swung around the curve with Roger Cummings and his wife, Gail, in the front and their ten-year-old twin boys in the back seat.

"Wow!" said Teddy, one of the twins. "This place looks like fun."

"It sure does," agreed the other.

"You boys haven't seen nothin' yet. Wait till you get a load of the river," said Roger, pride written on his face.

He'd worked nights at a second job for over a year for the money to buy the camper. It wasn't brand spanking new, but plenty nice enough for him to take his family to the places his father had taken him.

He glanced over at his wife. "You okay, Babe?"

Gail wasn't, but she nodded anyway. She hated that their campsite was going to be next to the river, but she was determined to appear relaxed. She'd heard about this place since she was a kid and there was something about it that intrigued her. Yet, she knew she was taking a risk in coming.

Bobby, the other twin, clutched his mother's shoulders.

"We're gonna have a great time, Mom. You wait and see. You're gonna like this a lot better than the ocean."

"I'm sure I will, honey," she said as she patted his hand.

"Wow! Look at that," said Teddy, pointing to the monolith that stuck out from the mountain like a chimney.

"Are we goin' up *there*, Dad?"

"We sure are, son. First thing in the morning. Grandpa took me and your Aunt Jeannie up there when we were just about your age."

They passed through town, and a mile out, on the curvy road chiseled out of the mountain at the edge of the river, they spotted a bridge and the sign for the Hickory Nut Campground.

"This is it, guys!" shouted Roger, almost as excited as the two boys.

He drove across the bridge and pulled up to a chalet style A-frame with an "Office" sign in front.

"You guys wait here. I'll be right out."

"Aw, Dad. Can't we come?"

Roger opened his door, slid his hefty frame from the seat with a grunt and started toward the office. Then he tossed his head, went back and let the boys pour out, whooping and holler-ing. A boxer greeted them at the door of the office and sniffed the boys as they passed.

The place was stuffed with shelves full of canned goods, candy and all the things that forty years in the business had taught the owner a camper might have forgotten to bring— suntan lotion, fishing lures, band aids, lantern oil. The place be-ing so close to the river and closed all winter caused it to have a particular musty scent that lingered in the air and added to the mysterious otherworldliness of the leafy gorge.

A trim woman in her late fifties clad in tee shirt and shorts emerged from an adjacent room that appeared to be living quar-ters. Roger signed in and asked to have their lot switched, while the boys looked around the store. The wide disparity of items squeezed together on the maze of shelves and tacked onto every available bit of wall space inspired awe in them.

The boys ran out after their father as he headed back to the truck.

"Mom. You gotta see that place! They've got everything,"

said Teddy as he scrambled in.

Gail didn't hear. She had put the window down while they were in the office, and the sound of the river was all she was listening to.

Roger reached over and patted her leg. "I got them to switch our lot to the mountain side."

Gail responded with a grateful smile.

It didn't take long to set up their fifth wheel camper; and as soon as it was leveled, Gail went inside to check it out. She was reluctant to leave the boys, since she'd promised herself she wouldn't let them out of her sight for one moment. Other than a few things tossed around, she found everything in order.

The kitchen light came on, signaling Roger had hooked up the electricity. She tried the faucet, but it just sputtered. Roger would have to get that going while she started lunch. Sandwiches would be easiest to make. She opened the door and stuck out her head to call the boys in, but no one was around. That's odd, she thought. She got out and went to the other side of the camper. Roger was fiddling with the water hookup.

"Where are the boys?" she asked.

"Aw... they're probably down by the river."

She took long, stoic steps across the roadway, drawn by the savage sound of a raging torrent that was jumping and dashing against enormous rocks. The air was so thick with vapor she could smell the water. Her eyes desperately scanned the river, but there were no boys. The tumbling roar twisted its way into her brain. This was the very sound that had tormented her in her dark dreams, and she felt herself being pulled into the mysterious world of terror.

But she won't tell anyone about the dreams, for no one will believe she could live without breath. She will keep the secret of how the world turns cold every time she hears the sound of water pounding on rocks or crashing on shore. She won't let anyone know she has died.

Moments later, Roger was crouching down and holding her in his arms. He looked down at the knee she had scraped when she fell on the jagged rocks and ran his hand lovingly down the side of her face.

"*Awww,* honey, I never should have let you talk me into bringin' ya here."

She looked up. "... the boys..."

"They're fine. I saw 'em. They're on their way back from the store." He looked in her eyes. "Baby, let's pack up and go find another place. We can find something in the Smokies that isn't close to water."

She grabbed his arm. "No! I can do this. I want to do this."

Suddenly Teddy and Bobby came running, clutching plastic tomahawks in their fists.

"Gee, Mom. What happened?"

The boys studied the scene and gave each other a look. They knew what had happened. And as usual, Bobby did the talking, for in their earliest youth, the twins had made a secret pact that he would be their spokesman.

"We're sorry, Mom. We thought it would be okay to go to the store. We promise we won't go anywhere again without tellin' ya."

The intensity in Bobby's eyes told Gail his heart would break if this vacation turned out like the last. She sat up and gave him a big smile.

"I know you will... both of you. I just wanted to take a look at the river and I slipped on a rock." She started to unlace a shoe. "It's hot and I intend to go wading."

The boys laughed the kind of forced laugh that was more relief than mirth.

"Not here, Mom. The lady in the store said there's a great place up the road. She says it's an eddy and the shore is nice and sandy."

"That's right, Honey. Let's put something on that knee and get the boys some lunch. Then we can go over to the swimming hole."

Teddy tugged on his father's shirt. "Dad, can we go into town first?"

Bobby pulled his wallet out of his pocket. "Yeah. We got the twenty dollars Grandma gave us."

"And it's burning a hole in your pocket," Roger teased as he ruffled both of the boys' hair.

"All right, but let's get some lunch, first. Okay?"

Back at the campsite, the boys settled for a peanut butter and jelly sandwich and needed no urging to finish their milk. The camper was locked up, then they all jumped into the pick-up and headed to town.

THE GLASS-PANED DOOR to Bubba O'Leary's General Store swung open, allowing the hinges to complain loudly. The rattling of small doodads strung across the glass harmonized with the banjo music coming from within. Georgie entered, and the hinges screeched again as the door slammed shut with a muffled bang. A barrel with a checkerboard sitting on top was next to the door. Two empty stools invited people to play. Georgie tried to see if Peter or Anne O'Leary were around, but the labyrinth of rustic shelving, loaded with everything from tee shirts to cast iron cookware, blocked her view.

The bare, worn floorboards of the old building creaked as two ladies worked their way along a wall of shelves packed with kitchen items that were a throwback to the '30s—oil lanterns, glass straw holders, tin cookie cutters, pie tins. They were stacked on shelves going halfway up the sixteen-foot-tall narrow tongue and groove slat walls. Built in 1929 as a movie house, the cavernous store was at least twenty-five feet wide and a good eighty feet long. Other than the slight slant to the floor, all traces of the theater were gone except for a "King Kong" poster, a relic from the last movie ever shown there.

Georgie made her way past an old bin with colorful jelly beans pressed against the glass panes, instead of the seeds it had once held. Large covered jars of red and black licorice and dark brown coffee beans sat on top. Ahead, a family was stacking their finds on the counter, and Peter was ringing them up on the cash register. Georgie could see the store was full of customers. Good, the O'Learys would be too busy to want to chat.

She had hardly known anyone she talked to all that morning, and it was eerie having to introduce herself to the young girls working in the stores and restaurants. They had no idea that she had practically grown up running in and out of every establishment on the street. It left her with a strange sensation, almost as if she were like Persephone, temporarily returning from the dead.

Peter and Anne would be different. Bubba O'Leary's General Store had opened in town when she was still in high school. Peter had been the manager of the park when he and Anne were married and the two of them decided to open a store on Main Street. The general store was followed two years later by Bubba O'Leary's Outfitters. In between the two store launches, the first of the three O'Leary kids made her appearance; and it wasn't long afterward that Georgie started babysitting her.

Georgie remembered how the new establishments and growing family sent a surge of hopefulness through the town. A young couple had moved in and invested capital, instead of leaving and taking their kids and money with them, as so many had done.

Georgie sauntered over to an old Coca-Cola cooler and lifted the lid. She'd get her mother a couple of Nehis while she was there. She picked up a paper bag from the stack and started putting in the old-fashioned things she knew would delight her—a Moon Pie, some Turkish taffy, a box of Smith Brothers cough drops.

Then she went over to an old circulating nail bin now used for candy, got another bag and grabbed a handful of Mary Janes and some Bit-O-Honeys. She stopped for a moment. What was she thinking? This wasn't going to do her mother's diabetes any good. Georgie tossed the candies back in the bin and returned the other items. Then she pictured her mother sitting alone in her room in her lounge chair searching her deeds for mention of the wolf den like she actually believed she was going to find it, and decided to pick up some sugar-free candy for her at Willow Creek instead.

She got in line at the counter with the Nehis, and after Peter rang her up, he signed the petition after only a glance. No doubt he'd already heard that she'd be coming around with it. When she found Anne waiting on someone, she was reminded that she needed a pair of zip-off pants for the hike with Ron. But she couldn't do it now. Even though Debbie was working at their store, she needed to get back to check on her mother's wound.

She got Anne's signature between customers, rushed back across the street and ran up the outside staircase to the apartment. Ali was at the sink in the kitchen cutting up vegetables.

"Where are the boys?" Georgie asked.

Georgie sensed something was wrong the way Ali kept cutting. Seeping into her mind was the possibility that Ali had gotten bad news about her husband who only had three months left on his hitch in Afghanistan. Georgie put her things on the counter, then went over and put a hand on Ali's shoulder.

"What is it, Sis?"

"We got a problem with Mom," said Ali as she kept chopping the carrots.

"What kind of a problem?"

Ali stopped and faced Georgie. It was apparent she'd been crying.

"I didn't mean to do it. I just wasn't thinking."

"What didn't you mean to do?"

Ali started back on the carrots and kept cutting, zombie-like.

"Debbie phoned that she needed some change, so I took it down to her. While I was at it, I checked the back cash register for singles and saw there were plenty. Well, you know Debbie. When she's upset, she finds some other excuse to get you engaged."

Georgie's brow wrinkled, fearful of where this was leading.

"It took me a while, but I finally got it out of her." Ali stopped chopping and faced Georgie. "This couple came in with two boys. Debbie said they were twins. Well, anyway, they bought a bunch of toys, and after they left, the woman came back in the store alone. She didn't buy anything. She just walked around in a daze until her husband finally came and got her. Debbie said it creeped her out."

Georgie slammed her fist on the counter.

"And you had to come upstairs and tell Mom."

"I didn't mean to," Ali said cowering. "She had asked me to find out how much Debbie had cashed in for the day, and when I went in to tell her, it just spilled out."

Georgie took a long breath and slowly let it out, sorry she had lost her temper.

"So, how bad is it this time?"

"The usual. She wants to call the police. She wanted me to go out and find the lady. I calmed her down by telling her I'd send the boys out to find you and have you track her down."

Ali dissolved in tears, then got hold of herself. "I hope this doesn't balloon out of control. I can't handle it. I can't handle the boys seeing it. That's why I sent them out." She let out a cynical little laugh. "I gave them some money and told them to get an ice cream cone. Do you believe that? Right before dinner, I sent them out to get ice cream."

She closed her eyes and threw her head back. "I never should have moved back here with the boys. Cal was the one who thought it was a good idea while he was in Afghanistan. It's my fault. I should have told him how bad Mom gets." She bit her lip to suppress another bout of crying. "I hate it. It's so unfair the way she carries on about Shelby. You'd think she doesn't have any other children. Doesn't she know what this does to us? Oh, how I wish Dad was here."

Georgie felt anger rising. How many times when they were kids had she held her sister in her arms in the darkness of their room and comforted her after one of her mother's episodes? No, she wasn't going to let her mother get away with doing this to another generation.

"Where's your purse?" asked Georgie.

Ali looked confused.

"Go get it and then go out and find the boys. Take them out for something to eat, then take them to my place for the night. I'll stay here with her."

Ali raced into her bedroom and came out a few minutes later. She reached for the doorknob and then looked back.

"I've got my cell phone. Call me if you need me."

Georgie went over and locked the door behind her while her mind spun. She had some lorazepam to give her mother if things got out of hand. Hopefully, it wouldn't come to that. She went to the cupboard, took out a glass, then found the bottle of her father's scotch. She noticed her hand was shaking as she poured herself a good shot's worth. She threw it back, then grabbed the petition and started down the hall.

She opened the door and breezed into the room.

"I got everybody on the street to sign it."

She ignored the tortured look on her mother's face and tossed the petition on the table next to her.

"Ali's gonna have to catch the folks who live in town Tuesday morning at the post office when they come to pick up their mail and then run up to The Hickory Nut."

"The woman. Did you find her?"

"Of course, Mom. How many folks are walking around town with twin boys?"

She took her mother's laptop from the rollaway table and put it on the bed, then she went over to the drawer where she kept her medical supplies and took out a wound kit.

"Well, damn it?!"

Georgie believed lying was one of the most despicable things anyone could do; yet, she had been an expert at it since she was a child of six.

"Mom, it's not Shelby. The woman said she was forty."

Flooding back at Georgie were all the grim times as she was growing up that she was forced to find out the age of girls with blonde hair who had happened into the store. She was amazed at all the ways she had devised to start a conversation with a complete stranger, and ashamed of all the times she had lied to her mother when one was the right age.

"How do you know she's not lying?"

"Mom, people subtract years from their age. They don't add them. Anyway, she had brown eyes."

She left the room to wash her hands, and when she came back, her heart sank at the sight of the empty stare she'd seen on her mother's face a hundred times before. She opened the kit, put on the sterile gloves and dressed the wound in silence while her mother sat clutching Shelby's picture. Another lie, another bullet dodged. She'd call Ali and tell her to bring the boys back.

CHAPTER NINE

GEORGIE COULD TELL it was going to be a hot, humid day the way there wasn't a single leaf stirring at sunrise. One could usually count on *some* kind of breeze that early, except on the real scorchers. Standing on the porch that her dad had screened in mostly so no one would fall off, Georgie looked down on Southside Drive and could see Route 74 across the river. Lights glowed from the sparse stream of cars and pick-ups already carrying mountain folks to their jobs in Asheville and Hendersonville twenty-five miles away.

Perfume from the huge wisteria vine twisting around the giant poplar below lingered in the air. She wondered what had possessed someone to build this cabin on a narrow ledge on the side of the mountain that took three flights of stairs to reach.

Right after her parents bought the place, Ali had found a black-and-white snapshot of a handsome mustached man. It must have been taken right after the cabin was built in the early 1900s. The man's sleeves were rolled up and suspenders held up his pants as he leaned on an axe as if it were a cane. Three flights of steps zigzagged behind him. She remembered lying in bed with Ali and staring at his broad, confident grin, and the both of them agreeing he had to have been a romantic.

She was running the brush through her hair when a voice on NPR drifted out from the cabin. Another senator was demanding another investigation. It had to be the five-thirty news. She twisted the rubber band tight around her ponytail and noticed the clouds were glowing pink from the sun that was still below the horizon. It gave her a surge of expectation. She had suppressed the anticipation of the trek all weekend, but now she let herself feed on the excitement. Oh, how she loved hiking the wilderness.

She rushed back in and put on the pair of zip-off slacks she'd picked up at Bubba's, then sat on the bed and put on her hiking boots. She'd gone on dozens of treks with her friends over the past year, but this one would be special. Those other hikes had been on established trails. She slipped into a sports bra and rifled through her dresser till she found her olive drab long-sleeved hiking shirt. Ron wouldn't want her to impact the environment with color even though they were going to be out in the middle of nowhere.

She finished stuffing her backpack and snapped off the radio. Just then, she heard a vehicle pull in the lot and she grabbed her gear and ran down the stairs, suddenly feeling like a kid again. Ron grinned at her from his truck, looking damn proud of himself for having come up with the one temptation she couldn't resist. She opened the door, swung up onto the seat and wedged the backpack under the dash.

"Well, where are we goin'?" she asked as she rolled down her window.

"Macon County."

"Do you think this old clunker will make it that far?" she laughed.

"Now, don't you go hurtin' Old Red's feelings. Once we start up that old loggin' road, you're gonna be plenty happy we got her."

She patted the dashboard and said, "Sorry, old girl," then relaxed against the door with her elbow thrust out the window like old times.

"Okay. What are we lookin' for?"

"A big ole Fraser magnolia. It's in a remote cove. Evidently a holdout that's escaped logging."

The truck rolled over the bridge and turned west down Main Street.

"Right now, the state champion Fraser magnolia is just two counties over in Haywood."

"How big is that one?"

"A hundred and five feet tall and one hundred and one inches around."

"Stop! Pull in here," she yelled as she pointed to the parking area in front of Medina's Café on the edge of downtown.

"Georgie, if we take time to eat, we'll ..."

Before he could finish, she had opened the door and slid out.

"I'll be right back."

She started toward the cafe, then quickly turned back.

"You still take your coffee black, no sugar?" His resigned nod made her laugh.

A few minutes later she emerged with a cardboard carton and climbed in. She took out a Styrofoam box and handed it to him, but wouldn't let go.

"Are ya gonna give it to me or not?"

"Do you remember what you use to say every time I asked you for your half of the money for the buns at Christy's Cinnamon Shop?"

He pulled the box free and was soon eating the warm bun smeared with cream cheese icing, while she settled the coffees in the cup holders.

They sat enjoying the treat for a few minutes, and then he started the truck and swung back on the road. A few miles up in Bat Cave, Route 64 split from 74 and headed south.

"Well, *do you* remember what you used to tell me?" Georgie asked as she licked her fingers.

He glanced over at her. "Give me a break. I was only a kid."

"Boy, I can't believe you made me pay for the buns just because we were using your aunt's car. Heck, you even squeezed half the gas money out of me."

"Squeezed is right! I'd never seen anyone so preoccupied with money in my whole life."

"Don't knock it. That li'l ole preoccupation, along with a good deal of help from the State of North Carolina, got me through nursing school."

He drove along Route 64 until it hit I-26 in Hendersonville, then headed toward I-40.

"I'm looking forward to this trek," she said as she collected everything from their little breakfast. "I really needed to get outta there... for a day anyway."

She didn't like the way that remark sounded and decided to change the subject.

"By the way, what's the deal with champion trees?"

"Well... the National Register of Big Trees lists the largest recorded living specimens of each tree variety found in the continental United States. They're called National Champion Trees. Then there's the North Carolina Champion Trees. That's the title we're goin' for first." He looked over at her. "But your job is gonna be jotting down all the coordinates of the trek, so the tree can be located again... and we can find our way outta there."

"Are you tellin' me you're the only one who's gonna do all the compass readings?"

"Don't worry, Georgie," he said laughing. "You'll get your chance on the trek out."

There was something about the way he said her name and his easy laugh that told her everything was going to be all right— that it didn't matter anymore, that the day after he proudly announced he had landed the job as the park naturalist and asked her to marry him, she took off without a goodbye.

She studied the face that had toughened since then. The jaw line was leaner and harder and his deeply tanned, lank muscular body testified to a harsh life spent challenging the mountains. It struck her, that even though they hadn't seen each other for all these years, it was as natural to be sitting next to him as if it were only yesterday that they'd been inseparable.

By the time the truck was sailing west on I-40, the direction of the conversation had drifted to the inevitable telling of their life stories. He spoke mostly about his career, giving her the impression that he led a lonely life and was more married to the wilderness than to Mary.

It was easy to see that all the things Ali had told her about him being crazy about his daughter were true. Yet, there was something about the way he wrinkled his brow when he talked about her, that gave the impression he was concerned about her. It touched her that the cause of his having to marry Mary had turned out to be the most cherished part of his existence. Almost like a reward for doing the right thing.

"My little Jennifer is quite an artist when you consider she's only eleven. Last summer I took her to Costa Rica on a project I was doing for the Department of the Interior and you wouldn't believe the drawings she did of the birds that hung around our cabana."

"What did you do with her during the day?"

"Took her right along with me. Heck, the little darlin' even put my field notes on my laptop for me."

Hearing him talk so lovingly about his only child suddenly made her jealous of Mary. If she hadn't run off after graduating, they'd now be comfortable married folk with their little girl chatting away in the back seat—not her sitting home alone every night wondering if she'd ever be a mother. Stop it! she screamed in her head. People like her didn't have choices.

As far as she was concerned, there were three kinds of souls—those who go through life experiencing all the normal ups and downs, those who are permanently marred by some horrific event that strikes from out of nowhere, and those who cause the horrific events.

As a certified wound nurse, she ran across a lot of unfortunate folks who experienced a tragedy like losing an arm or a leg or a loved one, yet somehow managed to get on with their lives. They added up the loss as a major bump in the road they just had to struggle past. Others spent the rest of their lives mired in resentment and self-pity, using the tragedy to feed an already existing inner wound.

Then she thought about the third kind: the people who cause the horrific events. Even though her psychiatrist, Dr. Benjamin Harold, who she dutifully visited once a month, disagreed with her, Georgie believed they spent the rest of their lives unable to forgive themselves.

The truck had left I-40 and had been sailing along Route 23

for a half hour, when Ron suddenly pulled off and onto a dirt road, jolting her out of her thoughts. She grabbed the armrest and braced a hand against the dashboard as the truck jostled along an old logging road overgrown with brush. The truck hit a deep rut, bouncing her so high that her head hit the roof. The truck kept climbing and eventually started twisting around an outcrop of granite. She stuck her head out the window and saw the front tire was on the very edge of the narrow ledge with nothing but treetops below.

"Shouldn't we get out and walk," she hollered over the noise of the engine.

"Don't worry. I've driven this road a dozen times."

"You call this a road!"

He laughed. "You ain't goin' soft on me, are ya?"

A steep, heavily forested cove suddenly appeared below.

"Good God! You're not driving down there, are you?" she cried out as the truck started its dissent.

She quickly tightened her seatbelt, then braced both hands on the dash and gritted her teeth. The truck slowly made its way over a series of rocks, swaying rhythmically from side to side in a bizarre dance. At the bottom, the truck was swallowed by thick undergrowth. Branches brushed against the sides and scraped across the roof. Now in the bowels of a dark hemlock grove, the logging road became more apparent. Up ahead, a wide, fast-moving stream sparkled in the dappled light as it rolled across immense slabs of flat rock. A steep incline rose on the other side.

"I've got to speed up if we're gonna make it up there," he shouted as he swung into a lower gear and stepped on the gas.

She closed her eyes and braced as they splashed through the water and started the climb. He cranked the truck into its lowest gear, unfazed by the adventurous ride, obviously used to driving through rough terrain as a matter of course.

Once they conquered the hump, they bounced along the contour of the mountain for a while until finally stopping next to a huge rock outcrop. She took a deep breath and slowly let it out before she let go of her grip on the dash.

"Okay, girl. This is where the game begins," he said as he

reached for a rolled up U.S. Geological map.

"*Aww...* You mean this joy ride is over?"

He laughed. "I see you're still full of your smart remarks."

She made a face.

"Now, don't you be complainin' none. Old Red just knocked a mile off this little jaunt of ours."

He spread the map open and pointed to an "X."

"See this place that looks like a cove? This is where the tree's been spotted by two different people. One from a plane and the other from a helicopter. I talked with both of these guys, and there're pretty sure of what they saw."

He pointed to another place on the map.

"This is where we are right now. I made a study of this preserve five years ago and I remember there was a waterfall in that cove. I'm surprised I missed the magnolia. I especially look out for that kind of thing."

He reached in his pocket and pulled out a notebook that had a pen attached to it with a string.

"Here, this is for you."

She took it, thinking this was no game for him. This was his unique way of life and she was being honored with the privilege of being allowed to share in it. She watched him study the map and recognized the boy she used to know. There was the same deliberateness, the same quiet force, except now his body was that of a man. He studied the map for a moment, then the terrain ahead as if he were memorizing everything.

"I've marked the old logging trail in pencil. It should bring us close to the tree. I've estimated this baby is somewhere around a three-mile hike from here. I average 5.6 ft. per pace. That amounts to about 18 paces per 100 ft. Normal walking is 2 miles per hour; fast walking on level ground can be 3 miles per hour. With those long legs of yours, you should have no trouble keeping up with me. We should be able to do two miles an hour, so let's figure two hours in and two hours out at the most and an hour to measure it and rest up a bit." He checked his watch. "It's a quarter to nine. We should be back by two, three at the latest."

He looked up at her and saw she was smiling.

"What?"

"You're taking a big chance with me. How do you know I can handle this?"

He gave her the devilishly amused look she hadn't seen since she was eighteen, and the missing of it made her think she was going to cry.

"Is something wrong?"

She shrugged. "No. I'm just happy, is all."

A smile flickered across his face.

"Okay, let's get started." He pointed to the notebook.

She opened it to the first blank page she could find.

"Okay, put down these coordinates: north 35.20732 and west 83.49794. I'll count the distances and holler them out to you."

He studied the compass again.

"I'm gonna adjust the background dial 4 degrees so we don't have to do any compensating for the declination."

"So, you still prefer working with the compass instead of GPS," she said as she got out of the pick-up and pulled out her backpack.

"You can't count on GPS here in the wilderness," he said loud enough for her to hear as he got out of the truck. "When the satellite moves behind the mountain you lose the signal."

He spread the map open on a huge rock as she came near.

"Here's where we are. See? This is the outcrop in front of us. The logging trail should take us down into this valley that's cut through with a stream and up and around to the cove with the tree." He pointed to a place with tight contour lines. "But we're gonna have to cut across at this point and climb to this high ridge so we can spot it. Otherwise, it could be quite a job finding it."

"It looks steep."

"The elevation change from that point is almost a hundred feet. It'll be strenuous, but it's our best shot."

She started to reach for her backpack when he grabbed it up. He held it trying to calculate its weight, then put it down, unzipped it and took out a gallon jug of water.

"I've got all the water we're gonna need in mine, plus there's gotta be plenty of springs up there, Calico."

Calico? She hadn't heard the nickname in years and was surprised he still remembered it.

He pulled a silky swimsuit from her backpack and looked questioningly up at her.

"I just thought we might want to take a swim."

He shook his head as he stuffed it back in.

"I remember when all you needed to go swimmin' was your underwear."

He zipped up the backpack, rose and helped her put it on, then checked to make sure most of the weight was evenly distributed at the bottom.

"That's okay, Calico. I can see you're quite the lady now."

She smiled to herself. This was the way it had always been between them. Since he was two years older than she was, he always seemed to be taking care of her. When he was getting his Associate's Degree, he'd come home whenever he could and take her hiking. It saddened her to remember, how every time they'd discover a dark cave, she'd want to curl up in it as if it were a womb and never go back to a home filled with regret.

They made their way to the top of the outcrop that overlooked a billowing sea of green below.

"Okay, our first bearing is 20 degrees west southwest," said Ron, reading the compass.

She followed close behind him as they made their way down the mountain. The old trail was overgrown and almost indiscernible. The brush was tall and she instinctively got closer to him so the branches wouldn't slap back on her. Suddenly he raised his arm for her to stop and turned with his finger to his lips, signaling for her to be quiet. He pointed to a small grassy opening. She wrinkled her forehead to tell him she saw nothing. He pointed to it again. Just then the little fawn raised its head. It instinctively lay where its mother had left it and wouldn't move till she came back. Ron continued on, and she tore herself away from the newborn.

After a good hour of trudging through the thicket, he stopped to study the map again. Large droplets of sweat had been dripping from her face all morning. She sat down on a rock and he handed her a bottle of water. She gulped it down and he laughed when she threw her head back and poured the last of it over her face.

"Mark down, direct west, girl, then let's get moving," he said as he put his hand on her shoulder.

She could still feel his hand on her shoulder even now that he was two steps ahead of her. She tried to shrug it away, but it stayed with her. They didn't talk on the walk, as if all they needed to say had been said on the ride down. The scent of the Deet that she had applied before they started hung in a cloud around her, but every once in a while she got a whiff of his manly scent, mostly some common brand of soap that went well with the balsam in the air.

The way he deftly made his way through the forest, it was apparent he was at home here, comfortable with his way of life. It showed in his slow, shy smile and his underlying mountain man strength. Everything about him reflected his North Carolina roots. He was the only person she knew who firmly belonged in two worlds.

The rhythmic way his wide shoulders moved as he walked, made her remember one of their torrid encounters in one of the rental cabins, when she'd taken off all her clothes for the first time and lay down on the bed next to him. Now, as she followed behind him through the forest, she wondered what it would have been like if he had yielded to her pleas and made love to her. When he suddenly turned to point out some poison ivy, she almost blushed and was glad he couldn't read her thoughts.

They scrambled down a long steep section of forest, shadowed by a thick stand of towering hemlocks. The ground was covered in a soft earthy-smelling layer of decomposed pine needles. During the descent they lost the logging trail, but the slope was too steep for them to go back and retrace their steps. He took another reading and she marked it down. They forged ahead to the other side of the small hollow, working their way around and over several granite outcroppings. While he cleared a path through some dog-hobble with a machete, she dug out her climbing gloves. The going was getting rougher off the trail and she needed all the help she could get.

Picking up their pace, they soon found themselves on level ground. When he suddenly signaled for her to stop, she was thankful for a chance to catch her breath.

"Can you hear that? The stream's right up ahead."

Once they reached it, they found the trail just around a bend. They traced it up a steep slope until it came alongside a wall of granite, honeycombed with colonies of trees.

"Okay, this is where we're gonna make the climb."

He studied the rise, then pointed to a series of trees projecting from the mountain at an angle.

"We can start off by climbing up those and then tackle the face. It might be tricky up at the top with that cliff cantilevering out like that, but I've got a maneuver that will work up there."

They made their way up and over all the tree trunks. Sprinkled across the face of the mountain were places where tree seeds had found their way into cracks and taken hold. They had created patches of forest along the sheer-faced rock ledges and provided a somewhat checkered path for them to follow. Ron carefully scaled them, always reaching down and across to give her a hand. Finally, he came to the point near the top where a huge rock overhung the edge. A couple of feet away, a rock face jutted out at a right angle.

"This one's gonna be a little tricky," he yelled down. "Watch how I grip this."

She could barely see up above, but caught a glimpse of him grabbing the overhang with both hands and almost effortlessly raising himself up. He got a foothold on a notch in the face of the rock jutting out, and thrust himself over the edge. Her heart sank. She didn't have the upper body strength to pull that off. Running through her head was how disgusted she'd always been when a patient told of some foolish risk they had taken.

A moment later, he yelled, "I'm going to lower a rope to you. Holler when you've got it tied around your waist."

"I don't think I can do this."

"Sure you can. Anyway, it'll be too hard going back down."

The rope was lowered and she tied it and checked it twice.

"Are you ready?"

She gave her gloves a tug, took a deep breath and moved up to the ledge above. She glanced below. He was right. It would be a lot harder going down. Sweat was now running freely down her face. She swiped her upper arm across the right side of her face and then the other arm across the left.

"I can't see you!" she shouted, shocked at how high pitched her voice had become.

"Hang on. I'll be right there."

He was suddenly crouching down and leaning over the ledge above.

"Okay, I want you to reach up and put one hand right here and grab my hand with the other. I'm going to lift you up, and as soon as you can get your foot on that notch up there to your right, give it all you've got."

"What about that maneuver you were talking about down there?"

"Don't worry. I'll never let you go."

The words rang with truth, and she looked into his cool blue eyes and wondered if they held a deeper meaning. Suddenly emotional, she imagined he'd been sending a message with everything he'd said and done that morning.

"Come on, girl. I'm ready for you."

She reached up on her tiptoes and ran her hand along the overhang to get the feel of it, heart thumping, nearly panting. Get a grip, she ordered herself. This is no time to hyperventilate.

"Okay! I'm ready!" she yelled.

She got a white-knuckled grip on the rock and reached for his hand. His grasp was solid. She didn't breathe as he lifted her. The surface above the overhang came into view. She steadied herself with her left hand and reached her foot over, feeling for the notch. Once she found a firm toehold, she thrust herself upward; and the next thing she knew, she was sprawled out next to him on the promontory.

He broke into a slow smile.

"That was my old 'tie 'em to a tree before you yank 'em up' maneuver."

"I'm impressed." She laughed a little breathlessly, not sure if it was because of the climb or his nearness.

Something in her face must have told him she felt uneasy lying there next to him, for he solemnly untied the rope from her waist and got up and looked down into the cove.

Her legs were a little shaky as she got up and stood next to him.

"This is beautiful," she gasped.

"Do you see the tree?"

He crouched down and took out a pair of binoculars from his backpack and handed them up to her.

"Look over to the far left."

She scanned the treetops until she spotted it in a clearing.

"That's a magnolia, all right."

It was at the bottom of the small craggy cove. A narrow waterfall tumbled down a series of granite ledges a short distance away.

"We'll go down and take a look and you can rest up while I measure it."

They made their way down in silence, the kind of silence that begged for her to say something. But she was afraid of what it might be. She knew enough about men to know he wanted her. She could see it in his eyes, in the way he moved. It was the kind of mating ritual a man of nature instinctively understood—the way a male bird puffs up its belly to show his brawn, or a stag fights to display his strength. He was showing her he could take care of her and was a deserving mate. All she could dare to say in response to his silent avowal was that she was sorry, but she knew that wasn't what he wanted to hear.

The climb up the rock face had already strained her beyond her limit. He must have noticed, because he took her hand and led her down, helping her over fallen logs and down from boulders, until they finally reached the clearing in front of the tree.

"Boy, that baby's big," he said. "It *juuust* might beat out the one in Haywood County."

He pointed to a giant poplar across their path. It lay in a jumble of trees it had taken down with it.

"That blowdown opened the place up. That's why they were able to spot the magnolia from the air." He turned and looked at her. "You look done in. Let's get you over by that waterfall and let you cool off while I get the measurements."

They reached the falls and she undid her backpack and dropped it on a big, smooth rock on the edge of a deep pool below the falls. She yanked off her boots and peeled off her socks, then started to unzip the backpack.

"Oh, to hell with the suit," she said as she shed her hiking pants and shirt and jumped in.

Within seconds, her head popped up from the water with her screaming from its coldness. He was busy going through his backpack for his tape measure, but she could tell by the way he was smiling to himself he had seen her jump in.

Once he left, she swam around for a while before getting out and onto the huge rock. The warmth and smoothness of it felt good under her feet. She took hold of her ponytail and ran her hand tightly down it to squeeze out the water, then pulled a shirt from her backpack and used the long sleeves to tie it onto her waist.

Shivering, she put on a dry tee shirt, spread her sweaty clothes on the rock to dry, and lay back against the warmth of the rock and faced the sun. With her head on her pack, she slowly dozed off.

She awoke with a start, gazing around her, a little disconcerted. It felt like she'd been asleep a long time, but judging by the angle of the sun, it'd probably only been about an hour. Feeling strangely alone, she quickly got dressed. While setting out the lunch, she was relieved to see Ron emerge from the forest.

He came over and put his foot up on the rock ledge, rested a forearm on his knee and took off his trekking hat.

"It's a champ, all right," he said as he ran his fingers through his hair. "Six inches more girth and a good four feet taller." He slapped his hat against his thigh. "I measured the height and crown spread using two different methods and came up with pretty much the same numbers."

While they ate, Georgie worried if she would be able to make it back. Every muscle in her body was aching and her feet hurt. From the way he had lifted her over the ledge, she took comfort in the belief that he had the strength to carry her out if it came down to it.

"With all the running I do, I figured this hike would be a breeze, but that climb up the rock face pretty much wiped me out," she confessed.

He didn't comment or offer a word as he ate, as if deliberately giving her permission to do all the talking. She scooted over to the edge of the rock and dangled her sore feet in the cold water and thought this is what heaven must be like: clear air laden with the smell of balsam, a sea of variegated green rolling in the breeze and framed by a cobalt blue sky, and the sweet music of bird calls sounding over the endless splashing of water on rocks.

He suddenly reached over and snapped up a frog from the edge of the pond. He held it with one hand and slowly stroked it with a finger.

"It's a mountain chorus frog. You only see these little fellas around this part of the state." He pointed to a stripe on the brown stocky creature. "See this? It goes from his eye to his groin on both sides." He carefully placed the frog back where he got it. "For quite a few years, they thought those little buggers were gone for good, then they showed up again in 2001."

She laughed. "Boy, you haven't changed any. I remember that menagerie you kept on your aunt's porch. You would feed them and study them until you knew everything about them. I don't know how your aunt put up with all those snakes and injured critters people brought you."

He fixed his eyes on her. "And you helped me. You never shied away from taking care of all those creatures... no matter how messed up they were. I knew then you'd end up as a nurse."

She pulled her feet up from the water and hugged her legs and thought about what he had said.

"I knew it, too. I guess it's a calling."

There was something about the magic of the moment that brought back the doubts that sometimes overtook her when things were going well with Ron. Maybe it was because she knew it couldn't last. Or maybe it was the deliberate way he was looking after her as if he had all the time in the world to wait for her to tell him what he had wanted to hear ever since they were kids. She pictured the dozens of times she watched him patiently lure an animal into a cage with all kinds of tactics. No, my friend, she said to herself. It didn't work. No matter how tired you get me, no matter how much you make me depend on you, I'll never let my guard down. I have kept my secret for all these years and it'll go with me to my grave.

RON SLOWED HIS PACE on the way back for Georgie's sake. She had refused the offer of his hat, so he had taken out his bandana and wrapped it around her head like a do-rag. They still had to chart the trek from the champion tree to where they had veered off the logging road. After that, they picked up a lot of their in-bound trail and the going got easier, except for the final climb out of the valley. The insects were thicker that late in the afternoon and the sun scorching. Georgie grunted and moaned aloud the last steep yards up to the ridge.

She had fallen behind, and as he stood waiting for her to catch up, she breathlessly waved the notebook.

"I've been counting your steps, Mister Eighteen Paces Per Hundred Feet, and you're off a couple on this painful little stretch."

He laughed to himself. Georgie was obviously reaching the limit of her endurance. He wanted to pick her up and carry her back to the truck, but he knew if he did it would kill him to let her go. She had lost the rhythm of their gait and kept bumping into him and grabbing onto his shirt to steady herself. When they reached the crest, she sighed audibly at the sight of the truck nestled next to the big outcrop of rock.

When she neared it, she unlatched her backpack and let it drop to the ground, then she reached out her hand and snapped her fingers several times—her signal for another bottle of water.

Shaking his head and laughing, he opened his backpack and gave her one, even though she had poured most of the last bottle over her head. He grabbed her backpack and helped her into the truck, then collected their gear and threw it into the bed before getting behind the wheel. He put the key in the ignition, but didn't have the heart to turn on the engine. He just wanted to sit there in the wilderness he loved with Georgie only a breath away. It made him ache to think that in a couple hours he would be dropping her off. There was so much he wanted to say, but it wasn't time yet.

He looked over at her and tried, but couldn't feel ashamed for taking her on such a vigorous trek just so he could be near her. She had collapsed against the door and hung an arm out the window. Her cheeks were a dramatic rose red. Somewhere along the trail she had braided her ponytail and it now hung limply across her chest, dark and wet from all her dousing. She'd taken off the bottoms of her slacks at the base of the mountain, and he was struck for the millionth time by the long, beautiful line of her legs.

Of all the creatures in the world he had ever wanted to make better, she was the most cherished, for, ever since the first week he rode the school bus with her, he knew she was tormented by something she had buried deep inside and couldn't let go. And of all the creatures he had studied and loved, she was the most elusive. He knew if she got away from him again, he'd never get over it.

CHAPTER TEN

THE FACT THAT THE DEED was made out to a woman caught Dinah's eye. Out of the two hundred or more she'd studied, there weren't three made out solely to a woman. Dated June 14, 1894, it was for two of her great-grandfather's downtown lots. She read the elegant script with interest: "... in the case spirituous or malt liquors of any kind whatsoever are manufactured, sold, bartered or exchanged; or offered for sale, barter or exchange upon the premises herein described, the title to the same shall become null and void and the property revert to the grantor or assigns..."

The lots in question were located across the alley from Dinah's bedroom window. Being the first time she ran across this wording in any of the downtown deeds, she wondered if the woman who was buying the lots might have been known to have had a shady reputation. The sale of liquor in the town had a checkered past and it wasn't until June of 2013 that the town voted to allow liquor by the drink even though "wet" townships surrounded them on every side.

The boys' toy cars hit the bedroom door with two thuds for the nth time, and Dinah yelled for them to stop their racing so she could get some work done.

Michael peeked in. "Sorry, Grandma."

"Oh, shucks, boy. Come on over and give me a hug."

He ran over and slid up on the chair's soft arm, clutching one of his racing cars.

"So, who's King of the Hill today?" she asked.

"Oh, Isaac again. He's got the fastest cars."

Michael made a face at the computer screen and commented that the writing looked weird, then casually ran a small car down his leg and onto the arm of the chair.

"Grandma, how come they don't run the King of the Hill races up Chimney Rock Mountain anymore?"

She sighed deeply and took off her glasses, thinking about the annual hillclimb weekends that had rocked the town every year from 1956 to 1995.

"Huh, Grandma? How come?"

"Oh, baby, things are different now. Back in those days when I was growin' up, heck... if you could think it up... you could do it. People were free to use their imagination 'cause there weren't all these regulations hamstringin' ya. And nobody knew enough to sue anybody. If you got hurt in the crowd when you were watchin' the race, you just got up, brushed yourself off and got on with what you were doin'. Today, everybody's lookin' for somethin' they can litigate; and then there's the wildlife folks. Things just piled up against it so much they stopped havin' it."

"Was it fun, Grandma?"

"Oooh, darlin', those were great times. I grew up watchin' those races on my daddy's shoulders. There were banners across the road and fans lined up at the switchbacks all the way up the mountain to the rock. The air would get blue with exhaust. The cars were all competing against the clock, so we only dared scoot across the road right after one passed. All kinds of people came from all over. You could honestly say the spirit was magic. Drivers, pit crews, fans, workers were all part of it."

She tapped her fingers on the black leatherette and let the memories flood back to her.

"When I was around ten, my sister Jackie and I took a short-cut through the woods to the top of the mountain and caught rides with drivers after they crossed the finish line. You should have seen us. We were like movie stars waving to the crowd all the way down."

"That sounds like fun, Grandma."

"Yep. That crazy Hillclimb brought together the park, this town and everyone involved in it in a way that none of us will ever forget."

Dinah ran her hand lovingly along the boy's face and looked in his eyes.

"But once me and my two sisters got to be twelve, we had to work in the stores. We'd see the cars come and go and we could hear 'em, but we never got to actually watch the race again."

Ali rushed in the room. "Mom, Georgie wants you out on the deck when Aunt Jackie and Aunt LuVerne come."

"Oh, hogwash. Georgie wants this and Georgie wants that. Can't an old lady just do as she pleases?"

Ali glanced over at Mike. "And you, young man, get in that bathroom and wash your hands and face, then put on the clean clothes I laid out on your bed."

"Can't a little boy just do as he pleases?" mimicked Mike in a sing-song voice.

Before Ali could get her hands on him, he escaped out the door.

"Where's that sister of yours?" asked Dinah.

"Oh you know her. She's out there puttin' on the dog for the aunts. She's gone and dragged out all your best stuff. I'm tellin' you, if any of that barbeque sauce gets on that linen tablecloth, I'm not cleanin' it."

"She's just like your dad. He'd fuss just like that whenever we had any kind of doins'."

Ali took a bright blue housedress sprinkled with yellow daisies off the hanger that was hooked on the door.

"Come on, Mom. You better put this on. Georgie pressed it special for you last night."

Ali helped her out of the recliner and Dinah started dressing. It was family get-togethers like this when she missed Jack the most. Especially since it was times like this that Georgie resembled him the most. She hadn't been her father's favorite when she was small, but by the time she hit her teens and it became clear she was his duplicate both in image and temperament, it was only natural for the two of them to stick together. Dinah could still hear him defending her at the dinner table when the subject of all her jobs was brought up after a hectic day in the store when they really could have used her.

The sudden sound of a commotion got their attention.

"Mom, your sisters are here. Let's get movin' before Georgie gets upset."

"Oh, the heck with her. I don't know what's wrong with you, gal. You've been doin' her biddin' ever since you were a kid."

By the time Ali got Dinah out on the deck, the two aunts were comfortably seated and sipping wine. Jackie, the eldest, was the only one of the three sisters who had kept her girlish figure.

"Well, there she is," Jackie announced as she spotted Dinah. "The answer to all our prayers."

Dinah made her way to the chair where Isaac was waiting to place the ottoman under her feet.

"And just what prayer am I answering?"

"Don't you remember? You're gonna take us for a trip around the world once you find great-grandpa's gold."

"I wouldn't recommend you start packing anytime soon," Georgie tossed out as she placed a pitcher onto the table. It held colorful orange ditch lilies she'd plucked from the alley.

"But Mike just finished tellin' us that this sweet sister of ours is gonna find that wolf den any day now," said the other sister, LuVerne.

Ali's voice boomed out from the house, wanting Georgie to come help her cut up the pork loin, so Georgie quickly finished arranging the flowers and left for the kitchen.

Mike was standing with his arm around Dinah's shoulder.

"And once grandma finds the gold, she won't have to sell the motorcycles anymore."

Jackie's eyebrow raised as she mulled the remark over for a moment. Dinah caught the motion and waited for her to get around to saying what was on her mind.

"That reminds me." Jackie's tone dripped with insinuation. "When Georgie told me you were putting the bikes on eBay, I mentioned it to my neighbor, but he couldn't find them."

"They're on there. He just didn't look good."

"I looked," said LuVerne, "and couldn't find them either."

"Well, there are so many listed, you just didn't see 'em."

"I searched just like Georgie had said; Jack's red Harley-Davidson Ultra Classic with the pack on the back, radio, CD player, CB radio and cruise control. Then for your Softail; and I couldn't come up with either one of them."

"Mike! Isaac! You two go and help in the kitchen," Dinah commanded.

"What will we help with, Grandma?" asked Mike.

Isaac went over and tugged on Mike's arm.

"Come on. Let's go get some of our cars."

The minute the boys were beyond earshot, Jackie leaned toward Dinah and whispered, "You haven't put them on eBay yet, have you?"

"And the emphasis is on the *yet*," piped up LuVerne.

Jackie gave LuVerne a stern look, causing her to throw up her hands and make a face.

"Georgie is overreacting again. Things aren't that bad," said Dinah.

"Sure," said LuVerne. "The sheriff will never find this place."

Dinah was beginning to feel cornered by her two sisters. They'd always been a team, even though LuVerne was at least ten years younger than she and Jackie.

"I don't want you two saying a word to Georgie about this. I'm just asking for this one single little favor."

LuVerne's mouth fell open. *"One single little favor?* We'd need a calculator to add up all the times we had to bury stuff on your account."

"That's enough, LuVerne. This isn't getting us anywhere," cautioned Jackie.

"Nor is it helping Georgie. That kid has taken four months off without pay to help out here. I know for a fact that she's in line for a big promotion. And I've been in nursing long enough to know that a leave of absence isn't gonna look good on her record. I so much as told her so, but she just went ahead and did it anyway."

Jackie rose and filled her glass.

"This calls for another drink." She waved the bottle at LuVerne. "Want some?"

LuVerne shook her head.

Just then, the boys came in, lugging a huge scrapbook.

"Georgie said you brought this over for us to look through," said Isaac.

The appearance of the scrapbook put a smile on LuVerne's face.

"Bring it here," she said enthusiastically.

She got busy looking through it with the boys, while Jackie extracted a promise from Dinah that she'd get the bikes listed right away.

Georgie drifted back out on the porch where both of the fans lazily whirled, generating enough movement in the air to make the warm evening pleasant. She poured herself some wine and pulled up a chair next to LuVerne. The scrapbook was opened to a large, somewhat creased black-and-white photo of downtown Chimney Rock. It showed the street packed with people and a flat-bed truck with a country band on it.

LuVerne pointed out a girl in a circle of dancers.

"That there's Dinah."

"I love that picture," said Georgie. "Mama looks so young."

Ali, who had just come in and put a platter on the table, came over and bent down between her aunt and sister to get a good look.

"Get a load of those clothes," she said. "Wow. Look at Mom in that full skirt and peasant blouse. Weren't *you* the cat's meow."

"I was wearing a crinoline petticoat, too."

"Ma, you look just like Kim Novak in *Picnic*," said Ali.

"Ha!" let out LuVerne. "She was more of a Susan Hayward in *I'll Cry Tomorrow.*"

LuVerne must have caught the look from Jackie by the way she self-consciously cleared her throat.

"When was that picture taken, Mom?" asked Ali.

"I was still in high school, so it had to be in the late fifties."

Dinah's thoughts drifted off as Jackie reminisced out loud.

"That Monday night street dance was one heck of a date night. Boy, people came from all over for those dances. Asheville, Hendersonville, Rutherfordton, from all around. Of course all the locals would come whether they danced or not. You got to remember, there was little or no TV, and hardly anyone had air conditioning in those days."

"What kind of dancing did they do, Aunt Jackie?" asked Isaac.

"Square dancing, boy. Nothin' formal. Some folks used clogging steps, but it was mostly a slide your feet kinda thing. They'd play tunes like *Turkey in the Straw* and *Cotton-Eyed Joe*."

"They'd just call out the figures," added LuVerne. "Do-si-do, promenade, right hands over, circle left. The whole street was blocked off and they sent all the traffic up Terrace Drive and back onto 74. It was pretty grand."

Dinah listened as the family oohed and aahed over the pictures, but she had no need to look at them. Every era of the town's history was vivid in her memory. All the talk of the street dances took her back to the dismal '70s when they were phased out, and the closing of the post office suddenly nagged at her.

But Chimney Rock, she thought, had weathered so many falls from so many highs, if charted, they would be as spiked as the Blue Ridge Mountains themselves. If she could come up with two words that would describe the place, it would be "surviving change." There'd been so many in her lifetime alone. In the '80s when the mills started closing, the fabulous Fourth of July weeks in town when the cotton mills closed for summer vacation came to an end. Then the King of the Hill races ceased in the '90s.

The whole phenomenon of the movie industry that flourished in the gorge during the first half of the 1900s was another boon that had evaporated. In those days, there was no Hollywood with its sets, so the moviemakers who were then located in the East had to find actual colorful, exciting places to film; and since there wasn't anything around more colorful and exciting than the Hickory Nut Gorge, it was used as a backdrop for over fifty silent pictures as well as a slew of films spanning every decade since.

Almost a hundred years before celebrities could hop a flight to exotic places like St. Moritz or Dubai, the gorge was luring stars like Gloria Swanson, Clark Gable, Douglas Fairbanks and Mary Pickford, all who vacationed at the famed Esmeralda Inn.

Dinah figured the nation's cultural changes impacted Chimney Rock more than elsewhere because the essence of the place itself was more dramatic.

But somehow, some way, this less than five hundred acres of rock and river from ridge to ridge had managed to keep coming back to life every spring. The legions of folks who loved and labored in the mountainous park for over 100 years, and the myriad of shopkeepers and restaurateurs that carried on business over the generations in the little mountain hamlet at its base, had come forth with renewed hope at the start of every tourist season since 1896 when Jerome B. Freeman bought the monolith from the Speculation Land Company and forged a path to it from the town.

Dinah sat deep in the past, enveloped by the sound of the kids' laughter and her sisters' storytelling. Suddenly she noticed Mike tugging on her arm.

"What are you thinkin' about, Grandma?"

"Oh nothin', baby. Nothin' at all."

CHAPTER ELEVEN

I**T FELT GOOD TO BE** behind the wheel of her Ford Escape and sailing up bucolic Route 221 on her way to Boone. Georgie was making the two-and-a-half hour trip for her monthly visit with Dr. Harold. By the time they would get through all the niceties and the update on what she was doing, she figured there wouldn't be but ten minutes of their one hour visit left for substantive talk. That's okay. That ten minutes was usually all the lifeline she needed.

She'd planned her trip so she'd hit Boone a couple hours before her appointment. That way she'd have time to check out the house. The car made its way past the plethora of shops and business establishments dotting the highway on the outskirts of Boone, then swung left toward the Appalachian State University campus. She made a right and wound into a neighborhood of well-maintained older homes occupied mostly by families of college professors and university employees.

She had bought the house when the neighborhood was in transition. Only twenty-three years old, yet determined to get her own place and rent it out herself, she found someone anxious to sell and willing to hold the mortgage. The owner, who in those days was considered a slumlord, had lived downstairs and turned the upstairs into cramped efficiency apartments for students.

Luckily, she was able to rent the first floor to a retired professor who wanted to be close to the university. The only trouble with this blue-chip tenant was that the woman was high maintenance. She would phone upstairs to Georgie if there was so much as a flake of snow on the front sidewalk, and Georgie would dutifully put on a jacket and sweep it off. Georgie couldn't count all the times she had to help the woman find the cat that she kept locked up in her flat. It had to be recaptured every time it came back looking for food after one of its escapes.

She pulled up to the front and got out. The gardener she had hired was evidently taking good care of the lawn and shrubs, and had gone as far as dead-heading the geraniums. The upstairs bay windows with their ruffled curtains gave the place a homey look and went well with the Wedgwood blue siding and cream trim. She wondered if any of her early tenants ever came by to see the old place, and if they did, what they thought of it.

She had lived in one of the upstairs apartments and rented out the other three to female students, with everyone sharing the bathroom at the end of the hall. There were no frilly swags from Country Curtains then, just the yellowed paper shades that came with the house. In those days, because she was still in school, it was important that Georgie earn enough on all her rentals to cover her living expenses and pay the mortgage and taxes.

She ran up the steps of the bungalow that she had since turned back into a single-family. She spotted two empty wine glasses on the table next to a couple of lounge chairs. Good. Her best friend's sister who was staying there for the summer was enjoying the porch. She unlocked the door and went in. The serenity of the large living room and nearness of cherished items triggered a yearning to be back home. She shook the feeling off. The last thing she needed right now was a case of homesickness.

She ran upstairs and checked out the ceiling in the back bedroom to make sure the roof wasn't leaking again. Everything was all right in there, so she gave the other rooms a quick glance. The guest bedroom held the only clue that anyone was living in the house. There was a stack of books on the desk by the window, a laptop sat open and papers were scattered about. The girl was doing research for her master's thesis and had to be spending most of her time at the library.

Next, Georgie wanted to change the air filter, then check the basement and make sure water wasn't leaking in there either. She'd been in the house for a half-hour when the doorbell rang. The lady next door had probably noticed her car pull up and would be coming over to say hello. She threw open the door and was stunned to find her ex-husband standing there.

She managed a casual hello, but the awkwardness of the situation flustered her. As a nurse, she couldn't help evaluating his health. His skin was a good color and the whites of his eyes clear. His dark curls glistened like they did in the old days, and most of his handsome good looks had returned.

"You look good, Butch."

"Thanks. So do you."

He looked around, averting her eyes.

"I'm sorry to drop in on you like this, but I knew you'd be in town to see your doctor on the third Tuesday of the month. Although, I'll never figure out why you waste your time seeing a shrink. I don't know anyone who's got their head screwed on as solid as you."

She said nothing, still trying to get her bearings. It didn't seem right to invite someone into a house they had lived in for four years as if they were a stranger.

"I flew in for my brother's wedding on Saturday. My mom said she runs into you at the hospital a lot and you're always nice to her."

"Why wouldn't I be, Butch? She was always nice to me."

He looked down and kicked the edge of the threshold with his foot.

"I just came to tell you I've been clean for almost two years now." He looked up at her and let out a brusque laugh that sounded hollow. "I knew it'd make you happy that all that energy you spent on me wasn't a complete waste."

"Come on in," she said as she smiled and motioned with her head to the living room.

He followed her to the kitchen and she pulled out a chair for him. A quick glance at the counters told her the two bottles of wine she had left were still there, but she didn't know whether she should offer him some.

He must have read her mind, for he said, "I don't touch that anymore either."

She pulled out a chair and sat down.

"My mother says your mom's been in an accident. I hope she's okay."

"She'll be fine."

He self-consciously looked around the room. "She says you're going with some doctor."

"Well... kinda. Yeah, I guess I am. His name is Phillip Griffin. I worked with him in the ER when I was in training. His wife died a couple years back."

"I hope you have a good life with him. God knows you deserve it after what I put you through."

Georgie wasn't going to tell him that she and Phil had decided to let their relationship cool while she was in Chimney Rock. He was sixteen years older than she was and wanted to get married. They were a good match, except he'd already had his family and didn't want any more children, and she did. Butch's mom, who worked in the hospital's office, evidently hadn't heard gossip about their not seeing each other over the summer, leading Georgie to believe Phil hadn't started dating anyone else.

Neither of them said anything for a while as Georgie, her shoulders slumped, sat with all the crashed hopes and dreams she'd had for Butch and her leafing over in her brain like pages in a family album. She'd never been able to tell him why she had to see Dr. Harold and wondered if it would have made a difference if she had. She swiped away a tear rolling down her cheek.

"Oh, gee, Georgie. Please don't do that," Butch said, wincing.

She waved her hand. "I'm fine. It's just that I'm so pleased to see you're makin' out okay, Butch."

She got up and pulled off a paper towel from the holder and blotted her face.

He looked around as if he were searching for something to say that would change the mood.

"I see you finally got your new kitchen."

She blew her nose and laughed. "You know me. Never satisfied."

"I've got to hand it to you. You've really done wonders with this place. I'll never forget the first time I saw it. Geez, I thought you were nuts." He barely laughed. "And all those girls you had living upstairs. What a zoo."

"I still keep in touch with some of them," she said as she folded her arms and leaned back against the counter.

They were silent again, each of them taking the other in. When her eyes landed on the dark curls peeking from his shirt, she had to stop an avalanche of memories from caving in on her.

She took a deep breath and said, "Your mom told me you're living in Wyoming."

He nodded.

"Are you married?"

"Yep."

"Any kids?"

"One on the way. My wife's father owns a big trailer park outside Laramie. I started working for him... and met her... and now the two of us are pretty much running the place."

He massaged his jaw like he was trying to build up courage to say something, then looked her straight in the eye for the first time.

"Georgie, I'm really sorry for everything, and I want you to know that I plan to give you back all the money I took."

"Don't worry about it right now, Butch. You've got a kid comin'." She smiled. "Unless you hit the lottery or somethin'."

Except for the shouts of children at play in the yard next door, the room fell silent again.

"I appreciate your signing all the papers without causing any trouble," she said.

"That was the least I could do."

The fridge compressor kicked on and it seemed to shatter the mood.

He slapped his hand on the table and started to get up.

"I better shove off. I just came to say my piece."

Suddenly cold, she hugged herself as she followed him to the door. It seemed otherworldly to her that the tall, handsome man with the wide shoulders that she had lain with had never really known her, and it sickened her that she had never let him.

They walked out onto the porch together, and just as he was about to descend the steps, he turned and looked at her. They slid their arms around each other and she buried her face against his. She felt the familiar wet curls at the back of his neck and recognized the scent of his shampoo.

They pulled away and he looked in her eyes. "Have a good life," he said, and then he turned and went down the stairs and to his car.

She looked up and down the street, but no one had been out. She was pleased this intimate moment between the two of them hadn't been intruded on by strangers. Now there would be no misinterpretations of the meaning of the two people in each other's arms. He had simply asked for her forgiveness and she had given it.

She watched the green Chevy that had to be his mother's disappear down the street before she went back in. She walked through the darkened rooms downstairs and strolled into the kitchen, now bathed in the afternoon sunlight. The clock above the stove told her she still had time before she had to leave. She got a glass out of the cupboard and poured some wine, then meandered back into the living room. She thumbed through her CDs and put one on, then sat on the sofa in front of the dark fireplace listening to Gregg Allman croon *Rendezvous with the Blues.*

BY FIVE, SHE WAS WINDING through the mountains heading back to Chimney Rock. She couldn't help thinking the session she'd just had with Dr. Harold had started a new chapter in her endless search for peace of mind. He had made quite a few notes this time, especially when she told him about Ron. When she said forgiving Butch had made her feel contented, the doctor had stopped writing and given her a look that asked her for more.

Then, when she told him she believed there was some unknown underlying reason she took a leave of absence and went back home, he gave her the look again. She was surprised to find herself readily admitting it had to be more than to take care of her mother. She could have easily made arrangements for satisfactory care. She struggled to put everything together as she told him about making the decision right after Phil's veiled ultimatum that they get married before his planned retirement at the end of the year.

"So why *do you* think you went back?" he had asked her.

As she drove along the highway, she still didn't have an answer that made any sense. After all, she was just where she wanted to be—with a successful career, financial security, a kind and good man wanting to marry her. Why would she jump back into the churning cauldron she'd worked all those years to escape from? She'd have to think about her doctor's calculating question. She wondered if she did find the answer, if she would ever tell him.

The heavy traffic out of Boone started to annoy her. Had to be commuters on their way home. She stepped on the gas to pass a beat-up truck loaded with lumber chugging up the mountain, and it dawned on her, that for the first time she could recall, she was anxious to get back to Chimney Rock.

CHAPTER TWELVE

I T HAD BEEN RAINING on and off for five days, giving Ron an excuse to come home to his cabin and work on his hawthorn book. Right after he got out of college, he'd built the place out of poplar logs on land his mother had left him and had kept adding on to it once he and Mary got married. Located on Shumont Mountain, which rose up on the other side of Round Top, on a road bearing his mother's family name, it was part of the 200-acre farm his great-great-great-grandfather had bought from the State of North Carolina in 1797 for a hundred shillings. The original survey and land grant, signed by the then Governor Davie, now hung over his fireplace.

He picked up the letter from the University Press with the imposing seal embossed at the top and read it again. There it was in black and white, stating they wanted him to cut the pages of his hawthorn book from five hundred to no more than three hundred. It was painfully clear to him they weren't using the same formula in publishing the book as he was in writing it. The press was evidently following a model that guaranteed they wouldn't lose money.

The reason he had spent ten years researching hawthorns all over the Southeast was to put together an accurate and complete book on the subject. And that couldn't be done in "no more than three hundred pages." He figured he needed to have 800 to 1,000 photographs to convey the range of variation for the 145 different types of plants he'd identified. Because of the wide range of leaf shapes, there was no way he could have just one picture representing each type.

He wished he wasn't so stubborn, but he wasn't going to cut the book down. He couldn't. He sat there looking at the neat stacks on his bookshelf. He had the text, the tables, keys, photographs, and drawings. Why not find a designer and publish the book himself?

After all, he'd spent hundreds of hours just straightening out the names. Over the years, botanists had come across already-named plants, and thinking they had found an undiscovered specimen, renamed them. He had carefully identified 145 different types of hawthorns, yet found 537 names.

His cell phone started ringing and he dug it out from underneath the papers on his desk. A slow smile appeared when he recognized the number.

"It's nice to see you calling *me* for once, babydoll."

"Dad, don't call me that. FGS, I'm almost twelve."

"What do you want me to call you then?"

"Jenni. Remember, Dad? I told you that last week. I'm spelling it with an *i* at the end."

He could hear her opening the fridge.

"How are you coming on your hawthorn book?" she asked.

"I'm actually working on it as we speak."

"How weird is that. You know, Dad, you've been drawing those hawthorns for as long as I can remember. When I was a little kid, I was so disappointed when I asked you to show me some and you took me to the woods behind the house and there they were, nothing but bushes with thorns."

"But think of all the food and protection they provide for animals."

"I know. In fact, I've been studying them a little myself, Dad. Did you know hawthorn is particularly deadly to vampires? You can only slay them with stakes made from hawthorn wood."

"Thanks, I'll remember that."

"Have you thought of a name yet for the one you discovered in that balsam forest you showed me?"

"Naming it isn't as important as getting it described. I've finished collecting the spring flowering samples from every place it occurs as well as the leaves. Now I've got to go back and get the fruit samples."

"Have you found it anywhere else?"

"Not yet."

"Dad, I was thinking about a name. You know how the first word for all of them is Crataegus?"

"That means hawthorn."

"Duh. I know that, Dad."

The echoing tone of her voice told him she had put the phone on speaker and was doing something in the kitchen.

"Well, I was looking through the list of them on the internet and I found one called Crataegus Jakii. That's with two 'i's at the end."

He started to laugh.

"It's not funny, Dad. It's got to have a name and what's wrong with Crataegus Jenni?

"If I did name it after you, it would have to end with 'ae,' because it's the feminine termination."

"Jennae. I like that. Oh, Dad, it would be *soooo* cool to have a tree named after me. Just think. It would be in all the books, on the internet, forever. In fact, I just might plant one of them myself."

"Why not? Think of how handy it would be for making vampire stakes."

"Really, Dad."

"How's your mom?"

"The same. The check you mailed her lasted one whole day. Good thing you sent me the money in that book. Thanks. I got Mom to take me shopping for art supplies like you said. By the way, what in the world are you doing with that kind of book? I started to read it and it was like trash. Totally."

"I picked up a whole box of them at a yard sale for a dollar. I just got them to send you money."

"That's a relief."

"That's what the lady who sold me all those romance novels

said when I told her what I wanted them for."

They were quiet for a moment before Jennifer said, "I really miss you, Dad."

Ron felt a lump in his throat and he had to swallow hard.

"It won't be long. I've got to leave next Monday for the Bahamas on a project for the Department of the Interior. I'll be gone for two weeks, but don't worry, I'll be back before you get here."

"Well, I need to get the dinner going so it'll be ready when Mom and Tim get home from work. I try to get something in their stomachs before they... well, you know."

He knew all right. Mary's drinking had been a problem since the early days of their marriage. He didn't want to let Jennifer go with her to New Mexico, but he knew his daughter would be broken-hearted if he had said no. The only good reason he had seen in Mary's going was that a new life with a new man might be what she needed to turn her life around. God knows he had tried everything else he could think of.

He had made sure that he talked with Jennifer daily, even if that meant driving somewhere to get a signal, and he had come to the conclusion that things weren't turning out for the best.

"Honey, I never should have agreed to let you go with her. When you get here, I'll arrange it so you don't have to go back."

"Dad, you know I can't leave her. If I wasn't here, GOK what would happen to her. Besides, it's not that bad. At least they make it to work every day. Tim isn't a bad guy. He's just... I don't know. He's like Mom. Neither of them are really grown up. Anyway, not like you, Dad."

The call ended with her saying LHK and him hoping it was a term of endearment.

As far as he was concerned, it was settled. Jennifer wasn't going back with her mother after the two weeks were up, and no amount of histrionics, arguments or pleading would change his mind. The only reason he had let Jennifer go in the first place was that he wanted to give Mary one last chance to straighten herself out. That job was hardly up to a loving little girl.

He checked his watch. Adam Bentley had talked him into

meeting him for dinner in Chimney Rock at six. A good thing. After that call, he needed some cheering up. Adam was always full of plans for hiking and rock climbing in the gorge. Belonging to the Carolina Climbers Coalition and the Friends of Chimney Rock State Park, he had his ear to the ground and knew a lot of the state's long-range plans. And from what Ron could gather, they were big.

He had watched as the state swallowed up the land on either side of Chimney Rock Village. They either owned, or some conservancy was holding for them, hundreds of acres of land on the northern slope, crawling all the way around the ridge to Bald Mountain. On the south slope and up over the ridge, they owned several thousand more acres, including the park and what was known as the World's Edge. In total, the state had accumulated 5,700 acres on both sides of the town.

They were equally active along the length of the ten mile gorge. They had already announced their plans for an eventual hiking trail going from Chimney Rock State Park, up the gorge to the continental divide in Gerton, across the highway and doubling back to Chimney Rock, then curling around Bald Mountain overlooking Lake Lure. In all, it would be a twenty mile hike that would take multiple days to accomplish and pass some of the most beautiful scenery on the face of the earth.

He pulled into town twenty minutes early and was tempted to visit Georgie at the store, but he had second thoughts after recalling how on edge she was when he had phoned and invited her to go with him to see *The Last of the Mohicans* at the park on Saturday. She'd always liked being in control when it came to her mother, and after Dinah's laughable performance on the phone, he took it as a good sign that Georgie wanted to meet him at the park entrance.

All the tables on the front porch of Medina's Village Bistro were already taken, so he went inside and sat at the counter. He had ordered a beer and was studying the menu when Adam slid onto the stool next to him. Adam was just six years younger than him, but he'd only recently gotten engaged. A lot of the hardcore climbers Ron knew took a year or so off after they got out of school and traveled around doing rock climbing and living on the barest minimum before diving into their careers. Then they'd keep at the sport intensively until they realized there was more to life than climbing. With his recent engagement, Ron figured Adam had finally reached that stage.

By and large, rock climbers were also hikers since they usually needed that ability to reach their destinations, so Ron had bumped into a lot of them in his activities all over the western part of the state.

"Have you ever hiked up Round Top?" asked Adam as he caught the waitress's eye and pointed to Ron's beer.

"Pretty much every inch."

"That's what we figured."

Adam's beer arrived, along with a menu.

"So, what are you guys cookin' up?" asked Ron.

"You know that rock face just up there behind the town?"

"Yeah, the south face of Round Top Mountain."

"I've never been up there, but they say it's awesome for climbing. Well, the coalition is thinking of buying a chunk of it. Obviously, we're going to have to develop some hiking trails, too. That's where you come in. The Carolina Mountain Club has folks with expertise in trail building we can use once we get it laid out, but right now we need you to work with us on sizing up the area so we can establish how much we need to buy."

The waitress appeared with her order pad.

"You fellas know what you want?"

Adam pointed to the chalkboard behind her. "That special looks good."

She jotted it down and looked at Ron.

"What's a Cassoulet?" he said as he scratched his head.

Adam laughed and told him he'd love it.

"Put us down for two specials and two more beers," he said to the waitress.

"At least I know I'm gonna like the beer," threw out Ron.

Keenly interested in what might be happening to Round Top, he asked, "Have you talked with the guy who owns it?"

"Yeah. And he's amenable. Especially when we told him we

were going to give it to the state." He took a gulp of his beer. "It's damn ironic. After the Revolutionary War, when North Carolina owned every inch of this gorge, they were selling it off at fifty shillings a hundred acres to anyone who wanted to buy it. Heck, that was six cents an acre. Now in some extreme cases they're buying back that very same land for as much as a thousand dollars an acre."

"If you can pull this off, what impact do you think it will have on the town?"

"Are you kidding? It would be a boon. Look at it this way, Ron. Right now, this town dies in the winter, and that's when we climb. Rumbling Bald next door is considered a world class rock climbing destination and draws climbers from all over the world. That section over the town is just as spectacular. Two sections that offer entirely different challenges will more than double the draw to this area. Hopefully, we can find a trail that will connect the two."

Their food arrived and they both dug in.

After swallowing the first bite and following it with a swig of beer, Ron chuckled, "I don't know why they didn't just call it sausage and beans."

CHAPTER THIRTEEN

W HEN THE PR GUY FROM THE PARK strolled into the store last month with a poster for a screening of *The Last of the Mohicans,* Georgie was struck with how much the picture of Daniel Day Lewis charging through the forest looked like Ron. At the time, she wouldn't have dreamed she'd ever be seeing the film with him, yet he had invited her and here she was getting ready to go.

She'd arranged for him to pick her up at the park entrance at seven-thirty to avoid an episode with her mother. What was going on between her and Ron was too fragile to be tampered with. She put her medical kit back in the drawer in her mother's room, glad she had been so cautious. The whole house was in an uproar over the boys having friends over for a sleepover.

Dinah was filled with anxiety over the kids spending the night out on the deck. Her blood pressure had shot up and Georgie had to give her a nifedipine. Her father had made the fence that surrounded the back deck secure from trespassers, but the only way they were able to settle her mother down was to promise Ali would stay out there with the kids all night.

Georgie had told everyone she was going to the movie with a friend, but by tomorrow there'd be talk about Ron and her, so in the morning she had to get around to letting her mother know just who that friend was.

She didn't know why, but she gave her sister a big hug before she left. She supposed it was because she was feeling Ali's pain at the boys' not being able to share the childhood memory of the sleepover with their dad.

Wearing shorts and a frilly top, Georgie skipped down the steps between the two stores and onto the street. Wisps of clouds zigzagged across the bright blue sky, yet the sun was low enough to dip the temperature to the comfortable seventies. All but a couple stores had closed, but there remained a sprinkling of people on the street. Mostly the dinner crowd going for a drink and something to eat at the River Watch or Laura's House.

A water-soaked family had come up from the Riverwalk. The mother wrapped a beach blanket around one of the shivering, barefoot kids while the father fluffed the other's hair dry with a towel. An elderly couple with a twitchy little Pomeranian sat watching on a bench across from them with approving smiles.

Cars were streaming into the park from either direction, yet they stopped to let Georgie and another couple cross the street. Spotting Ron in a Subaru at the curb, she jumped in and they joined the caravan of vehicles climbing through the forest to the ticket booth.

Vehicles jammed the huge flat meadow that was half-way up the mountain. People poured out from the parking area with blankets, chairs, picnic baskets. Up ahead, folks sat in a sea of canvas chairs in front of the forty-foot screen.

Georgie was surprised to see so many people at the annual showing of the movie that was shot using a lot of the park's spectacular scenery. There were picnics spread on tailgates, grills ablaze, tables covered with elaborate set-ups, families and couples lying on blankets laughing and talking. The mass of over five hundred people pulsed with kids and dogs and friends hollering greetings to each other.

She'd had no idea this was such a big event and wished she had thought to pack a picnic. Ron, with an army blanket under his arm, pointed to a spot on the lawn. They made their way, gingerly stepping over and around dogs, totes and backpacks. With barely enough space to spread out the blanket, their neighbors kindly rearranged their chairs to make room.

Settled, Ron tapped her on the shoulder and motioned with a curled finger for her to follow. They found the concession stand that was set up under a pavilion on the edge of the field, bought some food and started back. People were stopping Ron to talk at almost every step. She hadn't known anyone he introduced her to, but gathered that most of them were connected in one way or another to the park. It was impossible not to notice how surprised his friends were to see him, as if he never got out.

In spite of all the appraising looks she had to endure, it made her feel good that he was stepping out of character on her behalf, and the satisfied grin on his face when he introduced her made her feel like he was proud to be showing her off.

At last, darkness fell and the movie opened with Daniel Day Lewis agilely clambering through the forest chasing an elk. An ominous, pulsating drumbeat sounded in the background. It kept building in tension until the music exploded into a haunting Gaelic melody, stirring every drop of Scottish blood in her. The emotional lilt of the Scottish fiddle breathed life into the vivid imagery on the screen and gave her goose bumps.

At the intermission, the lady sitting next to them told her the movie's theme music was *The Gael,* which meant *The Scot.* How appropriate, she thought, since the gorge was settled mostly by the Scots-Irish. Georgie told the woman that she and her mother were in the movie and had been dressed as Indians in a crowd scene that was filmed almost directly across the gorge from where they were sitting. She'd seen the movie dozens of times, but unfortunately, had never been able to spot herself or her mother.

The movie started again, and she listened for *I Will Find You,* written for the movie by her favorite Irish musical group, *Clannad.* As she sat in the darkness of the gorge, the familiar words of the mournful song that she knew by heart swirled through her head. *No matter where you go, I will find you... if it takes a thousand years.* Her thoughts melted in her brain like snowflakes that fall on an outstretched hand. The hike, the movie, everything was a message. Her mother's accident, the agreement with Phil not to see each other over the summer, Ron's breakup with Mary—all fate. Yet she knew the only way Ron and she could go forward together was if she told him her secret.

She had come to the same conclusion the night he asked her to marry him, but she wasn't brave enough, strong enough to do it. It had seemed impossible back then to untangle all the lies and deceptions, and she knew it wouldn't have been right to drag her dead sister into their marriage. It would have rotted it just like it had her childhood. How many times as she had lain in his arms had he woven a story of one of his animal rescues that led to a perfect opening for her to spill out her story? He had kept doing it, and she had kept refusing to go there.

That was the beauty of her relationships with Butch and Phil. They started with a clean slate. No need for explanations or reasons for shame. She simply was who they saw. Both of those loves had suspected something was bothering her, but never made any demands; the sorry part was, that by her not opening up to them, they never got all of her. With Ron it would have had to be different. Complete.

She knew Ron wouldn't hold anything against her, but life had taught her enough lessons that she also knew her revelation couldn't stop with him. By returning to Chimney Rock she had put herself back in the crucible, and she sat there wondering why—and if this man who wanted her, could help her get through it.

Even though he had been careful not to sit too close to her, she could feel the heat from his body. She looked over at him and promised herself that tonight she wasn't going to offer herself the way she did all those years back. This time, it was he who had to come for her.

The movie ended and the haunting vocal harmonies lingered in her brain as they packed up and left with both of them knowing they were going to spend the night together. Her cheeks and ears were burning and she was aware of the heaving of her breasts from her ever-deepening breaths.

When the car got to the entrance on Main Street, she was reminded of her mother's condition, and she didn't want it gnawing at her during the night ahead. She put her hand on his arm and said, "Before we go to my place, I'd like to check on my mom. Her blood pressure was dangerously high this afternoon. I might have to give her more medication."

She looked into his eyes for a long moment and the longing in them excited her. He hit the steering wheel with his fist and flashed the shy smile before driving across to Terrace Drive and starting up the alley. They pulled up next to the fence door with Georgie telling him to wait in the car. He made a joke about her not getting rid of him that easily, and got out.

Through the slits between the wood slats, Georgie could see lights were on in the house. She started to put the key in the lock, when he put his arm around her waist, pulled her close and whispered in her ear to make it quick. The heat from his cheek made her heart stop.

Suddenly the door flew open, and the street lamp revealed cots and sleeping bags scattered over the deck. Most of the kids were still awake, and Mike was at the door grinning up at her.

In a sing-song voice, he teased, "Your boyfriend's here with Grandma. Your boyfriend's here. Your boyfriend's here."

Ali, with a tortured look on her face, appeared from out of the dark and couldn't take her eyes off Ron.

"The doctor from Boone is here to see you."

"You mean Phil?"

"Yeah. Phil. He showed up about an hour ago."

Georgie closed her eyes and groaned. She fought an urge to turn around and run back to the car.

"Where are they?" she finally asked.

Mike sang out. "Your boyfriend's in the living room with Grandma."

Ali reached over and grabbed him.

"Why don't you wait in the car while I take care of this," Georgie said, looking into Ron's eyes.

"Let's go on in," he said, and started toward the kitchen.

His terse response caught her off guard. She was frightened and at the same time touched that he was unwilling to stand down and determined to hold on to what he felt was his. Knowing his stubborn streak, she didn't argue.

As they went through the kitchen to the living room she wanted to stop and put her arms around him and tell him that he was the one, but the way his expression had hardened and his walk had turned into a stomp, she didn't dare. They found her mother sitting in a lounge chair with her feet up and a hand around a beer. Phil stood up as she entered, but the smile on his face dissolved the moment he spotted Ron coming in behind her.

Phil looked so yacht club in his crisp khakis and canvas dock shoes next to Ron in his wrinkled hiking shorts and tee shirt. It was like Ari Onassis meets Daniel Boone. The dark tan that Phil owed to all his golf tournaments complimented his gray side-burns. He was shorter than Ron and of a slighter build, yet Georgie wished he wasn't so damn handsome and prosperous looking. She introduced the two of them, and for a tense moment thought someone was going to throw a punch. Ron finally stepped forward and offered his hand. The handshake was long and firm and the body language savage.

"Sit down, boys," said Dinah, sounding a little worried.

Ron pulled up a nearby chair and said with solemn authority, "I'll take one of those beers, too."

Georgie said she'd get him one and quickly left the room. She found Ali in the kitchen looking haggard.

"You look like you've had a rough night, Sis."

"Oh, Georgie," she said as she handed her the beer she had already taken out of the refrigerator. "Donna Burgin called and told us she saw you get in a car with Ron, and the minute that guy showed up, I started praying you wouldn't stop by the house to check on Mom. I'd of gone up on the mountain and warned you, but I couldn't leave these kids. I must have called you on your cell a dozen times. Mom's done everything she could think of to keep him here until we got you on the phone. Georgie, what are you gonna do?"

"Ride it out, I guess." She smirked. "At least they didn't take a swing at each other." She took the beer and started back in and then stopped. "Mom looks awful. I'm gonna have to check her out and get her to bed."

When she walked into the living room, Phil was telling how

he had conservation easements on several pieces of land he owned, and she assumed he had asked Ron what he did. Ron was hunched forward in his chair with his forearms resting on his knees. He looked to her like someone on the threshold of fight-or-flight. She handed him the beer and went over to neutral territory next to her mother. Every time she glanced over at Ron he was looking straight at her, his face and neck darker than usual.

After a few minutes of her mother nervously rattling on about Georgie and Ron being friends since they were kids, Ron stood up like he'd heard enough and said he had to get going. Phil rose to shake hands but Ron ignored him.

"Are you coming, Georgie?"

She was temporarily speechless, then spluttered, "I've got to stay and help my sister with the kids tonight."

What she really meant, and didn't want her mother to hear, was that she was seriously worried about what all the excitement might have done to her mother's blood pressure. She also had to do something about Phil.

Ron stared at her. All the defiance had melted and a look of betrayal was etched on his face. If she had let herself, she would have burst into tears. He turned and left without another word.

Georgie started after him, but Phil grabbed her arm and held her back. She pulled loose from his grasp and ran after Ron, catching a glimpse of her mother who had clasped her face in dismay. Ali was standing in the kitchen with her mouth open. Once on the deck, Mike jumped in front of her and started to say he was sorry. She swiftly moved him aside and kept going toward the door. By the time she made it to the street, Ron's car was pulling out with a screech.

She threw her head back and stared up at the stars, remembering the pride on his face as he showed her off up on the mountain. She was suddenly frightened, and a sickening feeling of loss came over her. If only she had gotten his phone number. Somehow she had to get hold of him in the morning and explain everything. She took a deep breath, gathered her strength and went back in the house.

Phil appeared relieved to see her walk through the door, but her mother looked ill.

"I've got to take my mom's pressure." She swiftly left for the bedroom and came back with her paraphernalia. She got to work with cool efficiency. "Phil, her pressure is 250 over 200."

"You got any nifedipine?"

"Yes. I gave her ten milligrams at seven." She checked her watch. "That was four and a half hours ago."

"Let's give her another one and get her into bed."

It was a half hour before they were ready to leave.

"Did you get a room here in town?" queried Georgie.

"For Pete's sake, Georgie. I assumed I'd be staying with you," he said as they walked toward his car.

"Phil, you never should have come. You promised me you wouldn't."

He stopped and faced her, then tenderly took her in his arms.

"I went to dinner with a couple of friends after a conference in Charlotte and I couldn't keep from coming here. I couldn't get you on your cell, but I knew I could find your mother's place again, and figured she'd tell me where you were staying."

He kissed her, and when she felt nothing but remorse, she decided she might as well cap this nightmare off with the agony of telling him it was over.

"Okay, let's go."

The BMW zoomed down Terrace, then over to Southside. The motion detector triggered the lights as they pulled into the cottage's lot. He got his overnight bag from the trunk, and when they got upstairs, she pointed to the extra bedroom before going into the kitchen for two glasses of the Merlot she had planned to share with Ron. She had to bat back tears remembering the expression on his face when she said she couldn't go with him.

Phil had gone out onto the porch and was sitting in the dark.

"You sure didn't look happy to see me tonight, darling," he said as she handed him a glass.

She sank into a chair and sipped her wine, knowing he was waiting for an explanation.

"Well?"

"Phil, you are a great guy and one hell of a good catch for

some lucky girl."

"And you're about to tell me you're not that lucky girl."

"Phil, no matter how hard I try, I just can't see myself spending the rest of my life after you retire next year cruising around in a bikini on your boat in the Caribbean. It would be so purposeless. When I boil it all down, I'm a nurse and I need to be needed."

She gulped down the rest of the wine. "I'm glad you pressed me for a decision. It's made me think. I've been in survival mode all my life. Before now, I never took a moment to ask myself what I wanted out of life or where I was going. In fact, for most of the thirty-one years that I've been on this planet, I've been sloshing around regretting something I did years ago.

"I don't know if it's this gorge, my crazy mother, or your pressuring me for a decision, but I took an honest look at myself. And you know what? I'm tired of all the regretting. What I really want is to... to be happy in my own home, baking bread and having babies. You've had your family, and I don't blame you for not wanting another one, but I haven't. And I know if I marry you, I'll spend the rest of my life sorry I passed up my last chance to be a mother. There'll be no turning back the clock; no do-over. I love your kids, Phil, but they're almost my age. I want my own baby."

"I suppose with that Tarzan character you were out with tonight."

He made the statement with so little rancor that she knew he had accepted the situation and it was over between them.

"I better call it a night," he said as he rose and started inside, his voice dripping with fatigue and resignation.

She watched as his silhouette disappeared into the cabin, and the sadness in his walk made her fight an impulse to cry out for him. Tears streamed down her cheeks as the loss of him hit her. All she could think of was all the hurt she'd laid on two of the most decent men she'd ever known. As she sat softly crying in the dark, she had no reason to notice the car parked in the driveway across the street or the driver sitting inside.

CHAPTER FOURTEEN

"MOM, I WANT YOU to go easy on Georgie today and try and cooperate," said Ali as she finished getting her mother dressed and settled in her recliner.

Mike was playing with his cars on the floor.

"Mom, do you think Georgie is still mad at me?" he asked.

"No, she's not darling, but I am." She said it intending to reinforce the long talk she'd had with him.

He stood up and leaned against the arm of the recliner.

"I'm glad 'cause I really like her." He touched Dinah's arm. "Georgie's real pretty, isn't she Grandma?"

"I suppose so, but you should have seen my Shelby. Her hair was like gold and her eyes the deepest blue you ever did see."

"Georgie's hair is like gold and her eyes are real blue, too," said Mike.

"Mike, go out on the deck with your brother," snapped Ali.

A pout appeared on his face and he stomped out.

Ali picked up the towel she had used for her mother's bath.

"Mom, you have to stop doing that."

"What?"

"Every time anyone pays me or Georgie a compliment you tell them Shelby was better. Do you have any idea what that does to us?" She shifted her weight. "I'll tell you what it does. It makes us feel unloved."

"That's ridiculous. Of course you're loved."

"Well, I want you to stop bringing up Shelby in front of the boys." She bent down and picked up one of Mike's cars. "It was bad enough that Georgie and I had to grow up with a ghost."

Ali sank down on the bed in a thoughtful daze.

"I felt bad listening to her all day yesterday trying to get hold of Ron. She sounded so desperate."

"Why doesn't she just run over to his cabin on Shumont?"

"She did. Sunday morning. But he wasn't there."

"Well the whole thing's her fault. If she had answered her dad-gummed phone, this mess wouldn't have happened. That girl left us in a fix. When that doctor asked me where she was staying, I certainly wasn't going to send him to the cottage. We've had two killings in this township over situations like that. I figured I had no choice but to keep him entertained until you warned her."

"Yesterday, someone at the park told her Ron was in the Bahamas on a job."

"I don't like the sound of that. Him leaving without tellin' her."

Ali mulled that over for a moment, then as she got up, she remembered something.

"She told me she's got a physical therapist coming to see you today, so be prepared to cooperate. Okay?"

Ali left shaking her head, while Dinah sat looking out to nowhere.

It was getting close to ten, and Georgie still hadn't shown up. Ali decided she better go and open the store herself. She hollered for the boys who were watching TV not to leave the house and went downstairs. When she hit the bottom step, she saw Georgie at her mother's desk.

Georgie turned and looked up. "Hi, Sis. What time is it?"

"Almost ten."

"Time flies when you're having fun," she said dryly. "I've been here catching up on Mom's accounting since around seven."

Ali looked over Georgie's shoulder. "How bad is it?"

"Sales are good, but those damn credit card charges are

deadly." She swiveled around to face Ali and drummed her pencil on the arm of the chair. "It kills me to stand by while Ma pays the interest on nearly fifty-thousand dollars. We've done good enough this month to cut the principal down by five thousand, but that's not enough. I'm going to see what I can do about renegotiating the interest rates. If I offer to pay off a big chunk, they may go for it. But if I can't get better terms, I'll just pay off the one charging the most interest and close the account."

"How are you going to manage that?"

"I've got a bunch of CDs due for renewal that aren't earning more than a point and a half. That's why it ticks me off these banks have the gall to charge Mom fourteen, sixteen and twenty-two percent. She can pay me back when she sells the bikes."

Ali twisted her mouth to one side.

"What? What aren't you telling me?"

Ali threw her head back, stared at the ceiling and groaned.

Georgie snapped the pencil in half and tossed it across the room. "Damn it! She promised me!"

Georgie jumped up and headed for the stairs.

"Georgie, wait till you've cooled down!"

"Ha! Now's *exactly* the right time to see her. And believe me, *no more mister nice guy!"*

GEORGIE DIDN'T KNOW what she was doing in that madhouse as she took the steps two at a time. She raced down the hall and threw open the door, slamming it against the wall.

"Okay, Mom. Where are the bikes?"

Dinah got a cagey look, as if she were thinking fast.

"What do you want them for?"

"I know you didn't list them on eBay. So where in the hell are they?"

"In the garage down the alley."

"Where are the keys?"

Dinah dropped her head in her hands and started crying.

"Mom, you're wasting your breath. I've seen it all. People with arms and legs torn off, babies who have been raped. Believe me, I'm as hard as nails when I have to be." She bent down and looked her in the eye. "Now where are the keys!"

Dinah was suddenly composed, but it didn't surprise Georgie. She'd seen her fake tear jags for her father dozens of times.

Dinah folded her hands across her belly and leaned back in her chair.

"They're in the kitchen drawer."

Georgie raced out of the room and returned with the keys.

"Okay, Mom. This is the way it's going to be. I'm going to kick in twenty-five thousand of my hard earned dollars to clean up half of that credit card debt, and then I'm going to cancel the lot of them. Then I'm going to sell the two bikes, so I can get my hard-earned money back. And you..." She pointed to her mother. "...are going on a strict diabetes diet. I didn't think you were going to make it through the night on Saturday.

"When Cal gets back from Afghanistan in a couple of months, Ali's going to be shoving off. And so am I. But before I do, I'm gonna make *damn sure* you're in good enough shape to go it alone. And that means keeping the books. Dad's not here anymore, and you're going to have to learn how to do it. I can't keep coming back to clean things up. You're sitting on a cash cow with that store, and if you screw it up after I get you straightened out, you're going to end up living in a trailer on one of those damned lots that got you into this mess in the first place."

THE POSTER HAD BEEN UP at Heavenly Hoggs for just over a week when she got the call. There was a guy over there who wanted to take a look at the bikes. Georgie said she'd meet him in the alley in ten minutes. A surge of hopefulness swept over her as she phoned upstairs and told Ali to come down right away with the keys and take over the store. Once she sold the bikes, she'd get back the twenty-five thousand dollars she had sent to the credit card companies and was already starting to regret.

Moments later Ali appeared with the two boys trailing behind.

"You're not really going to sell them, are you, Aunt Georgie?" asked Mike.

Ali bent down, clutched his shoulders and whispered in his

ear. He threw his arms around her midsection and pressed his head against her belly and started crying.

Ali looked at Georgie with agony on her face and said, "Go on. We'll be all right," and handed Georgie the keys.

"No, we won't! Grandma was going to give Grandpa's bike to Daddy when he comes home. *I hate her!*" screamed Mike. He sobbed openly. "Grandma says it'll be bad luck on Daddy if she sells the bike."

Georgie's heart sank.

"*Go!*" demanded Ali.

Georgie grabbed the keys and ran up the stairs. She raced through the kitchen and onto the deck, then out the gate. A motorcycle turned up the alley as she reached the garage. Glad she had gotten someone to check out the bikes before she put up the poster, she unlocked the heavy metal door to the windowless cinderblock building and turned on the lights, then waited for him out on the street.

The man drove his bike up to the garage, rolled to a stop and shut it down. He took off his helmet and exposed a black POW/ MIA do-rag wrapped around his head. She estimated that he was somewhere in his forties as he hung the helmet on his handlebars, got off and slapped down the kickstand. His sleeveless denim shirt exposed a Marine Corps insignia tattooed on one arm. It made her wonder if he'd been in Afghanistan and knew Ali's husband.

He offered his hand. "It's very kind of you to show the bikes to me on such short notice. I appreciate it," he said as they shook hands.

"I've been looking for one for my fiancé and one for myself." He glanced at the one he had just parked. "That's my brother's."

"Well, come take a look."

She took off one of the custom covers concealing the bikes, and he the other.

"Do you mind if I crank it up?" he asked.

"Go ahead."

He thumbed the starter switch on her father's bike and the big V-twin roared to life and quickly settled into a rhythmic rumble. The sound echoed off the cinderblock walls, filling the room. As it sat there idling and vibrating, he circled it and listened.

A cascade of happy memories came flooding back to Georgie as she listened to the engine purr. She could see her father putting a helmet on her and lovingly adjusting it under her chin. She could feel her arms around him and smell his leather jacket as the bike sashayed around the curves as they rode through the gorge. She always loved the way he'd open it up at the bottom of the gap and cruise down the beautiful Fairview Valley straightaway.

The man cut the engine and the room became eerily quiet.

"Can I try the other one?"

"Sure."

He fired it up and let her mother's softail idle for a while before turning it off.

"It's a fluke that I stopped in that store in town, but these are exactly what I've been looking for." He massaged his jaw and looked at her father's bike. "How much are you asking for that one?"

Georgie could hardly believe the words coming from her mouth. "It's not for sale."

His forehead wrinkled. "I haven't done anything to offend you, have I, Ma'am?"

"No. It was sold this morning."

As he stood there with his arms folded, getting over his disappointment, her mind raced. She had better call Steve Gale and get her mother's lots listed right away. She'd have to wait until they were sold to get her money back, but if the rumors about some outfit buying the cliffs above the town for rock climbing were true, prices on the few pieces of property left in Chimney Rock would be going up. Suddenly it was important that she get the nineteen thousand for her mother's bike and clean up most of the debt.

"How much are you asking for the other one?" he asked.

"Nineteen."

He gave her the kind of look that said he believed her price was firm; yet he put forth a half-hearted attempt at bargaining.

"It's four years old... and it's got a few miles on it."

"Nineteen. Take it or leave it."

"Okay, lady. I'll take it. It's my fiancé's favorite color. In fact, it's got her name written all over it." He reached to shake Georgie's hand. "Do we have a deal?"

She nodded and shook on it.

He pulled out his wallet and found a folded check in one of the compartments.

"Here, let me give you a thousand right now to seal the deal and I'll bring you a certified check for the rest tomorrow. How's that?"

She nodded, and he wrote out the check and told her he'd be back with his trailer in the early afternoon the next day. She gave him her cell phone number, and they covered the bikes.

"Boy I sure would have liked to have gotten that Ultra Classic, too. Who's the lucky guy?"

"He's in Afghanistan right now, and God willing, he'll be home in a couple of months."

CHAPTER FIFTEEN

IT WAS EARLY in the morning and Georgie was standing on the porch of the cliff house trying to imagine what the street looked like when her great-great-grandfather, the illustrious James M. Flack, owned everything on both sides of the river.

Georgie, being her father's daughter, always felt distanced from the Flack legacy, but it was easy to see why her mother was so connected to it. Growing up, her mother and her two sisters had the run of the town. And why not, the family owned a big chunk of it. Her great-uncle owned the famous Esmeralda Inn where *Ben Hur* was written and movie stars came to stay, and her great-grandfather owned the Mountainview Inn on Main Street across from the chimney.

The summer places dotting the street had started off as family camps built out of logs or framed up and sheathed in rough-cut slabs of oak, with nothing but outdoor plumbing and spring water that trickled from the mountain.

Eventually, an enterprising character started a private water company. He ran a series of connecting pipes from a spring at the top of Chimney Rock Mountain and down along the surface until it hit the river, then he strung the pipes across by wire. With all the freezing and thawing, they were always coming apart, and there being no water, someone would have to call Mike Keyes who made the repairs. He'd grab his tool chest and trudge up the mountain till he found the break. It wasn't until 1991 that the town finally got incorporated and took over and modernized the water works.

That wasn't the only utility that had started out privately owned. In 1920, old James M. Flack diverted a section of the river and built a power plant at the foot of Southside, furnishing power for Chimney Rock and all of the surrounding area for 25¢ per month. It not only brought lights to his hotel, but hot water, a dishwasher, electric churn, mangle and washing machine.

Georgie stood there on the porch, wondering how she could ever fit in. How she could ever feel a part of this place like her mother did? Two painful weeks had gone by since the disastrous movie night, and she still hadn't heard from Ron. The not knowing where she stood with him was making her moods see-saw from lethargy, because she wasn't getting enough sleep, to near panic, because she feared she had lost him.

She went over, opened a drawer to her dresser and took out a small wooden box. It was the kind they sold in their store with a decal of Chimney Rock on top. She took off the lid and found the strip of pictures taken at a booth at the fairgrounds and flipped it over. *Calico and Ron* was written on the back.

He had called her Calico ever since that fateful ride on the school bus. She sat down on the bed and enveloped herself in the memory. She could see the bus come to a stop and the boys letting the girls on first. Ron was only thirteen and at the school for just over a week, but she could see he was already the heartthrob of every girl in the middle school. She was making her way to the back of the bus, when one of the Lake Lure kids yanked on her dress. She poked him with her elbow, and a sudden cacophony arose. *Georgie Porgie pudding and pie, kissed the girls and made them cry. When the boys came out to play, Georgie Porgie ran away.*

"You kids are a bunch of brats!" she yelled.

"And you're a big snob!" shouted the boy who had pulled on her dress.

She swung into the last seat and watched Ron from the corner of her eye as he quieted everyone down on his way towards her, slipping into the seat next to her. She looked out the window and concentrated on battling back tears. She usually ignored these kinds of taunts, but it stung to have this new boy witness the disrespect everyone had for her.

"Don't mind them. They just wanted to get your attention," he said.

She kept looking out the window, even though she wasn't seeing anything.

"I'm not a snob."

"I know that. You're just frightened."

She turned and glared at him. "I'm not afraid of anything!"

It was the first time she saw his shy smile.

"Well, you sure as heck remind me of the little calico cat that showed up at our house on Shumont. She wouldn't make friends with our other cat and only stuck around for the food. Every time our old tabby came near her, she'd snarl and strike at him. Heck, she would even run across the room and bat at him if he so much as looked at her. But I figured she wasn't mean. She'd just been so scared from being alone in the wild without a mother to look after her that she couldn't trust anyone."

Georgie smiled at the memory. Things changed for her after that day. His guardianship raised her stature on the bus, and she never heard the nursery rhyme again.

She turned the strip over and looked at the two in the photo. She was a senior in high school when it was taken, and he was finishing up his two-year course at college. If only she had trusted him enough to say yes when he asked her to marry him. But it had taken her thirteen years to sort the whole mess out in her head, and just when she was finally going to tell him her secret, Phil had to show up and ruin everything.

She couldn't let the not knowing where she stood with him go on much longer. She'd poured out her heart in a letter she left tucked in his door five days ago, after she heard he was back from the Bahamas. Since then, she had held her breath every time a phone rang or the store door opened. She'd been rolling over thoughts in her head about the flyer the park had put up at the post office. One of the events they had listed was an "Off the Beaten Track" hike for this afternoon with Ron leading it.

She rushed back in the cabin and checked the time. Only

eight. He wouldn't be going up the mountain until after ten. She could still catch him at his house, and if he wasn't there, she'd go up to the park and look for him after the hike. She started to slip on a pair of shorts, then tossed them on the bed and ran to her closet and got out the slinky pink flowered summer shift that had caught her eye in the window of April's Boutique in town.

She put it on and took a moment to study herself in the mirror. If this doesn't get him, she said to herself as she smoothed the dress over her hips, nothing will. She carefully combed her hair, and then found some white pumps and slipped them on. She grabbed her wallet, ran down the stairs and jumped in her car. It wouldn't take but twenty minutes to get to his place.

She drove down Southside, passing a couple who were jogging with their dog. Farther up, Suicide was sniffing a trashcan one of the summer people had left at the end of their drive. She crossed the bridge and made a left onto Main Street. Other than a couple of shopkeepers puttering in their planters, no one was out. As usual, the breakfast crowd was pouring into Medina's Café.

She turned up Route 9 in Bat Cave, then right onto Shumont Road. A pick-up coming from the other direction raced past her. She stole enough of a glimpse of the man behind the wheel to see it wasn't Ron. She turned onto a gravel road and went up a steep grade through the woods until she reached a clearing and saw his Subaru parked in front of his house. She pulled up beside it and got out. The air was already stifling hot and the only thing moving was a goldfinch teetering on a sunflower on the edge of the driveway.

Other than her shoes clacking on the stone walkway, it was eerily quiet. A sudden high-pitched screech from a blue jay startled her as she reached the door. She smoothed her dress and hair before lifting the hand-wrought knocker. She tapped several times and waited. A chorus of bird songs suddenly rose as if she had woken up the whole neighborhood. She started to knock again, when the door swung open.

Years had passed since she had laid eyes on Mary, but the pitch black curls and white porcelain complexion were unmistakable; yet, it was shocking how much she was showing her age. She was clasping a silky robe around herself with enough of her voluminous bosoms exposed to make it apparent she had nothing on underneath.

Georgie was stunned.

A snide smile spread across Mary's face, as if she was pleased at the effect her appearance had made on Georgie. Mary stood with a raised eyebrow, eyeing her up and down.

"I'm afraid you've caught me and Ron at an inconvenient time for a visit, Georgie." She pulled her robe together tighter and added, "We're kind of occupied," she winked. "If you know what I mean." Her voice turned coarse. "So why don't you just turn your pretty little self around and go back to wherever you came from."

The door closed and Georgie walked stoically back to her car. The only sounds she heard were the ringing in her ears and the echoing of her footsteps on the stones. She numbly got in her car and pulled out of the lot. Once she reached the safety of the woods, she let the car roll to a stop, dropped her head in her hands and wept.

WHAT A PIECE OF GOOD LUCK, thought Mary as she lit a cigarette. Ron being off in the back of the property with Jennifer just when that Haydock bitch showed up. She hadn't planned this trip back from New Mexico a moment too soon. She pulled out the empty tuna fish can from under the sink that she was using as an ashtray and laid her cigarette in it, then went over to the table next to the couch, opened her purse and took out a powder-blue envelope. She tapped it on her cheek and thought.

Recalling how unlike himself Ron had been since she arrived, she worried about what he might do if he found out she had kept Georgie's letter from him. Yet, she didn't want to burn it in case she might need it as evidence in a divorce proceeding. Right now, she had better find a safe place to hide it; the two of them would be back any minute.

She hurried into her bedroom, slapped her suitcase on the bed and started to open it. No, this won't do. Jennifer might want to use it to put in some of her things. She rushed back into the living room and scanned the furniture, stopping at the encyclopedias. Perfect. No one ever opened them anymore. She rushed over and pulled one out, tucked the letter in and slipped the book back in its place.

That done, she went over to the fridge and got out a beer, then picked up her ashtray and went outside. It was hot and sticky on the porch, but she didn't want to risk being caught smoking in the house. No, she wasn't going to be the one blamed for marring Ron's happy reunion with Jennifer. She took a deep drag of her cigarette and savored the episode with Georgie. As long as she lived, she'd never forget the thrill of seeing the hurt expression on her face.

Watching her through a part in the curtains, she had delighted at the unsteady way she had walked back to her car. Mary had dreamed of a moment like this ever since her father took her to live in that dumpy trailer in the alley behind the stores, and she had to watch Georgie tease and flirt with Ron as they all waited for the school bus. It had been easy to see how smitten he was with Georgie; yet, one day when it was raining and they were all on the corner waiting for the bus, he left the shelter of Georgie's umbrella, took off his slicker, wrapped it around her, and said something nice about not wanting the pretty dress she was wearing to get wet.

Recalling the part in the letter where Georgie said she regretted not marrying him, she got angry all over again. That was the one irrefutable, bitter pill she could never swallow. Ron had actually chosen Georgie, while the only way she had gotten him, was to seduce him when he was on the rebound.

After they were married, he kept insisting that Georgie didn't mean anything to him anymore, but she knew better. One night, right after they were married, he was tossing in his sleep, and she reached over and touched him. Moments later he was making love to her and moaning Georgie's name.

For the past twelve years, she had felt like she was some kind of booby prize—the price he'd had to pay for his cherished daughter. She was suddenly heartsick thinking about Jennifer.

She was the only decent thing she had produced in her entire life. How strange, she thought, it turning out the way it had. The darling little soul was the light of each of their lives and the chain that kept them attached.

She looked around at the forest circling the house and it was as if she had never seen it before. It certainly looked a lot better than the view of the parking lot they had from that apartment in Albuquerque. Running off with Tim hadn't panned out as well as she had hoped. He was turning out to be as boring as Ron. Only, Ron had always been a good provider.

Snippets of the letter kept sneaking up on her. *She was sure she could get a job in Hendersonville.* How far had their relationship advanced for Georgie to make such big plans, she wondered. And wasn't that just like Georgie, to assume she could have anything she wanted.

She took a deep drag on her cigarette and stared off into the distance. Why do I hate Georgie so much, she asked herself. Was it because deep down she knew she didn't deserve Ron? No matter how loving he was to her, she'd always resented that he had wanted Georgie instead. She had been white trash and no amount of glossing over would erase that fact. And why was she drinking so much? Was it to punish herself for not being good enough and so much less than what Ron and her precious Jennifer deserved?

She put out the cigarette and got up. Whatever it was that made her do all those things wasn't important right now. It was thrilling to think she could finally get her revenge on all the uppity people in that town. But most gratifying was that she was going to make sure Georgie would never get what she evidently wanted most. As long as she had her daughter, she had a way of controlling Ron. She smiled to herself. Getting pregnant with Jennifer was the one jackpot that kept paying off.

CHAPTER SIXTEEN

A HAZE CLOAKED THE TOWN as Gail drove down Main Street. The gray sky clearing far in the distance made her hopeful the sun would be coming out soon. At least, the asphalt, dark and wet from the night's rain, gave the town a freshly washed look.

Not yet noon, and half the parking spaces in front of the stores were already filled. A man was opening a hatch-back and pulling out a stroller while his wife held a squirming toddler. Next to them, a woman struggled to get an elderly lady out from the front seat of a sedan and into a wheelchair. They were all hurrying as if they were afraid they might be missing something.

Gail wanted to make sure this was the only place she got that eerie feeling, so she continued driving westward through the town to the campground where they had stayed. The farther away she got, the more the feeling ebbed. She found a place to turn around, and drove back into town, passing through it again. The village boundaries imperceptibly merged with the town of Lake Lure a half-mile up the road. By the time she reached the Lake Lure Inn that sat across from the beach, the sensation had diminished again. She was now convinced the answer to what all the flashbacks meant lay in that quaint little village.

Now, back in town, the sun emerged from behind one of the clouds dotting the sky like puffs of smoke from a steam locomotive. She stopped at a crosswalk to let a family pass and noticed a street between two stores to her left. She craned her neck and saw that it led to a single-lane, steel trestle bridge over the river. When the last of the family trooped past, she let her car creep onto the street and found herself at the foot of the bridge.

A web of steel beams and braces crisscrossed and encased the narrow structure that ran for a hundred yards or so. She stopped and let down her window, listening to the river and wondering what she would do if someone came from the other direction. Stop! she screamed in her head. If you don't watch out, you're going pass out like you did at the campground.

She started across. The thumping of the tires on the bridge and the raging of the river made her tighten her grip on the steering wheel. Her shaking hand fumbled for the button to raise the window and extinguish the sound. The bridge spilled onto a lane that ran along the river. She wiped, first one, then the other of her sweaty hands on her jeans, already dreading the thought of having to go back over the bridge again. Huge poplar, oak and black locust trees reached skyward all along the street, and sprinkled on each side were neat, nicely maintained little cottages that looked mostly like summer residences.

The street led to a dead end, so she turned in a driveway and started back. She looked around and searched for something that might evoke a memory. A cabin perched way up on a ledge on the mountain side of the road seemed odd to her. Then, there it was again: the bridge. Only this time, people were milling around taking pictures and watching the river race underneath. She decided to wait until everyone got off before crossing, but when a tradesman in a pickup pulled up behind her, she started across. A man on the bridge noticed her and alerted everyone, and they pressed themselves against the rails as she crept past.

Once back out on the street, her heart stopped pounding. She cruised past the row of stores and turned right onto what looked like another street. A sign read "Terrace Drive." It wove around the back of the stores and resembled an alley. She went up a short distance and then stopped, her heart suddenly pounding. Why was this innocuous little street bedeviling her so much? Nothing but tall wood plank fences lining one side to give privacy to the small backyard spaces behind the stores. The other side rose almost straight up the mountain, with a garage and a couple of houses tucked in. The street was deserted except for a lone black cat slinking along the fence. It shot a look at her before darting through an opening in a chain link gate.

The alley had to be directly behind that store she'd felt she had been in before. Yet, her mother had insisted she'd never stepped foot in Chimney Rock until Roger brought her there three weeks ago. She continued up the lane. It climbed the mountain, then followed its contour, weaving up and down until it spilled out onto Main Street across from a motel. She read the marquee aloud: Carter Lodge. It didn't mean a thing to her.

She drove back into town and found a parking space in front of the Olde Mountain Emporium. It wouldn't be good to go in there again after the way the clerk stared at her the last time. Instead, she meandered into the store next door. When she realized it specialized in American Indian items, the name, Featherheads, suddenly made sense. She browsed a stack of postcards with photos of American Indian chiefs, while keeping an eye on the woman who was waiting on a young couple. Seeing that the shopkeeper was finished, she picked out two cards she thought her boys might like and took them up to the counter.

"This is a nice store you have here," she said as the woman rang the sale. "I'll have to bring my two boys to get some books." She eyed the woman. "Do you own it?"

"Yes, I do."

"How long have you had it?"

"Around fifteen years."

Gail made an expression as if she found that interesting.

"Who owns the store next door?"

"You mean the Mountain Emporium?"

"Uh-huh."

"Dinah Haydock."

"Oh," she said, as if that too was of interest. "How long has she had it?"

"A long time. She told me she even worked there as a kid."

"Do you know how old she is?"

The woman's eyebrow rose slightly as if she was sensing she was being asked too many questions.

"Maybe in her late fifties."

Then the woman abruptly reached out her hand for a book that someone behind her was waiting to buy, causing Gail to move aside. Assuming that was a signal that the woman wanted to end the conversation, she left the store.

Across the street, over an entrance to a staircase, a sign read "Riverwalk." She crossed and glanced at the rustic stairs leading down to the river. Recognizing something in its muffled roar, she was convinced it had something to do with her phobia of water. She clutched the handrail and started down. Tightness gripped her chest.

The stairs led to a park-like path that meandered along the river's edge. A small footbridge lay ahead. A feeling of other-worldliness swept over her as she went on the narrow structure that led to what looked like a small island. Feeling as if she were detached from her body, she looked over the railing and spied the clear green water rushing over the rocky bottom, slapping the sides of the huge boulders at its edges.

She studied the island. It was nothing but a jumble of huge chunks of granite of every size and shape laying askew as if they had tumbled haphazardly from the mountain. There was no formal passage; however, the exposed roots of the trees clinging onto the surface bore witness to the hundreds of feet that had tramped a rugged path over them.

She had to fight off an intense need to escape before she could force herself to step out onto a rock. The sun slipped behind a cloud, and it was as if the light had been turned down with a dimmer switch, making it suddenly cooler. Ahead, a huge boulder the size of a car cantilevered over a stretch of rapids. Two small boys stood on it, frolicking. Her eyes darted around. Where on God's earth were the parents? The youngest of the two boys leaned over the edge on his tiptoes and twirled his arms around, pretending he was falling in.

Suddenly a strange numbness traveled through her body. She grabbed a tree and held on as she was blanketed in darkness.

All she could see in her mind's eye was the river calling out to a little girl... the little girl skips onto a huge rock. Someone is gripping the little girl's hand and pulling her back.

"Let me go. I want to dance on the rocks."

"No! Mama will kill me if anything happens to you."

The big girl is bossy and grasping her hand so tight it hurts. The rock is slippery, and then the water instantly ice cold. The current is dragging the both of them. There is terror on the face of the big girl, yet she keeps her grasp on the little girl's hand. The big girl holds onto a limb of a tree that has fallen into the river. She listens to the little girl's screams as she floats to her death.

"Georgie! Georgie!" she cried out.

With the scream, Gail's awareness returned. She buried her face in her hands and sobbed as an avalanche of loss over-whelmed her. A woman was kneeling next to her, and her husband and the two boys were staring down on them.

"Is Georgie your husband?" the woman asked. "Ma'am, is that your husband? Do you know where he is?"

Gail saw the concern on all the faces, yet she did not answer.

The woman looked up at her husband for assistance. He reached for Gail and helped her up while the woman wrapped an arm around her waist to steady her.

"Is there someone we can call?" she asked.

"No. I'm all right."

The family insisted on helping her back up onto the street. After they walked her to her car, she smiled reassuringly and started the engine. She watched in the rearview mirror until she saw them disappear into a store, then she turned off the engine and sat motionless. Who was Georgie? What on earth had she been doing in this town? On that river? She wished her mother was stronger so she could talk to her about it. Ever since she told her about their vacation in Chimney Rock, she'd been more nervous and agitated than usual. Her condition being so delicate, Gail would have to tread lightly, but one thing for sure, this was the place in her nightmares and she was going to find out why.

CHAPTER SEVENTEEN

K IM SHERRILL AGONIZED for two days before calling Dinah about the lady who had come into her store and asked so many questions. Nagging at her was what happened the last time Dinah had thought someone was her missing daughter. The detective interviewed everyone on the street, but nothing had come of it except a lot of embarrassment when she turned out to be the sister of a girl who worked at Chimney Sweeps.

It had been years since her neighbor's daughter had gone missing, and the last thing Kim wanted to do was tear open the wound one more time, but the resemblance between the woman and Dinah's oldest daughter was too striking to ignore.

"What did she look like?" asked Dinah after Kim told her about the encounter.

"Blond, blue eyes, tall. Nice looking." Kim didn't dare mention the woman's uncanny resemblance to Georgie.

"How old would you say she was?"

"Somewhere in her early thirties."

Kim winced at the sound of the strained breathing as Dinah thanked her before slamming down the phone.

GEORGIE KNEW SOMETHING WAS WRONG the minute she came into the house and laid eyes on Ali. Her hair was mussed and she had the dazed look of an automobile accident survivor that Georgie remembered from her days working in the ER.

Please God, she said to herself, not Cal.

"That woman's back," Ali said as she folded her arms and sank against a counter.

Georgie let the groceries slip from her arms onto the table.

"What are you talking about? What woman?"

"The same one who was here last month. She went into Featherheads and asked Kim all kinds of questions about Mom. I thought Mom was going to have a heart attack after Kim called her. I had to give her one of the emergency pills you left with me."

"How is she?"

"Passed out."

"What makes you so sure it's the same woman?"

"First of all, she told Kim she had two boys. But mostly, Kim said she was a dead ringer for you." Ali tossed her head and let out a humph. "Thank God, she didn't tell Mom any of that. I had a hard enough time keeping her from calling the police as it was. Sis, if it wasn't for that foot of hers holding her back, I'd never have been able to handle her. She was like a raging bull. I had to toss her phone out the window or we'd be dealing with the police right now. When that pill finally kicked in, she barely made it into her chair. I know we're both going to be bruised tomorrow."

Ali took a deep, weary breath. "The boys were just coming back on their bikes so I sent them to find the phone. It's there in the drawer." She sank onto a chair. "I don't know how Dad stood it all those years."

Georgie grabbed a strainer off its hook and started rinsing the grapes she had just bought. It took every bit of the restraint her medical training had instilled in her to appear calm. She had no clear idea of how she was going to handle this latest scene in the pitiful drama that had played itself out over and over again for the past twenty-five years.

"I'm sure that woman's not Shelby." Georgie took pains to sound relaxed. "She's probably going through some stressful event. The story was in every paper in the state. She's probably heard about it somehow, maybe from an article at the library, and is just sick enough to believe she's Shelby."

"I don't know, Georgie. Don't you think it odd that when we questioned Debbie about the woman who came into the store, she said she looked just like you? At the time, I thought you were a little heavy-handed, but now I'm glad you stressed to her how important it was for Mom's health for her to keep her mouth shut about it. I don't know what we would have done if Mom found out you had lied to her about the woman having brown eyes and being in her forties."

"How long ago did you give her the pill?"

"A half-hour."

"Where are the boys?"

"I sent them up to your place."

Georgie glanced at her watch. "Mom should be asleep until around ten." She aimed for nonchalant as she put the groceries away, but her mind raced. "You're going to have to spend the night at my place. Go over there now and take the boys to Genny's for something to eat. I'll handle this."

"You don't seem very worried, Georgie." Ali nervously wrung her hands. "When I asked the boys to find the phone, Mike knew something was wrong and ran down the hall to check on Mom before I could stop him. Thank God, she was out cold."

Ali clasped her hands to her chest. "I don't think I can do this anymore, Georgie. If the boys had been here, I would have had to call 911. I was going to pack up and take them to Cal's mom's the last time, but after all the sacrifices you've made to help out, I couldn't go and leave you alone with her. I'm sorry, Georgie, but I'm having a hard enough time coping with Cal being in constant danger. I can't take this, too."

Georgie hugged her, and as she listened to her sister sob, she was overcome with how unfair it was that Ali and her mother, after all these years, were still being dragged into this kind of trauma. How much longer, she asked herself, could she let the whole family suffer this way rather than take a chance of being hated for what she did. How many more times must she let her mother's hopes be rekindled and dashed? So many pivotal things had happened that summer, she wondered if that deranged woman wasn't sent by some higher power to finally tear the wound so wide open that even she, the master deceiver, wouldn't be able to come up with a lie big enough to cover it over.

She'd known all along that some deep craving within her had driven her to come home this summer, and she suddenly realized what it was. She was there to heal more than her mother's foot. She had come to heal the whole family's wounds. It was high time and she was ready.

"Hang in there, Sissy. I promise you won't have to go through this again. I'm going to put an end to all this tonight."

Ali gave her a strange look as she drew away, but before her sister could say anything, Georgie told her to go pack a few things for the boys, and then rushed her out of the house.

Georgie continued putting away the groceries. She fastidiously checked to make sure she'd bought everything she needed for the meal plan for her mother and Ali that she had taped to the cupboard door. It wouldn't hurt to have her sister looking a little trimmer when Cal came back.

After five minutes of fiddling with the food in the cupboard, she realized she was mindlessly switching the same items around. She slumped into a chair and pictured her mother lying drugged in her recliner, and a deluge of shame overwhelmed her. After years of lying, pretending and conniving, the inevitable moment when she had to admit to her guilt had finally arrived.

She got back on her feet and went down the hall to check on her mother. She found her lying in her chair with her mouth sagged open. Seeing the room in disarray, she started straightening it up, but paused when she spotted her mother's scrapbook lying open on the floor.

She bent down and was about to close it when the picture of Shelby on the front page of the Hendersonville *Times-News* caught her eye. She had always detested the tome that functioned as Shelby's final resting place. In all the years since her sister's disappearance, she had never once looked through it, but the night ahead challenged her to finally face the specter that had haunted them all. She had always been able to block out all the talk about Shelby, but the sight of her was a killing thing.

THE SCRABOOK LAY closed on the kitchen table next to an empty glass, the bottle of scotch nearby. It had grown dark, and Georgie was barely able to make out the time on the clock on the wall. Past ten. She had better start her mother's dinner. She'd be waking soon.

Georgie stood up and felt herself sway, and for a moment thought she would fall. Her aching head made her wish she hadn't had that last drink. Blindly, she made her way to the wall switch and turned on the light. She carefully prepared a tray and started down the hall. She nudged open the door to her mother's bedroom with her elbow. There was just enough light from the kitchen to reveal her still asleep in the recliner. She put the tray on the table next to her mother, went over to the drawer where she kept her medical bag, and dug out the bottle of tranquilizers. She'd give her mother one the minute she woke.

Disturbed by the light, her mother suddenly sat up, calling out Georgie's name.

"I'm right here, Mom," she whispered.

Georgie went over to the corner and turned on the floor lamp. Its small 20 watt bulb barely cast enough light to illuminate the room, leaving everything mostly in shadow.

"What time is it?" her mother said groggily as she looked around. "And where are Ali and the boys?"

"She took them out for dinner, and they wanted to spend the night at the cliff house."

She adjusted the recliner so her mother would be sitting up, then pulled her rollaway table nearer.

"Here, Mom, I brought you something to eat." She took a pill from a bottle she pulled from her pocket and picked up a glass of water from the tray. "But first, I want you to take this."

Dinah lashed out at her. "No!"

The pill went flying across the room and the water splashed all over the table.

"I know what you're up to. You think I'm crazy! That woman *is* Shelby. I know it! And I know you lied to me about the last time she was here."

"Mom, don't do this to yourself. She's not Shelby."

"Gimme a phone! I've got to call the police."

Anxiety had distorted her mother's face, already puffy from the drug Ali had given her. Georgie quickly shook another tranquilizer from the bottle. "Mom, take this. It's for your own good."

Dinah thrust the rollaway table away with enough force to crash it against the dresser, then she reached for her walker and struggled to get up.

"What are you doing?"

"I'm gonna get in my car and drive down to the police station in Rutherfordton to make a report. We gotta get that detective over here to question Kim. That woman wouldn't have come back and asked all those questions unless she had a good reason."

"Mom, sit down. I'm not going to let you drive to Rutherfordton. You'll just make a fool out of yourself. Listen to me, she's not Shelby."

Dinah took a labored step toward her. The sneer on her face shocked Georgie.

"You're a pretty cool customer, aren't you? Just like your father. He never believed Shelby was still alive, but I knew she was 'cause I felt it in my bones. The only way I'll ever believe Shelby's gone, is if they prove it to me." She turned and started toward the door. "If you're not going to let me drive, I'm gonna go down on that street and find someone to take me. And if I can't find anyone to take me, I'll walk. Someone's got to fight for that little girl of mine."

Georgie jumped up. "Mom! Stop! I know for sure that woman isn't Shelby."

Dinah slowly turned her head. "What do you mean, *you know for sure?*"

"Sit down and take this pill and I'll tell you."

"I'll sit down, but you're not shoving any more of those damn pills down my throat. I intend to keep my wits about me."

She turned and teetered. Georgie was near enough to help her to her chair, but feared she might lash out at her again and hurt herself. Her mother flopped down on the recliner and looked stone-faced at Georgie, waiting for her to speak. The house was quiet except for the soft rattle of the katydids outside and the hum of the heat pump that had just kicked on.

Georgie went over to the window, pulled aside the curtains and looked down at the shops on Main Street. The sodium vapor street lamps cast an eerie pinkish glow through the mist that had settled on the town. Up above, a spotlight shone on the chimney with the Stars & Stripes waving in the gorge's eternal breeze.

Everything seemed so peaceful. No one would suspect that the apartment over the little store in this quaint little village was reeking with twenty-five years of regret. No one would feel the undercurrent of years of agony that couldn't be acknowledged lest the whole fabric of the family unravel. No one would know what had happened to the poor souls who had been tortured for twenty-five years not knowing what happened to their beloved child, unless they too were plagued and twisted by the worst fate that can befall a family.

Georgie spoke in a solemn cadence with her back to her mother, knowing her mournful words were bandits hiding in the shadows waiting to rob her.

"The morning Shelby went missing, she had crawled in bed with me. I can still hear her whispering in my ear, 'Let's go down to the river and dance on the rocks.'" Georgie wiped the tears streaming down her cheeks. "You know how she was. I never saw anyone so appealing in my whole life. I couldn't say no."

She swallowed hard and took a moment to steady her voice.

"No one was up, so we quietly dressed and tiptoed through the house. We unlocked the kitchen door and ran across the street to the Riverwalk. It had rained and the air was clean and fragrant. I can still smell the gardenias blooming on the landing. She wanted me to pick her some and I said I would on the way back. To this day, every time I see a gardenia, it's as if they're scolding me for not keeping my promise."

Her mother's pitiful wails suddenly filled the room, but Georgie kept on. "We got down to the river and I could see that the rain during the night had made it spit and roil. It looked like an angry dragon and it frightened me. I wanted to go back, but

Shelby pleaded, 'Please, let me go dancing on the rocks this one time.' I held onto to her hand as we crept onto a huge boulder that was leaning into the water."

"Oh, God, no," her mother cried out.

Georgie doggedly continued.

"Shelby lost her footing on the rain slick rock and started sliding. I was gripping her hand and got dragged along with her. I can still feel how icy the water was as the river swept us away. It was dark under the bridge, and as we shot out from underneath, I suddenly caught hold of a limb of a beached log." Tears streamed over the skin of dried tears on her face. "Mama, I swear I was holding onto her so tight I had no feeling in my hand..."

Sobs arose from a well of sorrow. "I've felt that little hand being torn from mine a million times." Georgie kept catching her breath in heaves with a heart-wrenching rhythm as her mother wept with her hands over her face.

"I heard her screaming my name above the river's roar. Then she suddenly stopped and I never heard her voice again. I climbed up on a limb and saw her bob down the river like a leaf floating on its surface until she went under. I stared at that river until I was shaking so hard I couldn't stand on the limb any longer... and I never saw her again."

The room was quiet, except for her mother's deep rasping sobs. Georgie went over to the dresser for a fistful of Kleenex and blew her nose. With zombie-like motion she dutifully got out the apparatus to take her mother's blood pressure. She went over to the drooping figure and reached for her arm. Suddenly she was shoved against the bed.

"Get your hands off me!"

Stunned, Georgie went over and looked into her mother's eyes. The hate and hurt in them sickened her.

"Mama, please! Don't do this."

The slap across her face echoed in her ears.

"You little bitch! How could you have lied to us all those years? Your father went to his grave wondering what happened to our beloved little Shelby."

Georgie had promised herself that no matter how badly her

mother took the news, she wasn't going to lose her temper, but those three words made her snap.

"*That's exactly* why I lied to you all these years, Mama!" Georgie's face twisted with resentment. "I was only six, Mama, but I was old enough to know if you and Daddy found out I had gotten your *beloved little Shelby* drowned in that river, no matter how hard you tried, you'd never be able to forgive me."

Dinah threw herself back in the recliner and pounded on the arms. "All the searching and prayin' to the Lord. How could you have been so heartless to let the guilt for not locking the kitchen door eat at me all these years?" She looked at Georgie who was sitting with her face buried in her hands. "Look at me, you little liar. I'm glad your father died without knowing what we had under our roof... what we'd raised. Girl, tell me! Why in God's name did you let it go on so long?"

Georgie raised her head.

"You want to know why? I'll show you why." She ran out of the room and returned with the scrapbook and flung it on the bed. "That's why!" She pointed to it. "That was the only person you ever cared about, Mama. Tonight I read every newspaper clipping in that book. And you know what? All you ever told those newspapers about was your precious little Shelby." She pointed to the album again. "In all of that, you didn't mention Ali or me *one single time!*

"Do you know what it was like growing up thinking that you didn't count? I deserved it, but not Ali. That poor kid has had to pay for my sin. I used to pray for the day I could escape from this mausoleum. Why do you think I worked so hard? You think it was for the money? Didn't you ever ask yourself why I took off the minute I graduated? You played the role of the martyr to the hilt, Mama, but Ali and I were the real victims. But don't you worry. I'm over it!" She buried her face in her hands and wept out loud for all the hurt. Finally she staggered to the dresser for more Kleenex and blew her nose.

She went over and looked out the window again. Two cats were staring at each other on the sidewalk under the street lamp with their backs arched. Finally, one of them slowly turned and walked away. Was that how this was going to end? Her turning away again? She knew they had to forgive each other or part forever. The edge on her voice faded.

"That's a lie, Mom. The only reason I had all those crazy jobs was so I'd have the money to run away if you and Dad ever found out. I wasn't that manic little overachiever just because I wanted to get ahead. I did it because I was scared, Mama."

Her mother's pained sobs tore at Georgie. She went over and got down on her knees and slipped her arms around her, never needing her mother's love more.

"I'm so sorry the river took your baby away, Mama. Please forgive me."

She buried her head in her mother's lap and wept.

Suddenly she was thrown to the floor.

"Get out of here. I never want to lay eyes on you again."

"But, Mama?" pleaded Georgie.

"What makes you think I'll believe a filthy little liar like you? Shelby's not dead. Someone pulled her out of that river and stole her."

"Mom, that's crazy! Who would ever do that? I tell you, she was under the water too long to have survived. You're in denial, Mama."

"Don't use those highfalutin' nurse terms on me!" She took hold of the tray on the table and flung it at her. "Get out and take this shit you've been feeding me with you. And get out of this house!"

Georgie staggered to her feet and went back to the kitchen with her brain groping for her next move. She never dreamed her revelation would devastate her mother the way it had. She couldn't leave her alone in this state. She glanced at the clock. Eleven-thirty. She'd have to get Ali back there right away. She wiped her nose on her sleeve and phoned. Ali answered after the first ring.

"You've got to get over here, Ali."

"You sound terrible. What's wrong?"

"I can't tell you over the phone. Just come."

"Is Mom all right?"

"Yes, but she needs you."

"I can't leave the boys."

"Call Nikki next door. Tell her it's an emergency and she'll come right over."

Within the hour, Ali came rushing through the kitchen door. Before she could ask what happened, Georgie pulled out a chair and told her to sit down, then stared mindlessly into space as she related the story.

Ali sat stunned. "I was only five, but I still remember how you changed after Shelby disappeared. I knew it was something more than just the shock of it all. You can't sleep in the same room with someone and not know when something's bothering them."

Ali hugged herself and seemed to be searching for answers.

"All those nightmares for all those years. Now that I look back, there were other things that should have made me suspicious. I remember thinking it strange when I was around eight and Dad told us to get our room ready for the new twin beds he'd be bringing home. I was so excited to be sleeping in my own bed that I yanked our old mattress off and saw that withered dress practically rusted right onto those bare springs. The way you grabbed it up and stuffed in your drawer I knew that something was terribly wrong about it." She looked at Georgie. "Was that the dress you were wearing when Shelby drowned?"

Georgie barely nodded.

"I bet if I had told Mom or Dad about it, they'd have gotten to the bottom of this a long time ago."

"Why didn't you?"

"I guess it was the fear I saw in your eyes. I didn't know what it was all about, but I knew if I said anything, you'd be in troub..."

Ali was suddenly interrupted by her mother screaming out her name. She quickly jumped to her feet and started for the hall. Georgie grabbed her arm and held her back.

"You've got to take over now, Ali."

"What do you mean, take over?"

"Mom doesn't want me near her."

"Do you blame her?"

Her mother screamed Ali's name again. She answered that she'd be right there, then glared at Georgie.

"I can't believe you never told us what happened. It would have been painful, but we would have gotten over it a lot better than we did." She tossed her head. *"Huh!* And I thought you took off right after you graduated just to get away from the sadness in this place. You were just escaping from the mess you made."

"Ali, please. I was only six, for Pete's sake."

"Yeah! For one year."

Georgie looked into Ali's eyes just inches from hers and for the first time in her life saw hate in them. She felt as if she'd been slapped for the second time that night, but the nurse in her was still in charge.

"You're going to have to go in there and take her blood pressure. We might have to do more than just give her some nifedipine. Whatever she needs, you'll have to get her to take it."

Once Ali left, Georgie phoned Nikki and told her that her mother wasn't feeling well. She was relieved when Nikki offered to stay the night. Georgie paced the kitchen until Ali reappeared with her medical kit and her mother's pressure reading. Thankfully, a nifedipine to control her high blood pressure and angina would be all her mother needed right now. Ali went back with the pills, while she sat at the kitchen table praying Ali would be able to get her mother to take the medicine. Finally, she heard footsteps in the hall and glanced at the clock. It was already two-thirty.

"Did she take it?"

Ali nodded and put her finger to her lips. "We've got to be quiet. I put her to bed and told her you left to take care of the boys. I held her hand until the medicine kicked in, but heaven help us if she wakes up."

Ali shuffled over to the counter and poured herself a cup of the coffee Georgie had just brewed.

"Let's go out on the deck, so we don't wake her."

They went out into the night and were swallowed by the darkness. After sitting silently for a while, Ali said, "What are we gonna do now? Mom will go crazy if she sees you in the house."

"I'll get a home care nurse in here as soon as I can."

"I'll ask Mom not to say anything to the boys, but you know her. They're going to know something's up, and Mike, sure as hell, is going to ask her about it."

The silence held for a while, then Ali spoke.

"Sooner or later we're going to have to call the police."

"I know."

"There'll probably be something about it in the papers."

"I know."

"At the very least there'll be talk."

They fell silent again. The chorus of katydids filled the air and every once in a while two whippoorwills called out to each other in the night.

"Remember the two we used to hear when we were kids?" asked Ali.

"Yeah."

"Boy, Georgie," Ali finally exploded. "When you phoned, I knew something horrible had happened, but in a million years, I'd never have guessed it was something like this. Do you have any idea how all those years of wondering what happened to Shelby has messed Mom up? I don't think she's ever going to forgive you for it. In fact, I don't know if I can. I went through my whole childhood with a mother who was so mired in grief, that I was invisible. Somehow, I don't think it would have been that way if you had only told the truth."

They sat there for a while longer, until Ali slapped her knees and got up.

"I'm gonna lie down in Mom's recliner. Why don't you lie on one of the boy's beds and try and get some rest. I'll come and tell you when she wakes."

After Ali left, Georgie listened to the sounds in the night. When she had made the decision to come back to Chimney Rock, she never dreamed the move would change her life. The whole depressing litany ran through her brain—finally facing up to what happened to Shelby, her mother and sister confirming her worst fears, the clumsy breakup with Phil, falling desperately in love with Ron again and then losing him. The whole mess was all about love—wanting it, giving it, rejecting it, needing it.

GEORGIE LEFT TO RETRIEVE the kids around six the next morning. Her nerves were raw and every sound seemed magnified. Even the blue sky vibrated as she drove to the cabin.

She thanked Nikki and explained that her mother had just had a bad bout with diabetes. Nikki was in her seventies and had seen enough woe in her days to recognize it when she saw it. She acknowledged the explanation with a nod; however, her eyes said she didn't believe a word of it. That's what you would expect in a town with just over a hundred permanent residents. Everyone knows everyone well enough to tell when they're lying. Thankfully, Nikki was gracious enough, not to press what she could surmise was a delicate issue.

Georgie took a quick shower and piled the sleepy pajama-clad boys into her car. Ali met them on the deck, and before putting them in bed again, explained that their grandma was sick and they had to be quiet.

Georgie ran downstairs to the store. She had to call her mother's doctor as soon as his office opened so he could give the insurance company a referral for a skilled wound nurse. It had taken a month for them to okay the visits for the therapist, but now that they had that set up, it shouldn't take more than a week to get in a nurse.

She checked the calendar. Good, Debbie wasn't scheduled to come in that morning. It wouldn't take much to arouse her suspicions. That woman could smell trouble a mile away, and they had to keep this quiet until things settled down. Thank God she had taught Ali how to take her mother's blood pressure.

She sat there thinking that maybe she should go back to Boone as soon as they got a nurse. She had faced up to the fact that Ron was a lost cause days ago, and with her mother not wanting to have anything to do with her, there wasn't much sense in her sticking around. She couldn't help thinking that her past was a rodent gnawing on the bones of her dreams.

CHAPTER EIGHTEEN

R ON CAREFULLY LACED up his hiking boots in anticipation of the strenuous trek he'd be taking on Round Top.
It was going to be challenging, especially with Mary along. The
cup of coffee he'd taken into her room before dawn to get her
roused must have worked. He could hear the shower running.
They hadn't shared a bedroom, or a bed for that matter, since he
discovered the batch of letters from New Mexico. They'd never
fought over it, he'd just left them lying on her dressing table
where he found them and moved his things to another room.

He peeked in on Jennifer, surprised when he saw that she
was awake. It was good to find her in the bed that had been
empty for too long. He sat down next to her and ran a hand
along her face.

"You gonna get up, baby?"

"Yeah, Dad. Terri's mom wants me over there by six-thirty
so they can get an early start for Cherokee. It's gonna be fun."
She touched his hand. "I'm glad you're taking Mom with you
today. She's really looking forward to it."

A week ago, when his friend from the Carolina Climbing
Coalition tried to reach him, he'd been too deep in the wilderness
to receive a signal. When Adam called the house looking for
him, Mary was told about the expedition to the foot of Round
Top's face to plan out a parking lot space and trail for the land
they had just purchased.

151

Ron had returned late that afternoon, and when he told her he didn't want Jennifer going back to New Mexico, he was surprised to find her so agreeable. In fact, he noticed her voice had taken on an uncommon warmth as he sat in an easy chair and glanced quickly through the mail.

"You're right, Ron. She's better off here among her friends," Mary said, handing him a beer. By the way, I might stay on a little longer... just to make sure she's settled in school."

"You don't have to do that. I can call the school."

"There's more to it than that, honey. Girl things. She'll need some new clothes and a couple pairs of shoes... and her backpack has seen better days."

"I can take her to the mall. She's old enough to shop for herself."

"You don't have time for that kind of thing. I'll be happy to do it."

"What about your job?"

"Oh, heck. The kind of jobs I had are a dime a dozen in Albuquerque."

He studied her for the first time since he'd gotten home and thought it curious that she was wearing shorts and a tee shirt instead of one of her usual flimsy dresses cut too low at the neck and too high at the knees.

She sauntered over and sat on the arm of his chair and put a hand on his shoulder.

"Ron, I want to go with you on Monday. Remember how you used to take me hiking up there at that deserted frontier town?"

He leaned his head back and looked up at her.

"That was years ago, and forgive me for saying it, but you're in no shape for a strenuous climb."

She stood up and ran her hands slowly along her hips.

"What's wrong with my shape?"

He rolled his eyes. "I didn't mean it like that."

She sat down again and put her arm around his shoulder.

"Ron, it would be like old times. Remember the way it was when we first got married? I promise I won't be in the way. I'll just stay at the base camp and get the lunch ready for everyone."

"We don't need lunch. We'll work right through till we're done."

"Aw, come on, Ron. Let me help out. While you boys are working, I'll hang out in the meadow and scratch around for old bits from that frontier town. Maybe I'll even find something from the Indian village they set up there for that movie."

That was three days ago, and now as he stood in the kitchen refilling his backpack, he dreaded having to take her along. Two big coolers Mary had insisted on packing were loaded with food and drinks. The team wasn't coming out there looking for a picnic, but he'd learned long ago it was easier to go along with her than get dragged into a heated discussion, ending with her swearing and slamming doors. He had to be especially careful since he didn't want to say anything that might change her attitude towards leaving Jennifer with him.

Ron loaded the truck, wondering if Mary would last long enough to serve up the sandwiches, or if he'd have to take time out from the expedition and bring her and the food home again before noon. He looked up as he heard the door open. Mary came out wearing the new hiking boots and slacks she had picked up at Bubba's with Jennifer.

His daughter proudly put her arm around Mary's waist.

"Doesn't she look great, Dad?"

It was suddenly worth the bother of bringing Mary along to see his daughter's face light up like that.

"She sure does, honey," he answered, smiling around the dread of having to tell his daughter that she wouldn't be going back to New Mexico with her mother.

They dropped Jennifer off at her friend's house and started for Chimney Rock. As they drove through the town and passed the Olde Mountain Emporium, Mary casually glanced out the window.

"Somebody mentioned your old flame's back in town," she said.

Ron knew better than to get lured onto that slippery ledge, so he ignored the remark.

"Have you run into her?" she asked.

The last thing Ron wanted to see was Mary in one of her moods, and he was willing to lie to escape it. The day was going to be rough enough as it was.

"No."

"Have you heard any of the talk goin' 'round?"

He glanced over at Mary, and when he saw her smile to herself, he became curious.

"No. What are they saying?"

"Nobody knows anything for sure, but from what her mother told Kim over at Featherheads, Georgie knew a lot more about what happened to that missing sister of hers than she's been letting on. They had to get a nurse in there because her mother won't let her near her. I guess she's not as high and mighty as everybody thought."

As Ron turned onto Terrace Drive and passed the back of the Haydock place, his mind churned with Mary's news. Just as he had thought. He'd always known Georgie was hiding some grim secret, and he'd figured it had to have something to do with her missing sister. It wasn't normal that she'd never once mentioned her.

He swung onto Silver City Road and started climbing, while Mary continued with her gossip.

"They say she's fixin' to go on back with some doctor she knows."

Ron's heart rate quickened as he pictured the man Georgie chose over him. Ever since he'd sat in his car across the street and watched her take the doctor up to her cottage, he hadn't been the same. He'd spent the night staring at the BMW, weighed down with the knowledge that he'd lost her again. It had been three weeks, and he still hadn't been able to shake the feeling. Images of what had probably happened up on the cliff kept clawing into his mind and shredding him apart.

He mulled over Mary's words. How sad that Georgie's mother didn't want anything to do with her. The closest Georgie had ever come to pouring out her heart was when he asked her what she wanted most in the world, as she lay curled up in his arms in one of those musty old rental cabins so many years ago. He still remembered how chilling it was when she answered, "For my mother to love me."

Now, it was even more haunting, for although his own mother had passed years ago, he still clung to the comfort of knowing how much she loved him. It was a buoy that had held him afloat through every crisis he'd ever faced.

That was the main reason he had put up with Mary all these years. He wanted his little Jennifer to have the same unshakable security of knowing a mother's love.

As much as he wanted to hate Georgie, he couldn't. Instead, he wanted to hold her in his arms and comfort her just like he had that frightened little calico cat that fate had wrenched from its mother.

As the truck climbed the curvy mountain road, his thoughts lingered on Georgie's phone messages. They'd stopped, and it was probably for the best. He had to keep thoughts of her out of his head or it would devour him. Besides, it wasn't his place to comfort her anymore. She had the doctor, now.

MARY SMILED TO HERSELF as the truck crawled along what barely resembled a road. *No. He hadn't run into her.* It angered her to think that if she hadn't read that letter she would have believed that lie. She had noticed a flicker of a wince when she told him about Georgie's mom, and she supposed he was now thinking over the little scenario she had painted. That letter was a god-send. She'd never have been able to throw in the part about the doctor unless she had gotten her hands on it.

Tonight after the trek, she'd offer to give him a massage like she used to when he came back with sore achy muscles after days of trekking through the wilderness. If all went well, she'd have him back in her bed and asking her to stay before the end of the week. And if things didn't go that well, she would stay anyway. After all, they were still married. Yet, to make sure everything went smoothly, she had better enlist Jennifer's help.

DEBBIE WAS IN THE STORE waiting on a customer while

Georgie sat in the storeroom, making out a list of items they needed. Georgie looked up to see Debbie holding a doll.

"A woman out there wants one of these, only in a pink dress. Is it okay if I get her name and number and tell her we'll order it?"

"Do you think she'll come back for it?"

"Oh, yeah. She buys from us all the time."

Georgie told her to go ahead, and then smiled after her. Her mother was lucky to have someone like Debbie to depend on. In her late fifties, she made a perfect sales clerk. She naturally liked people and always had a smile on her face. Separated from her husband for six years now, she'd worked on and off for her mother for the past twenty years and thought of the Olde Mountain Emporium as her second home.

Georgie added the doll to her reorder list and straightened the desk. It had been almost two weeks since her mother had banished her. With the help of the physical therapist and the home nurse who finally showed up, things had settled into a sort of 'new normal.' When the nurse stopped in downstairs and told her that her mother's foot was coming along beautifully, but that she had concerns about her being depressed, Georgie assumed it was to be expected. She and Ali were feeling the same.

It was strange, she thought, the way things had turned out. The only relief she'd had from this nightmare turned reality was when she relived the times she'd spent that summer with Ron. She smiled to herself. He hadn't changed a bit from that confident, easygoing young man with the shy smile who had always called her Calico. If anything, he was more confident.

She couldn't recall him touching her, except for the time on the hike when he put his hand on her shoulder and that night outside as she was unlocking the fence door when he urged her to hurry. She rested her forehead on her fist and groaned. Would these memories be all she would ever have? Would they have to last her for the rest of her life?

What was she doing to herself? She'd go crazy dwelling on what could have been. She had to concentrate on getting back to her job in Boone, the one pure, undeniably worthwhile occupation that made her proud of herself. As she sat there, something kept drawing her thoughts back to the strange events of the summer, and she wondered if she would ever sort them out.

She'd never been one to rely on any kind of an organized religion, even though she'd tried, many times. However, in all her years of nursing, she had seen too many prayers answered not to believe there was a God. She'd never found Him, but the way the guilt and shame she'd carried with her all these years was slowly dissipating, she was beginning to suspect He had found her. Her memories had always been a flock of vultures that pecked at her as she ran helter-skelter for cover in the woods. Ever since she'd told her mother the truth, they seemed to have been chased away.

She was startled by the sound of someone coming down the stairs. Isaac bounded down the last three steps in one long jump. Georgie smiled to herself, recalling how she and Ali used to do the same thing.

"Hi, Aunt Georgie."

"Hi, yourself, kiddo. How's everything up there in the ivory tower?"

He came over to her desk and rested a comforting hand on her shoulder. It felt good, especially after he said he missed not seeing her upstairs anymore.

For the first couple of days after her big revelation, the two boys had looked at her with a jaundiced eye. All that seemed to be behind them now; yet, the boys were aware things weren't right between their aunt and grandma. Georgie presumed they had mentioned that fact to their playmate down the street. That had to be the reason why their friend's aunt, Postmaster Carrie Owenby, had called her twice trying to get her to go to lunch—a sure indication that there was gossip on the street.

"The nurse just left," said Isaac. "She told Mom that Grandma will be walking real good by Christmas."

"How's she doing with the cane?"

"Good enough to go after a garter snake with it. Mike let one loose in her bedroom."

Georgie laughed. "How'd that happen?"

"Oh, he thought it would cheer her up if he showed it to her, but when she started screaming he got scared and dropped it. Don't worry Aunt Georgie, I caught it and took it back outside."

Georgie sat biting on the eraser end of her pencil, wondering when her mother would be able to tackle the steps. With all the credit card payments gone, they could easily manage more hours for help. She'd worked out a budget that would allow her mother to be in the store mornings and Debbie afternoons, with two people scheduled over the busy weekends, but it would require her mother to be able to navigate the steps before it could go into effect. As soon as that happened, she could go back to Boone.

Mike came hurling down the steps breathlessly yelling, "Aunt Georgie! Come quick! Grandma's bleeding! Ma needs you!"

They raced up to her mother's bedroom and found her sitting in the recliner with her foot up on a cushion, her bandage soaked in blood. Ali looked distraught and her mother, ashen with fear. Georgie quickly took away the cushion, retrieved her rollaway table and got out a wound kit. She rushed into the bathroom and washed her hands, then opened the wound kit, hurriedly arranged everything and put on a pair of gloves.

As soon as she told the boys to leave, she unwrapped the bandages. It looked good except for a troublesome section that had pulled apart. It was less than a quarter inch long, but blood trickled out at a consistent rate. She took off the gloves, put on a sterile pair and compressed the wound with a gauze pad. She looked up at her mother.

"What happened?"

"I bumped it bad on the corner of the bed."

"It's nothing to worry about. It'll be scabbed over by tomorrow morning."

When the bleeding finally stopped, she put on a fresh bandage, then collected all the refuse and put it in the bag she had hung on the table. She took a deep breath and slowly exhaled.

"There. You'll be fine now."

It was as if the air had been sucked from the room as the two women sat facing each other. There was so much Georgie wanted to say, and yet there were no words that could express what she was feeling. There was no anger or hate in her mother's eyes now. Just sorrow. It made Georgie want to reach out and put her arms around her, but she didn't dare.

Instead of telling her to leave, her mother sat silent. It made Georgie feel as if they were standing across a huge abyss from each other, and her mother was reaching out to her. She kept still for fear of breaking the spell.

Her mother finally broke the silence.

"Ali told me you didn't sell Dad's bike."

Georgie ripped off the gloves and tossed them in the bag. She understood the unspoken gratitude in her mother's words.

"Cal deserves it... and Dad would have wanted him to have it. I can wait until the lots sell to get my money. It wasn't earning anything sitting in the bank."

Silence fell on them again, and then Dinah finally asked the question that had been hanging in the air.

"What are you doing about that woman?"

"Nothing."

"I want you to find her."

"We won't have to find her. She's gonna find us. And when she does, I'm going to march her right up here so you can talk to her yourself."

It was obvious they both wanted to find the woman, but for different reasons. Georgie had seen her sister disappear in the river with her own eyes, and knew the woman wasn't Shelby, but she could see her mother was still in denial. Talking to the mystery woman might finally prove it to her once and for all. If that happened, maybe they could finally put Shelby to rest. Right now, however, Georgie was concentrating on getting everything running smoothly, so when the woman did show up again, she could get out of there and head back to Boone where she belonged.

"What if she goes to the neighbors again?"

"I've talked to Kim at Featherheads and Barbara at Chimney Sweeps and they both promised to call me right away if she comes into their stores again."

Georgie reached for the bag hanging on the table.

"We can't go to the police just yet. If we do, this whole mess will hit the papers... you know it will... and it could scare that woman away for good. I'm convinced she's someone with psychological problems, and I'm gonna make sure she gets some help once we straighten her out."

She got up and studied her mother's face. She had aged ten years in the past two weeks. Her cheeks were drooping and eyes swimming in dark pools. Georgie put her hand on the knob and started to open the door.

"You look tired, Mom. Try to get some rest."

Georgie left her mother's door ajar and went to the kitchen sink and poured a glass of water. She went over to the window, leaned against the sill and stared out onto the deck. The mention of the newspapers made her recall all the furtive looks she was getting from everyone in town. News traveled fast in a little place like Chimney Rock; like a virus, person to person and house to house, infecting everyone along the way. She laughed bitterly at the thought of how inured she'd become to it. After what she'd been through the other night with her mother, it would take a lot more than a few covert glances to rattle her. She was on a mission and nothing was going to deter her.

She had no doubt, that by the time this was over, she would have spent a good deal of time in purgatory and gotten more than a glimpse of hell. But it was a drop in the bucket compared to the gnawing shame of hiding behind a lie for twenty-five years. She laughed again when she realized that all her life she had wanted to belong to this iconic little village, and now she was getting her wish. The irony wasn't lost on her. Once this hit the papers, no one was ever going to forget Georgie Haydock.

CHAPTER NINETEEN

S TANDING AT A CLEARING on the rim of the gorge, Ron put his foot up on a rock and wiped the sweat off his brow. He glanced at his watch and saw it was a little past eleven-thirty. He checked his cell phone again, hoping he'd be able to call Mary. But still no signal. One of the guys on the team was the chief of the town's fire department and had brought some walkie-talkies, but they didn't have an extra one to leave with her. Ron imagined she'd spent most of the morning scavenging around for remnants of the old frontier town, and by now, was busy setting out her picnic on the truck's tailgate.

He felt bad about not being able to make it down for lunch. Mary was evidently trying hard to build some kind of bridge between them, and he didn't have the heart to thwart the effort she was putting forth, no matter how self-serving he figured it was. His team had planned to break their climb into two parts and hadn't expected the first part to move as fast as it had. Now they were too high up to turn back.

He decided to radio the team laying out the parking lot and trailhead. He'd ask them to relay the message to Mary when they got to the base camp for lunch. They'd tell her that he and his crew were going to keep going until the end of the shift at four. It was probably the coward's way out, but he didn't want to tell her himself when the guys got there with the radio. He knew how easily she got upset and didn't want to take a chance on her blowing up and saying something everyone would hear and they'd both end up regretting. Hopefully, she wouldn't fret when they told her.

"Sure," Ronnie Wood answered as soon as he was asked the favor. "I'll be glad to tell her."

Ronnie was a local guy who operated a small contracting business and also happened to be Chimney Rock's fire chief.

"Thanks," Ron replied. "And tell her, if she wants to go back after you guys finish eating, she can take the truck and I'll catch a ride home."

Ron's team, which included Adam, was made up of hikers and rock climbers from three counties. Their task was to chart a path along the base of Round Top's cliffs. Ron hadn't been up there for a couple of years, but he had dug out his notes and studied the county's aerials, all of which gave him a pretty good idea of what they were up against.

Adam had gone so far as to print out pictures of the entire south face and laboriously numbered every one of the over two dozen cliff sections at the top, as well as the dozens of additional rock outcrops sprinkled over the face. They were hoping to eventually weave together some of the hunting paths and old logging roads that crisscrossed the chain of mountains. They could curl the trail around the far side of Round Top, all the way to Bald Mountain, thereby linking the two rock climbing locations.

Adam came up behind him with a couple of guys from the coalition. Looking for a place to rest, they drifted over to a shady spot next to a huge slab of granite and peeled off their backpacks. Ron took out a kerchief and wiped the sweat pouring from his face and neck, then he got out a bottle of water, leaned against the rock and gulped it down.

Directly across the gorge was the meadow located half-way up Chimney Rock Mountain. The massive bald granite mountain, with the monolith sticking out from it like a chimney, wore a scarf of green over its top. From this vantage point, Ron could see the entire bald-faced escarpment, only interrupted by the cascading Hickory Nut Falls that plunged four hundred feet in a long narrow white ribbon.

Memories of the night he took Georgie to the movie sent a wave of melancholy through him. He shook it off and concentrated on Jennifer, a sure way to cheer himself up. It had been good to see her so happy this morning, and he suspected it was in large part due to their little family being back together again.

For the past couple of days, it had become obvious that Mary was angling for an invitation to stay. She'd even gone so far as to keep her drinking down to one or two beers a night. Ron knew her well enough to believe her change of heart had little to do with any feelings she might have for him, but more a realization that she was better off with him in North Carolina than with her boyfriend in Albuquerque.

He had faced the fact years ago that Mary would always be a burden he'd have to carry. Like it or not, his daughter's happiness relied heavily on her mother's well-being. It would certainly be easier to keep tabs on Mary if she were back home. Not ideal, just easier. He leaned against the rock and rested his eyes on the meadow across the gorge again, his thoughts automatically going back to that night at the movie. After all those years of yearning for a glimpse of Georgie, she had actually been only a breath away for two whole hours.

He swallowed a lump in his throat, then pushed himself away from the rock.

"Okay guys, let's keep going. I think we're gonna lick this thing today."

WASN'T THAT JUST LIKE RON not to show up, thought Mary as she led the men to the tailgate where the lunch was laid out.

Ronnie Wood loaded a plate and meandered over to the shady side of the truck where he spotted a rusting, bent-up tin sign leaning against its side. *Silver Slipper Saloon* was barely legible across the face in faded elaborate letters.

"Hey, guys. Get a load of this."

The four men finished filling their plates and went over to take a look. Mary smiled as she listened to their comments.

"I pretty near killed myself diggin' that thing up," she said as she strolled over to them. She pointed to a knoll covered with brush. "I was up there where they bulldozed everything away once they closed down the Silver City frontier town. I saw a small section of painted metal and got curious. It took me all morning to pull the dang thing out."

"Now, you want to be careful," warned Wood. "There's rattlers and all kinds of stuff you've got to watch out for."

"Oh, don't worry about me," Mary laughed. "I can take care of myself."

The men, who were volunteers from a hiking club out of Asheville, found places underneath the shade of a huge hickory and chowed down while listening to Wood ramble on about the meadow's history. His trademark red kerchief do-rag was wrapped around his head. He was long, lean and rugged looking, and spoke with a mountain twang. Even his face was thin and rugged, emphasized by a small gray goatee and ragged mustache.

"Back in the seventies, they put up a western boom town right here where we're sittin'. Even had ponies the kids could ride." He pointed to two huge steel columns in the distance. "Them thar was part of a double chairlift that brought folks up here from town."

"Isn't this where they filmed the Indian Village scene in *The Last of the Mohicans*?" asked one of the men.

"Yep. That was in the nineties." Wood flashed a mischievous grin. "I got an idea for the next movie they can make up here." He looked over at the men and winked. "Rescue on the Rim."

Mary's attention drifted from Wood's rendition of the two rescues on the Round Top cliffs that the fire department had executed in the past two years. Things weren't working out the way she had planned. She was especially irritated about Ron saying she could pack up and leave if she wanted. It was as if he didn't care if she were there or not.

Wood seemed to be enjoying having everyone's ear.

"I'll tell you, that woman who was stuck in that crevasse for four days without food or water would have been a goner if she hadn't clawed her way onto that rock to get warm just when the helicopter was making its last run. When we finally got her outta there, her fingers were so raw they were bleeding."

Mary couldn't care less about some lady stuck on a rock. She couldn't stop thinking about the part in Georgie's letter where she wrote that she knew Ron had taken her on that trek just so he could be alone with her, and how safe she felt with him after he lifted her up onto the cliff. It was burning a hole in her brain. If Ron had brought Georgie along with him today, he wouldn't have left her in the meadow. No, sirree, she'd be right at his side. That bastard would carry her on his back if he had to.

"Are there many bears up there?" one of the men asked Wood.

"B'ars? Plenty of 'em. It ain't nothin' to have a five-hundred-pound b'ar killed on that mountain."

"Someone told me there were still panthers up there, too."

"Heck, yeah. Panthers... mountain lions... whatever you want to call 'em. I know there are some big ones 'cause I've tracked 'em. They can leap fifteen foot without even touchin' the ground. I've heard them critters in the morning and late in the evenin'. They make the ha'r stand up on the back of your neck when you're up in a tree stand at daybreak huntin' deer. Their cries sound like a baby squealin'. I never caught a glimpse of one, but a buddy of mine has. He said it was black with a long tail."

The men, now finished, thanked Mary for the lunch and headed back to their jobs. They were soon swallowed by the forest, leaving her alone in the meadow. She had half a mind to pack up and go home, but Georgie's letter kept needling her. Whether Ron liked it or not, she was his wife and had every right to be there. Besides, when he and the men did come down, they'd be grateful for something to eat besides energy bars. That ought to win her some points. That sign she'd dug up would impress her husband as well. He was a sucker for anything old.

After the food was carefully put back in the coolers, she dug around in the knoll for more memorabilia, but after an hour she didn't come up with anything more than a few rotting chunks of wood that had to have been part of the old buildings.

The crickets and cicadas were starting to drive her crazy and made the place even lonelier. Every once in a while a cool breeze would sweep by, but for the most part, the sun was so hot she had to stay in the shade of one of the towering hickories at the edge of the meadow. She glanced at her cell phone. Not quite two. Ronnie said they'd be working till at least four. Not getting a signal, she couldn't call Ron. Sighing, she slipped the phone back into her pocket.

She grabbed a bottle of water out of the cooler and decided she'd follow the trail and see what the guys were doing. She could wait with them. Anything would be more interesting than sitting in the truck for the next two hours.

She started into the woods and began climbing a trail that had obviously been bushwhacked that day. It led to what seemed like an old logging road. She followed it for some distance, expecting to meet up with the crew around every turn. She was confused when it suddenly ended without her running into anyone. Somehow, she must have missed a turnoff. She started back, but, from the other direction, everything looked different. Where was the huge rock that looked like a pyramid she had passed on the way up? There was no way she could have missed that. Nothing looked familiar... nothing!

She came around a hemlock and suddenly found herself on a giant granite drop-off, and for the first time, was frightened. She had better retrace her steps and find that logging road right away. But, backtracking, she became even more disoriented. With a shaky hand she pulled out her cell to call Ron. Maybe she was high enough now to get a signal.

Damn! Her battery was dead. Now she couldn't even find out what time it was; but she was sure she'd been walking for at least an hour. Noticing her breathing had become rapid and worried that she was on the verge of panicking, she inhaled deeply and slowly let it out.

She had to get hold of herself and think. She'd been climbing uphill all along and getting nowhere. What if she headed down, instead? She'd have to end up somewhere on Highway 74, or the western side of the lake. Right? She started down and came to a stream in a small cove. After crossing it, she continued the descent only to end up at another giant granite drop-off behind a thick drift of laurel. She could see the northwest arm of Lake Lure in the distance, and realized she must have hiked around the face of Round Top. She was now behind it on the Shumont cliffs. A shiver ran down her spine as it suddenly dawned on her how lost she really was.

Okay, she told herself, going down is obviously going to be more dangerous than going up. If she could make it over the Shumont Mountain ridge, there was an old Jeep road on the back side that Ron had driven her on years ago. All she had to do was keep climbing up and she'd run into it.

She made her way over and around rock outcrops for what seemed like another hour and was heartened when she met up with a narrow overgrown trail she figured was used by hunters. Deciding to follow it, she was making good time when it came to a place where she would have to jump across a sheer drop-off to get to the other side. It didn't look like more than four feet, but the view over the edge made her knees wobble.

In her tired condition, it was too risky to attempt the leap. She had no choice but to abandon the trail and keep climbing. She had finished her water, but had hung on to the bottle, hoping she'd come across another stream. The terrain started to get steep and she had to claw her way up. She looked around for something strong enough to use as a walking stick. Finding a broken tree limb, she tossed the bottle and used both hands to dig the staff into the side of the mountain and pull herself up.

By the time she reached a knoll where she could rest, she was so exhausted she couldn't go any farther. She curled up in the shade and closed her eyes with the intention of catching her breath. Her breathing slowed and deepened, and within moments she was fast asleep.

RON AND HIS GROUP emerged from the woods at the trailhead a little after four-thirty. As the two teams started conferring with each other, Ron tapped Adam on the shoulder and said, "Come on. Let's get some eats."

They made their way to the meadow half expecting to see Mary setting out food at the back of the truck, but she wasn't there. Ron started shouting her name.

Noticing the concern in his voice, Adam radioed Wood.

"Hey, is Mary with you guys?"

He listened for a moment, his brow wrinkling.

"When's the last time you saw her?" Adam snapped off the radio and looked solemnly at Ron. "They haven't seen her since around one when they finished lunch."

THE MEN ASSEMBLED and began searching for Mary while Ron sat in his truck, feverishly trying to get her on her cell. Wood took charge of a search and sent a group westward with instructions to stop at the power line.

"Once she made it to that clearing, she would have been able to see the town below and would have headed in that direction," he told them.

He sent another group eastward to search all the way back to the Silver City Road they had come up on in the event she had decided to walk back rather than use the truck—a scenario he didn't think likely since she didn't leave a note. But anything was possible. He insisted that Ron stay with his truck and keep trying to reach Mary on her phone, then suggested he call around and get someone to go to the house to see if she was there. He purposely didn't want Ron to have one of the radios. If this turned out to be a missing person incident, the last thing he wanted was a close relative in on the search.

He left one of the guys with Ron and told him to phone if anything turned up, then started with his group up the old logging trail. Of all the potential routes she might have taken, he feared this one the most, especially since his team had tramped all along it that morning exploring.

Missing persons were his least favorite incidents. True, they never got a call unless someone needed help, but when they were missing, it was worse than finding a needle in a haystack. At least when it came to a haystack, you'd know that *that* needle was in *that* haystack. Running through his head were the rumors he'd heard that Mary liked to drink. It was possible she was nowhere near the mountain, but down there in Chimney Rock sitting in a bar having a beer. Or she could even have phoned a friend and met up with them.

As the fire chief in Chimney Rock, he was the lead on the search, but if it went on for too long it would roll over to the county. He'd instructed everyone to look for clues—cigarette butts, footprints, broken branches. He emphasized for them not to disturb anything and to try to get back to base as soon as they finished their route.

The minute he got out of earshot from Ron, Wood radioed 911 and gave them a heads up on a possible missing person. He told them they were fanning out in the immediate vicinity, and if they didn't come up with her in the next half hour, he'd call for additional resources.

That was one of the most important caveats his training had taught him: the longer you wait to mount a search, the harder it is to find the person. It was now past five and they hadn't seen Mary since one. Potentially, she already had a four hour jump on them. And if she were moving, she'd be going a lot faster than a rescue team would.

Wood's team searched all the way to the end of the logging trail, with no results. When the other two groups radioed him that they hadn't come up with anything either, he put in another call to 911. They would notify the county sheriff's office, round up all the Chimney Rock firemen and get the Lake Lure Fire Department in on it, too. Wood had four guys besides himself trained in high angle rescue, and Lake Lure had six.

By the time Wood's team neared the base on their return, they could hear the sirens from the fleet of rescue vehicles weaving up the mountain. Wood emerged from the forest happy to lay eyes on Ron Morgan, the chief of the Lake Lure Fire Department. He was a career firefighter, and unlike Wood who was part of a volunteer department, led six paid firemen.

The two departments worked as a team on most of the twenty-five or so rescues Chimney Rock got called out on every year. And if this search didn't come up with anything in the next couple of hours, Morgan, who was also the district Emergency Management Director, would be taking the lead.

The men from both fire departments were starting to pour in. They milled around, pulling out and checking their gear while they waited for assignments. The hikers and rock climbers stood around looking grim. The sheriff, who had gotten the story from 911 and had been listening to everything on his radio, pulled in, got out of his car and trudged over to Morgan and Wood. He tossed his head toward Ron who was sitting, bewildered, on a rock. Adam was standing next to him, coaxing him to drink some water.

"Is he the husband?"

Wood nodded.

"He was up on top with his crew the whole day. Me and my guys were the last ones to see his wife." He proceeded to relate what happened during lunch, and then added, "This guy's an experienced outdoorsman who knows these mountains, and we've had a hard time convincing him that he's more help here than up there. There's nothing worse on a rescue than having a member of the family in on it. They get emotionally driven and take chances, and before you know it, you're lookin' to rescue two people."

"I hear ya," said the sheriff. "Okay, let's go talk to him."

The sheriff took off his hat and ran his fingers through what little hair he had left as he lumbered his hefty body behind Wood and Morgan. His enormous belly was tugging on the buttons of his shirt and his step was a little labored, but his almost thirty years of experience with this type of situation made him a coveted asset.

Ron stood up and shook the hand the sheriff offered.

"That's all right, son. You just sit down there." He gave Morgan a quick glance before he proceeded. "I want you to understand that we have to ask you some questions we know are delicate, but it's all so we can help you find your wife."

"I understand."

"What frame of mind would you say she was in when you saw her last?"

He tossed his hands. "She was fine."

The sheriff nodded. "Has she ever done anything like this

before? Like wandering off?"

"No. Not like this."

"What do you mean... *not like this?*"

It was now over two hours since Ron discovered that Mary was missing, and the stress was beginning to show.

"Well, she left me a while back and went to New Mexico, but she came home two weeks ago... and I think she was planning on staying."

"Do you have any children at home?"

"Yes, our daughter. She's eleven."

"Does your wife have any health issues... or *any* issues that we should know about?"

"No. She's healthy. The only thing is... she has had a drinking problem. But I don't think she would have brought anything up here."

"Do you mind if we look through your truck and check?"

"No. Go ahead."

The sheriff signaled with a nod to Wood to take a look, then continued getting the description of everything Mary was wearing as well as her hiking and health history. Out of the corner of his eye he saw Wood shake his head, letting him know he hadn't found any alcohol in the truck.

"That'll be all we'll need right now," said the sheriff. "Do you have anyone at home to look after your daughter?"

"I called the folks she's been visiting and they're going to keep her for the night."

"Is there anyone who can let one of our volunteers into the house so we can get items your wife has worn out of the laundry basket without contaminating them with other scents? We don't want to confuse the dogs."

Ron nodded and looked at the sheriff as if the potential for tragedy was finally dawning on him.

The sheriff squatted down next to him.

"Son, believe me, everything is being done to find your wife. The guys who are out there right now know their stuff, and we need you to stay put right here in case we want you to identify any pieces of clothing we might come across. They'll be trying to get dogs on this search, so right now you'll really be helping us out by setting it up so one of our guys can get some of her clothes. Okay?"

He patted Ron on the back and then he and Morgan walked back to where Wood was giving instructions to the crews.

Seeing him, Wood said, "Ron Morgan is now heading up this deal and wants to say a few words."

Morgan looked over the crowd. "Well, Wood has pretty much given you the facts, boys. She's thirty-one, weighs about 140 pounds and is in good health, but not an experienced hiker. We want you guys going out in teams of three or four and paying attention to the radio. Get plenty of water and energy bars out of the fire trucks. Enough to last you all night. This operational period will end at seven tomorrow morning. Make sure your head lamps and flashlights are working and you've got extra batteries.

"Our planning section chief has made up grids for you guys to work in and he'll be handing them out. He's got some hunting paths and a couple logging trails marked, but we don't know all that's out there. If you can get your GPS to work and can make those notations for us as you go along, it'll be a big help tomorrow if we don't find her tonight."

While everyone was getting teamed up and assigned, Morgan and Wood started making plans for the next day.

"I got hold of Southern Pride. They're gonna get three dogs here tomorrow morning by seven," said Morgan.

"Can't they get us anything tonight?"

"I already asked. They just came in from a big search in Georgia and the dogs need a night's rest."

Wood tossed his head toward the group that had been clearing the trails.

"What do you want to do about them? Most of 'em are willing to stay on and help."

"We've already got experienced volunteers coming from Bills Creek and Bat Cave. They know all our protocols and have all the rescue gear. Plus, face it, this woman doesn't look like someone who would be attempting those cliffs. Let's get their contact info and see where tonight's search gets us."

Morgan took a long look at the mountain in front of him.

"If she's somehow gotten around that mountain and into the cliffs of Shumont behind it or Bald next to it, we just might need them tomorrow. There're so many cliffs up there, our guys will never be able to search every nook and cranny." He glanced back at Wood. "But right now, I don't think I can justify putting these folks on a rope and having them rappel down a cliff just so we can say we've looked at it. We aren't gonna go that route until there's some likelihood that she's in a particular area."

"All right," said Wood. "I'll go tell 'em, then I'm gonna team up with my boy and my nephew and go out. We've hunted up thar for years."

Morgan checked his watch. It was already nearing eight. He expected the county's incident management team to assemble at the site within the hour and they'd divide up responsibilities for the next operating period. Meanwhile, he'd see about getting a helicopter there for the morning.

As Morgan waited to hear back from the highway patrol about the helicopter, he took a moment to study the mountain that had summoned them. A towering hulk veiled in a smoky blue haze during the day, it could look deceivingly innocent and inviting. But by nightfall it was like a chameleon beast waiting for its next victim. Now at sunset, its true colors were starting to come out. The granite glowed a vivid orange, brazenly reflecting the crimson sun sinking in the west. It cast deep, black shadows across the cliffs, exposing the jagged scars that millennia of the earth's movement had mercilessly wrought on its craggy face.

Morgan knew the cliffs would only be this vividly orange for ten minutes or so and was the sun's parting gesture before it sank behind the horizon. The meadow where he stood was already in complete shadow. This dark blanket would soon cover the forest and reach for the cliffs like a monolithic sundial. This eerie shadow seemed to be warning him that Round Top was a beautiful, but wild, animal that you never dared turn your back on, especially at night.

CHAPTER TWENTY

THE CALL TO DONNA'S HOUSE came in at seven-thirty that night. She gently lifted her big orange cat off her lap, grabbed her cane and made her way to the phone that lay on a counter cluttered with papers waiting to be sorted. Ronnie Wood was on the phone notifying her of the search for Ron Elliott's wife, Mary. Donna had heard the sirens on the mountain behind her house and was praying it was some minor incident that would be over the minute they carried someone off to the emergency ward with a sprained ankle or cut knee.

"How many do you think you'll have up there tonight?" she asked.

"It looks like thirty... maybe forty."

She glanced at the clock. "We should have something together by nine-thirty, unless you want it sooner."

Nine-thirty was all right with him, besides they both knew the food could be picked up sooner if it were ready. She hung up and reached for her list and started calling the ladies of the Women's Auxiliary. It would take almost an hour for Barbara Meliski, the town's mayor, to run up to the grocery store and pick everything up, so Donna told everyone to meet at the firehouse by eight-thirty.

Her feet and her back were killing her, but she'd hurt just as much at home as she would at the fire house. At eighty-two with a body riddled with arthritis, she wasn't getting around near as well as she used to, but she could still make sandwiches as good as the next person. After all, she'd been doing it since '75 when they started the auxiliary.

She took a dozen or so halting footsteps to her bedroom and started unbuttoning her faded and frayed housecoat. There was no question it had seen better days, too, but no one ever saw her in it, and she wasn't about to part with the last gift her husband had given her before he passed.

She could pretty much recite a list of all the major fires and searches Chimney Rock had experienced since she was in her early fifties, yet she never got used to the feeling of fear and worry that overtook her every time anyone in their little community was threatened. Locals or tourists, it didn't matter; her level of concern was the same. She just wanted to help in whatever way she could.

It wasn't as if the ladies considered it any kind of sacrifice to provide the food for the firemen; it was more like they were just doing what was expected. They always made sure they had enough in their bank account from all their bake sales, yard sales and pecan and cookbook sales to buy what they needed.

Besides, a person couldn't live in a place like Chimney Rock and expect things like fire fighting and town business to just get done like it happened in the big cities. A small place like Chimney Rock didn't have anywhere near the tax base to do more than provide water and sewer and light up its three streets at night. The rest got done when the folks who lived there got up and did it.

Donna pulled the polyester slacks she'd hung up earlier off the hook in the bathroom and fought with them until she finally got them on. She slipped on the same tee shirt she'd been wearing earlier that day, all the time thinking about the woman who was missing. She'd never cared much for her, especially with the latest rumor that she'd run off with someone out west and taken Ron's little girl with her. But all that was water over the dam when it came to the town taking care of its own. They may let every little thing that anyone ever did wrong bother the heck out of them and gossip it to death, but all that stopped at the firehouse door. Everyone pulled together, because everyone understood they weren't perfect either, and if they were in trouble, they'd want to be helped, too.

THE SUN WAS NOW behind the mountain and Mary woke to a coolness in the air. What she wouldn't give for a drop of water! Her parched throat barely managed a groan at the thought of all those drinks back at the truck. She lifted herself onto her elbows and every muscle in her body screamed in agony. She was pretty sure she had twisted an ankle by the way it felt. She finally managed to sit up, but sank back down when she started feeling woozy, afraid she'd pass out and hurt herself even more. She recalled all the times Ron had stressed how water was the most important item on a hike. She was in trouble and she knew it.

The darkened sky told her it was getting close to nightfall. She decided she was better off staying where she was. Stumbling around in the dark was just asking for it. At first light, she'd start again. Maybe there'd be some dew on the leaves then. A rash had started circling her left wrist and she was certain it was poison ivy. The itching was unbearable, but she knew enough not to scratch.

Sitting up for that brief moment had exhausted her. She rolled onto her side, pulled up her knees and rested her head on her arm, wondering what was going on at the base camp. They had to be out looking for her. Thinking back, she realized she should have stayed put the minute she couldn't find the logging trail. The way she'd wandered all over those mountains, it was going to be a lot harder for them to find her. What had Wood said about the lady who was spotted from a helicopter? Wasn't it something about her climbing onto a rock? Maybe that's what she should do in the morning. Find a huge bald rock and wait for a rescue.

But right now the only way she'd keep her sanity through the long night ahead was to concentrate on Jennifer. A fleeting thought that she might never see the sweet little face again made her eyes well up. Jennifer was the only perfect thing in her messed-up life. In fact, she was the only thing she could point to that justified her existence. Of all the rotten moves she had made, no one could accuse her of being a bad mother. She'd cherished that little girl from the moment she laid eyes on her. She still couldn't figure out how anything that perfect, that adorable could have come from her.

Then she thought of Ron. She was ashamed of all the ways she had done him dirty. The sickening part was that none of it was his fault. He had always treated her like a lady, unlike her father who had always managed to make her feel soiled. It had been years since she'd thought about the day Ron kicked in the door of that rundown trailer and took her away from him.

She lay curled on the ground, remembering being in that wretched place as clearly as if it were yesterday. It was early in the morning and she was bent over puking in the bathroom when her father started banging on the door. She had to open it before he kicked it in. The rage on his massive stubbled face frightened her. He grabbed her and flung her on the bed.

"You're pregnant, aren't you?"

He started unbuckling his belt and she made a run for the living room. She grabbed the phone and feverishly dialed Ron. But before she had a chance to say anything, her father grabbed her, threw her down on the couch and started beating her.

"I'll teach you to get pregnant, you little whore!"

She rolled into a ball and screamed as he thrashed her. To this day, she could still remember the way her whole body throbbed with pain after he stopped. She could still picture him sitting in the chair drinking a beer and listening to her sob. Finally, he got up and loomed over her.

"You're nothin' but a goddamned hillbilly like your ma, and I've decided to give you just what she got. And when I get through with you, that boy ain't gonna want to be seen with you. Maybe then you'll remember your place is here takin' care of me."

The thought of the hideous scar across her mother's face sent terror through her. She could hardly breathe as she watched him go over to the table and get his hunting knife out of its sheath. She got up on the couch and started backing up into the corner as

177

he came at her. She put her hands over her face and started to scream when the door suddenly burst open and Ron rushed in. He raced across the room, grabbed her father's wrist and twisted until the knife fell to the ground.

Ron looked him hard in the eye.

"Don't you ever lay another hand on her." He slowly let go of her father's wrist and reached for her hand saying, "You're coming with me."

She cautiously climbed off the couch without taking her eyes off her father who was standing with his mouth gaping open.

"Don't you want me to get some of my stuff?"

"You don't need anything from here."

He helped her into his truck and she sat clutching her torn nightgown as he drove through town. He stopped in front of his aunt's store on Main Street, deserted that early in the morning.

"Aren't you gonna take me to your place? I'm not dressed proper for your aunt."

"You're gonna need a woman's hand until we get married," he had told her.

Now, as she lay on the mountain, aching and hungry, she was still able to smile to herself. Wasn't that just like Ron. He'd never asked her to marry him; he'd just picked her up and took care of her like one of those injured critters he was always finding in the woods.

She curled up and wept. Ron was barely twenty-one at the time, but a bigger man than her father ever was.

With the sweet woodsy smell of decayed oak leaves and pine needles surrounding her, she lay reliving how she'd kept looking up and down the street that morning while scampering up the steps to his aunt's apartment. The minute she walked in the door, the lingering scent of lavender caressed her. Standing in her bare feet with her nightgown blotted with blood from her swollen welts, she felt safe for the first time in her life.

"Aunt Lucy," he said, "this is Mary. We're getting married and need your help."

Even now, achy and sore, she smiled remembering how he looked the other way when his aunt took off her gown before helping her into the sudsy tub she had scented with sweet smelling herbs.

"You get on to work, boy," his aunt had said. "I'll take care of her."

That was another thing no one could accuse her of. She'd made a good home for him and their baby. She'd put up ruffled curtains in the cabin and kept everything clean and sweet-smelling, just like at his Aunt Lucy's house.

Oh, Ron, how did it all go so wrong? Why didn't I think of these sweet things when the meanness came over me? She thought back to the sixth or seventh year after they were married. At first, after the house was all clean and dinner started, she'd have nothing more than a relaxing couple of beers on the couch while she waited for Jennifer to come home from school. However, the habit had insidiously turned into three or four more beers after she had put her to bed. If only Ron hadn't had to be away so much, or if she'd had family to share with, things might have been different.

The more she drank, the dirtier she felt, and the dirtier she felt, the more she saw herself as something less than Georgie Haydock. Why this fixation with Georgie? Never once in all the years they were married did Ron bring up her name, other than that night he'd whispered it in his dreams.

She lay there realizing it wasn't Georgie; it was what she represented. She could still see her long golden ponytail swishing over her shoulder. Standing perfectly still, Georgie oozed enough confidence to make anyone believe she had the world by the tail. And then when Georgie got off the school bus, she would run laughing to her place over her parent's store with Ron chasing after her, while she had to return to the dingy trailer and pick up her father's empty beer bottles, hoping he'd keep his hands off her.

At that time, she never dreamed of Ron ever noticing her. It wasn't until that lucky night in the park after she'd finished cleaning the bathrooms up in the Skyline shops. She had been too late finishing up to catch her ride back to town and had no choice but to walk the three miles down the mountain. That was when he pulled up in his truck.

"You don't want to be trying this alone, gal. Hop in."

Sitting in his truck, all she could think of was the gossip about him being in the dumps over Georgie taking off without so much as a by-your-leave. In fact, he was the *only* thing any of the girls who worked with her at the park ever talked about. She'd tried to chat with him when he came to get a sandwich at the concession stand next to the gift shop, but he would just make a friendly comment and then drift off.

"I heard you're building your own log cabin up on Shumont," she said.

He glanced over at her, and she could see she had finally hit on something that got his interest.

"I'd love to see it. Can you show it to me?"

"Well, I don't know. I was plannin' on finishing up a shed tonight."

"Heck, you can still do that. I'd love to watch; and if you want, I'll make ya somethin' to eat. Do you have any food up there?"

What had started off as a lonely guy with nothing better to do, ended up with him spending half the evening showing her the plants he had collected since he was a boy, while she did everything she could to seduce him. She was amused by his prudishness, but she soon got past that; and he put to rest her fears about his manhood the three times throughout the night he indulged himself with her, convincing her it was the first time he'd been with a woman. Up until the time she read Georgie's letter, she was certain he hadn't known anyone else but her, but now she was tormented by the possibility that this assumption was no longer true.

Lying there on the ground with her clothes sticking to her skin and body aching, her thoughts kept floating back to Georgie's letter. Hints about her missing sister had been there all along, but she never noticed. Not until everyone in town had started talking about the uproar at her mother's place did she wonder what the story was. She could now see all Georgie's airs were a smokescreen to cover up some shame she was hiding.

How ironic, she thought. Life was a dark forest filled with people playing peek-a-boo.

Then she remembered Georgie's words. *I love you and want us to be together more than any truth I might fear.* A sickening panic suddenly seized her. If anything happened to her, Georgie just might get what she wanted. And Jennifer... the thought of her little girl in Georgie's arms made her want to scream. God, she pleaded, please, please let me get home. If you give me this one last chance, I promise I'll be good.

FINISHED WITH THE TIN of fried chicken his son had brought him, Wood wiped his hands on a kerchief he pulled out of his pocket.

"Man, for someone as skinny as you, you sure can put the food away," said his nephew, Jonathon.

Wood was glad to have had the meal, since he hadn't eaten since noon and the sandwiches and coffee wouldn't be coming for another half hour. By the end of the night they'd have their fill of energy bars. He looked up at the sky and could see darkness was coming on and there were too many clouds to get any help from moonlight. He checked the pen light on his hat and then his flashlight, before clipping his radio onto the harness he'd strapped to his chest.

"Are you guys all set?"

His son, Jarrod, and his nephew both nodded.

They trudged across the meadow and onto the trail that led to the logging road that by now was trampled flat. Wood was convinced that, since Mary hadn't shown up in town or at home by now, she was definitely somewhere up on that mountain. Running in his veins was the blood of four generations of mountain men whose very survival had depended on their ability to track their quarry.

He thought back to the lunch and remembered the look on Mary's face when he'd told her that her husband wasn't going to make it down. Then there was the spread she had put out that had surely taken a lot of effort. She would have had to spend a good deal of time the day before just making that potato salad.

And she sure didn't look like the kind of gal that would be digging in a brush pile.

He put it all together and came up with a picture of a woman who was trying hard to please her husband. There'd been talk at the fire house about her coming back with the little girl for a visit; and then Morgan had told him that Ron had said something about her planning on staying. If that were the case, she sure wasn't going to try and walk back to town or go wandering west beyond the meadow. Sure as shootin', she was gonna look for the base crew and wait with them for her husband to show.

She didn't strike him as a particularly athletic woman, but she had a steely kind of strength to her. Yep, that gal could move fast if she took a hankerin' to it. He checked his watch. Nine. She had a possible eight hour jump on them. He traced back his team's movements after lunch. They had been working on the parking lot up until around two. If she were walking on that logging trail around then, she'd have heard them. So, that put her setting out after that. Let's see, he calculated. She wouldn't have taken any food because she wasn't planning on getting lost, so she wouldn't be good for moving around much after six or seven. He figured five hours was about it.

He tapped his son on the back.

"Jarrod, if this gal went to the end of this loggin' road and got lost, how far do you think she could travel in five hours?"

Jarrod thought about that for a moment.

"Heck, if she hit one of them huntin' paths she could make it all the way around Round Top."

Then his nephew chimed in.

"I'd hate to see some Sunday hiker on that trail. It's riddled with granite drop-offs."

Wood was thinking the same thing.

MORGAN HAD JUST DISPATCHED a rescue team from Bat Cave to walk the power line at the west end of the meadow that led down to the town. It wasn't that probable of a route, but it was possible Mary might have gone that way and gotten into some kind of trouble, and therefore it had to be thoroughly searched and eliminated.

He went over and poured himself a cup of coffee from the thermos the ladies had sent up and picked up another ham sandwich. He looked up when the truck pulled in. The passenger door flew open and a young girl slid down, clutching a framed photograph. The halogen lights that they had rigged up on a pole and operated from a generator in one of the fire trucks, cast a deep shadow on her porcelain face like in a chiaroscuro painting; but it still didn't hide the fear.

She ran to her father and buried her face in his arms as he crouched down and hugged her. Morgan could see the flashing blue lights from the sheriff's patrol car reflecting off the tears running down her face.

He had been standing next to her father when he was talking to her on the phone, and it had been apparent the child knew her mother was missing. Morgan had been able to tell from Ron's one-sided conversation that he was going to let her come up to the base camp. It was a development he should have discouraged, but he didn't have the heart.

Morgan watched as the sheriff went over to where the little family was huddling and reached for the picture frame the little girl started to hand him. There was something about the way she kept holding on to it, that explained why he and all those men were going to be searching up and down those mountains until they found her mother.

IT TOOK A GOOD HALF HOUR of careful searching for clues for Wood and his team to reach the end of the logging trail.

"Okay, let's make a wide circle and start looking," Wood told them. "I asked all the guys on the afternoon work team if they'd come down this far. They said they had and that they had fanned out and looked around, but hadn't gone more than twenty or so yards from the trail."

They took thirty paces into the woods and started circling. They hadn't gone ten yards when his son found a trampled path heading north. Now pitch black, they brought out their high intensity flashlights and started following the lightly trodden trail.

It started climbing west, then switched directions as it went around a huge rock outcrop. Finally, it led smack onto a solid slab of granite. Wood flashed the light ahead and saw they were on the top of a drop-off so steep that it gave him goose bumps. He carefully examined the ground leading to the promontory, but could find no other path leading away.

Wood was starting to get worried that there wasn't going to be a good outcome to this search, when his son hollered out.

"Pa, look here. See how this brush is bent forward toward that cliff."

Wood took a few steps and crouched down.

"Now look. See how these are going in the other direction? I think whoever made this track, turned around and went back the way they came."

Wood examined the trail for several paces and came to the same conclusion.

"Okay, boys, let's go back, but keep your eyes peeled. She might have veered off somewhere along the way."

They went a few more paces.

"Look! The brush is trampled up this way," shouted Jonathon.

Wood studied the path. If these were Mary's tracks she might've been trying to get back on the logging road. She must have gotten confused and taken the wrong turn.

They continued climbing, but kept losing the trail every time they got to a rock outcrop that had to be climbed over or around. After a couple hours, they reached a hemlock thicket and lost the trail completely. They made another arc with his nephew in the lead.

"I got it!" Jonathon yelled out.

"I'll be damned if this isn't going back down again," Wood told the boys after he took a look at it.

He checked his watch. Past two. He better call Morgan and give him a heads up.

"Anybody got anything yet," he asked Morgan.

"No. Just a lot of deer and bear tracks. How about you?"

"Well, I think this is turnin' into somethin'. These tracks

we've been following have gone way past what one of our trail builders would have made. They're zigzagging all over the backside of Round Top. Just like someone would have done if they were lost."

He told Morgan where he was and asked him to keep the searchers off the Shumont cliff area as well as the far backside of Round Top, so no one would disturb anything.

"When the dogs get here, call me and I'll give you my coordinates. Meanwhile, we'll keep on this."

Wood took off his backpack and let it slide to the ground.

"Okay, boys, let's take a rest. We better fill up on water and chow down some of those energy bars." He knew how important it was to keep hydrated in order to stay alert. They were about to go tramping all over the Shumont cliffs. All it took was one careless step, and someone could go over.

"I think we're on to her," said Jonathon as he threw a package of crackers over to his uncle.

Wood snapped it up with one hand.

"I think so, too. Yep. She's up here all right."

As soon as they had refueled, they started up again and followed the tracks down to a small stream. There, on the edge, they found clearly defined footprints made by hiking boots, too small to be a man's. This was the strongest clue they'd had all night. Energized, they moved at a rapid pace until Wood swung around a huge hemlock and stopped dead in his tracks. He was staring out onto a huge abyss.

"Phew! We sure came on that fast," he said to the boys. This time he was really worried. "Jarrod, get out your GPS. You should be able to get the coordinates on this open ledge."

His nephew crept along the area with his nose almost to the ground.

"Look over here. Doesn't that look like she's going back up again?"

Wood smiled. "Boy, do you have hound blood in you?"

"You still want those coordinates?" asked Jarrod.

"Yeah. Get 'em just in case."

By now it was going on four-thirty. Off in the distance they could see a faint white glow at the horizon. The sun would be starting to come up anytime now.

After a few more yards, the path wove its way back to the hunting trail.

"I know where we are now," said Wood. "I've been on this trail a dozen times. That gal's headed for the top of Shumont."

MARY DIDN'T WANT TO OPEN HER EYES, but the hip she'd been lying on was sore and so was her shoulder. The katydids had died down, but crickets were still chirping. It was light enough, that when she sat up and started to brush herself off, she could see the pus oozing from the rash on her wrist. She reached around, found her staff in the brush and managed to struggle to her feet.

The way she had become so weak in less than a full day, told her she had to think clearly if she wanted to get off that mountain alive. Her ankle was sore, but not broken. That was good. She felt stronger than she had last night, but she wasn't going to make it over the mountain to any Jeep trail. They've got people out looking for me, she reassured herself. The best thing was to find a bald rock and sit there until she was spotted from a helicopter.

Right now she was in too dense of an area for anyone to locate her. She better get moving while she still had the strength. Hopefully it wouldn't take too long to find a good spot. It would break her heart if a helicopter went by before she was in position.

WITH THE COMING OF DAYLIGHT, Wood and his boys found they were moving much faster. They were hoarse from calling out Mary's name all night, but when they reached the spot on the trail that ended at a chasm that had to be jumped across, Wood went over to the edge and gave another holler. For the nth time there was no answer.

It was solid rock across the abyss, so there was no way for them to tell if someone had recently been across.

"Okay, boys, you wait here. I'm going to go see if there are any signs of her over there."

He backed up several paces, took a run and leapt across, landing in a crouched position. The two boys found rocks to perch on as Wood disappeared behind a stand of rhododendrons. Before they knew it, he came leaping back across, startling them.

"No sign of her," said Wood. "She either made her way out of here..." He threw a thumb over his shoulder. "...or she's down there."

Jarrod tossed up his hands. "I know. You want me to get the coordinates."

Wood nodded to Jonathon. "Let's see if we can find where she might have gone from here."

He didn't want to tell the boys he was worried that with the coming of the light, she might be on the move again.

MARY HAD BEEN CLIMBING along a rock-strewn stretch for over an hour when the woods suddenly became so dense she could hardly get through it. The only way she was going to get past the hemlock branches sweeping the ground ahead was to crawl under them on her belly. Thank God, Jennifer had talked her into getting the hiking pants along with the boots.

She got down on the bed of pine needles and was scooting herself forward on her stomach when she thought she heard something that sounded like a rattle. Shivers ran down her spine and she wiggled through the underbrush as fast as she could. She breathlessly grabbed hold of a limb and pulled herself up.

She froze. Writhing on the ground next to her was a timber rattler. It had to be four feet long and at least five inches around. It had evidently struck out at her, but had bitten into the padded leather rim around the top of her boot instead; and now it couldn't free itself. In a lightening fast involuntary reaction, she shook her foot, but couldn't flick it off. It writhed in the air and then wrapped its body around her leg. In a purely reflex action, she reached down, took hold of it and yanked it off, flinging it into the air with a scream.

Gasping for breath and afraid she might have crawled into a viper nest, she crouched down and slowly backed out from under the hemlock, all the while straining her eyes for anything on the ground that moved. Without any warning, she felt herself slipping. She snapped her head around and saw she had backed onto a steeply slanted slab of granite. She tried to leap off, but gravel had washed out onto the rock and it was like trying to get a grip on a surface of ball bearings. Her feet flew out from under her and she came down spread-eagle onto the granite.

Still slipping across the rock, she frantically fumbled and clawed for some kind of crevice to grasp with her nails. She was desperate for any kind of handhold to stop her descent, but there was nothing! Gravity was relentlessly dragging her down. She could sense her feet going over the edge, then her knees, her chest, and finally her grasping hands. As the tips of her fingers parted from the stone and she tumbled into nothingness, the only thought running through her brain was a prayer to God, begging for a second chance.

WOOD HAD BEEN EXAMINING the bottle Mary had abandoned when Jonathon said he thought he heard what sounded like a scream coming from somewhere up on the ledge in the distance. Neither Wood nor Jarrod had heard anything, but Wood was beginning to put a lot of trust in his nephew's wilderness skills.

"Let's go, boys," he shouted, and they started racing helter-skelter up the mountain.

Suddenly an eerie moan that sounded like a fading siren, made them look up. A body sailed through the air no more than a hundred yards in front of them. The three men stood motionless, unable to move.

Wood repeated "No, no, no," over and over again. Finally, he got out his kerchief and wiped his eyes, then solemnly folded it and shoved it back in his pocket.

He switched on the radio.

"Morgan, you better prepare her husband. We're gonna need the basket."

CHAPTER TWENTY-ONE

T HE SWEET AROMA of warm peaches swirled around Gail like the sinuous arms of an exotic Siamese dancer as her car rolled down Route 9 on her way to her parents' house. Proudly lined up on the back seat were four bushels of what her mother always insisted "were the best tasting fruits on the planet: the Spartanburg peach." She loved the way her mother could always emphasize things with some kind of hyperbole. Maybe it was because of her unique name, Pearl, that she always put an interesting twist on things.

"There are more peaches grown in South Carolina's Spartanburg County than in all of Georgia," her mother always bragged. Renowned as the "tastier peach," the state agriculture folks claimed it was the work of Mother Nature herself. The hot days and humid nights, along with the slightly acidic soil in this county that lay at the foot of North Carolina's mountains, were purported to create this unusually sweet peach with its own special tang. And Gail and her mother were looking forward to putting up a hundred quarts of them in the following week.

Gail smiled to herself, remembering the first summer her mother had let her help. At eight, she was given the job of peeling the peaches. She calculated that they'd been doing this for eighteen years, and she decided to have a little get-together with Roger's and her parents on Friday and make a family celebration out of it.

Gail had dropped the twins off at Roger's parents' house late that morning and wouldn't be seeing the boys again until they all got home that night. All week, their dad would drive over to his parent's house after work and they'd have dinner together with the boys while Gail was with her mother, canning; when it came to peaches, the two families had a symbiotic relationship. While Gail and her mother canned, Roger's mom watched the boys and fed the family, and in turn, was given a generous supply of the golden treasure so she could produce her delicious peach pies, cobblers and breads for both families all winter.

Gail had mixed emotions as she turned onto the rolling country lane she'd grown up on. She almost expected to see her horse, Brownie, racing along the fence like he used to do every afternoon, looking for a treat when she got off the school bus. She was filled with the warm expectation of working side-by-side with the mother she loved in a tradition they both cherished; but at the same time, she could taste the poison of rebellion.

She didn't know how she was going to do it, but by the end of the week, she planned to get to the bottom of what had happened to her in Chimney Rock. That was practically all she thought about anymore. Ever since she'd returned from that last trip, she'd been distracted, and she knew Roger and the boys were noticing.

She had mulled over several scenarios. The most logical was that her mother had taken her down to that riverwalk and she had slipped into the river and almost drowned. That made sense. It also explained her lifelong fear of water and the strange way her mother acted. With her mother's delicate sensitivities, it was only natural she would never want to think about the event again. The only piece of the puzzle Gail couldn't find a place for was the bossy little girl who wouldn't let go of her hand. The girl named Georgie. Who on earth was Georgie?

When she thought back to the stressed way her mother had always reacted to her phobia for water, she was more convinced than ever that her mother held the answer to this puzzle. Gail hated that she had to bring all this up at a time during the year that held such a hallowed spot in their hearts. But she had to seize this chance, since it was the only time they were ever alone and totally uninterrupted. And her mother's health wasn't what it used to be. She had to find out before it was too late. No, she couldn't wait any longer. This would probably be the only time her mother would be able to handle it.

Every year, in spite of being frail and weak, her mother, who was raised on a peach farm in Alabama, managed to muster the considerable stamina it would take to wash, skin, halve, and pack the peaches, and then process the jars day after day until her cupboards upstairs in the kitchen and pantry downstairs in the basement were filled. It was almost as if it were the only way her mother could prove her worth—the one thing that excused all her frailness and need for special consideration the rest of the year.

Gail pulled into the garage space her parents still reserved for her, and got out. Her mother, donned in her apron, was waiting with the kitchen door open as she went up the steps with the first box of peaches.

Her dad would have helped if he weren't at work. He was well past the age he should have retired and let his store go, but Gail suspected he kept working so he could continue to lavish her and her family with all the things he was determined to give them, like the time he had insisted on going with them to pick out an RV. When she and Roger decided on a small one that fit their budget, her dad had said, "Go ahead and get the bigger one," and written out a check for the difference.

She put the box on the folding table her father had set up for their week's project. The familiar sound of the Open Bible Hour floated from the radio on the fridge, telling her it was past noon. Her mother had been listening to the ministry of WTBI's Tabernacle Baptist Church in Greenville every afternoon for as long as she could remember.

The two women worked in tandem all afternoon, with Gail washing and dipping wire baskets of peaches into boiling water until the skins were loosened, and then cutting them in half and pitting and peeling. She'd toss them into a huge vat of a citric acid mixture where they floated until her mother was ready to pack them into jars and get them into the canner for a half-hour boil. All afternoon the two women had something cooking on the stove's four burners, plus the two on the hot plate on the counter.

By five, the last of the jars they were processing for the day were put to boil in the canners. The two women pulled out chairs and sat down with glasses of iced tea for the first time that afternoon.

"Your dad's going to pick up a cooked chicken for us tonight on his way home, and I've got some potato salad made. How about some pork and beans, too?" Pearl asked.

"That sounds good," responded Gail as she gazed at the rows of jars filled with peach halves. She felt the special kind of pride experienced by those who lovingly preserve nourishment for their families for another day. She let the sense of accomplishment envelop her for a while, until Pearl got up and started to push her chair back under the table.

"Wait, Mom. I want to talk to you."

"About what?"

"Mom, last week I drove over to Chimney Rock."

Her mother took hold of the skirt of her apron and clutched it to her flat, wisp of a chest.

"You promised you'd never go there again."

"I know, Mom, but there are questions that are bothering me real bad, and I know you have the answers."

"The only answer I have is that I love you, Gail. And I don't want to ever talk about this again." With that, she turned and went over to the canners, switched off all the burners and started getting food out of the fridge. "Why don't you set the table while I get the dinner ready? Your dad will be pulling in any minute."

It suddenly dawned on Gail that this was going to be a lot harder than she had imagined. For the first time, the words her mother always uttered every time she was asked about their past had a strangely ominous overtone.

Like most only children, Gail shared a special kind of intimacy with her mother. Gail knew her so well that she could carry on a conversation with her even when she wasn't around, because she always knew what she would say. They had made an unspoken agreement way back when she was a little girl: Gail wasn't supposed to be curious or speak about anything in her parents' past. Once Gail accepted this premise, it became a habit, a fact, something she never questioned. Her father was in on the scheme too, but refused to actively participate. "Ask your mother," was all he ever said.

The only concrete fact about their past that Gail had ever laid eyes on was her birth certificate. It said she was born to Pearl and Raymond Braycroft in Blue Springs, Alabama. When she was in high school, she had looked the town up at the library and discovered it was near the Georgia border and had a population of 129. But other than that, she knew nothing about where they came from.

There was one question that gnawed at her since she was in her teens that she never dared ask. How come she looked so different from her parents? Neither of them were over five feet tall, and she had shot up over their heads as early as twelve. And then there was their coloring. Before her mother's hair turned gray, every five weeks she'd go to the beauty parlor and have her brown roots bleached blond to match hers.

The squeal of the automatic garage door going up got their attention. "There he is now," said Pearl in a relieved tone.

Gail sat in thought as her father entered, put the chicken on the counter and came over and kissed her on the top of her head. Ray strolled over to the table that held the jars and put his fists on his hips.

"You girls sure have been busy today. I could smell those peaches all the way out in the garage."

As was his habit, he kissed his wife, picked up the mail and newspaper and went into the adjoining den and sat down on his rocker to read. Gail rose and took three plates from the cupboard and set the table while her mother readied the meal.

A deluge of doubts kept swirling through Gail's mind as the three sat at the table and ate. It was eerie the way her mother acted as if nothing were wrong, as if she had never been asked about Chimney Rock. As Gail watched her mother cheerfully

193

put potato salad on everyone's plates, a sickening sensation shot through her. This fragile little woman was putting on the very same act she had repeated since Gail was a child. Yet, now it seemed too well practiced, too deliberate, too wrong. All the doubts she had buried in the past began clawing their way up from their graves.

All her life, her mother had put her questions to rest with the same response she had given her this afternoon. *The only answer I have is that I love you.* And she had complied by totally accepting that her mother loving her was all the logic she needed.

With dinner over, her father went back to the den and the two cleared the table. Then they started getting the jars out from the canners with tongs and lining them up with the rest. As they stood straightening the rows of jars, Gail sensed that the mood in the room had changed. She no longer felt the comfortable ease that had enveloped her all afternoon, and she could see this change reflected in her mother's posture and in her eyes. Gail wrapped her arms around her and wanted to squeeze her with all the love she felt for her, but knew she'd break if she did.

That night as she drove home, Gail determined that she would try again with her mother on Tuesday. She had no choice but to find out what all the flashbacks meant. They'd been increasing in frequency ever since the summer when Roger took her and the boys to the beach. They'd had to cut their vacation short because the ocean frightened her so much she'd kept blacking out. And she'd hardly had a decent night's sleep since that episode on Chimney Rock's Riverwalk.

But she and her mother had been playing this game of 'let's pretend' for so long she wasn't sure if her mother knew how to stop. Gail had known there was something wrong with this veil of secrecy from the time she was twelve when she found herself glibly throwing out evasive answers to her best friend who had asked her where her parents were from. Gail suddenly caught herself playing the same game her mother had taught her. When had she bought into it? Was it just the repetition? No, it was more than that. It was all tied to love. She played the game with her mother to prove that she loved her.

CHAPTER TWENTY-TWO

"WHERE'S THAT GEORGIE!" Dinah hollered.

"You don't want her in this house anymore. Remember?" said Ali.

"This is different. The only way we're gonna squelch all that gossip that's goin' 'round is if we all show up at the funeral together."

Dinah looked up and saw Georgie in the doorway dressed in the navy blue suit she hadn't worn since her father's funeral.

"I figured you'd want me to go with you," Georgie said.

Her mother responded with a "humph," and then yelled out, "Where are those boys?"

Isaac and Mike poked their heads out from behind Georgie.

"Get in here and let me see what you two look like."

They were wearing long pants and white shirts and their hair was combed and slicked down.

Dinah nodded her approval and then used her cane to get up. She, too, was wearing the same navy blue outfit she'd worn to her husband's funeral.

"Okay, let's get going. Whose car are we taking?"

"I've got mine parked in the alley," responded Georgie.

That got another "humph" from her mother, and when Georgie tried to help her into the front seat, she shooed her away with her cane. Ali got in the back with the two boys, and they took off for the Chimney Rock Baptist Church.

"Donna told me they're putting his wife in the plot next to his Aunt Lucy," said Dinah. "There was a big to-do about a funeral service for her, since she hadn't been to the church in five or six years... and all the talk about her... well, you know." Dinah let the subject drop and gazed out the window.

"From what I hear," said Ali, "that little girl of theirs is taking this pretty hard."

"Why wouldn't she?" snapped Dinah. "What an awful way to go. Donna said when they found the body, all her bones were broken and sticking out of her."

"Mom! Not in front of the boys!"

The two boys snickered.

Georgie pulled off the highway onto Boys Camp Road just past downtown. She could see the parking lot was almost full. Two cars behind her pulled off the road and onto the grass. Georgie planned to do the same after she dropped everyone off, but her mother would have none of it and pointed to a space.

"Go over there. We're all walkin' into that church together."

CHIMNEY ROCK BAPTIST CHURCH wasn't the biggest church in town or the one with the largest congregation; it was the *only* church in town. And technically speaking, it wasn't even in the town, but on its very edge in Lake Lure. It was moved there in 1926 when the valley was flooded to create one of the first resort communities to spring up in the South.

Lake Lure was developed with the same entrepreneurial spirit that infected the early speculators who were mesmerized by the beauty of the Hickory Nut Gorge and inflamed by its potential. Around the turn of the century, Lucius Morse, a doctor from Missouri, bought Chimney Rock Park from Jerome B. Freeman. Then, in the heady spirit of the Roaring Twenties, he accomplished the extraordinary feat of buying up all the land in the nearby valley, moving everyone out, building a dam and flooding the land to create 27 miles of winding shoreline and a new town.

The economic boom that followed WWI ignited a renewed spurt of growth and risk-taking in the village of Chimney Rock. And in 1929, when the Wall Street Crash ended the era and brought on the Great Depression, it was sorely felt by the Flacks, Freemans and the Morse family, as well as the many area folks who had engaged in land speculation in anticipation of the growth they believed the new resort would bring.

But before the valley was flooded, the Chimney Rock Baptist Church was given a piece of land on Boys Camp Road and the graves were moved to the cemetery at its rear. And today, Mary Elliott would be buried there in Ron's family plot.

NIKKI SATTERFIELD HAD gotten up at six to make her potato and bean salad for the visitation that would take place before the funeral that morning in the Chimney Rock Baptist Church. This was her seventh year of preparing that dish for the three or four funerals they held every year, and she always made sure she had the ingredients on hand so she'd be ready at a moment's notice.

She got the bowl she'd covered with foil from her car, took it in the side door and slipped past the kitchen to the fellowship hall where the ladies of the dinner committee were already busy setting up a buffet. There was a hushed silence in the room, with the only sounds coming from the clinking of glasses or an occasional thump on the buffet table as someone set out another bowl of food.

Nikki could almost taste the pall in the room, for there were too many tragic circumstances around this death. And piled on that was the way some of the elders had kicked up a storm over holding a service in their sanctuary for someone who was now considered out of the congregation. Then there was that business that everyone remembered about them having to rush their wedding. His aunt had tried to put a good face on it, but everyone knew it was a situation of Ron and Mary having to get married.

Thankfully, the pastor was able to cite several of Mary's good deeds in the early years of her marriage as well as enumerate the many years of service Ron's Aunt Lucy had given to the church.

Nikki dreaded having to offer Ron her condolences, and promised herself that for his sake she wouldn't cry when she spoke to their little girl. She remembered Ron always being so polite and reverent when he came for the Sunday school classes she taught. Mary had come to church regularly with Ron and his aunt for several years, but after Lucy's funeral, the only time anyone saw someone from that family was at Christmas and Easter when Ron brought the little girl 'round. None of that mattered right now, though. Ron was one of their own, and the decision had been made to take care of him and his in their hour of need.

Nikki offered to stay in the kitchen and pass whatever they were running low on through the window during the visitation. It would start any minute now. She was listening hard for the pastor's office door to open, signaling that the family would be coming down the hall. She was at the refrigerator when she heard it. All it would take was a quick glance for her to catch a glimpse of them, but she didn't have the heart. She went over and leaned against the wall so no one would see her, and then listened.

The pastor's voice was just above a murmur as the little group of mourners slowly moved past the doorway. Nikki finally went to the door and watched Ron and his little girl hold hands as they formed a reception line. Even that was sad. They were going to be the only two people who would be receiving family and friends. Nikki was relieved when she saw the pastor's wife come in. She with her husband would make it four.

After a nod from the pastor, an usher opened the door to the outside and people started shuffling in. Nikki recognized several people she knew from the park as they passed her, and assumed all the younger visitors were in the same line of work as Ron. She waited until most of the crowd had made their way through the reception line before going over. She was shocked when she got to Ron. He'd always been such a handsome man, but today his eyes were sunken bloodshot orbs and his face drawn.

She only had a fleeting moment to talk with him, because the woman next to her grabbed his hand and started gushing with condolences. Nikki looked down on Jennifer who was huddled against her father. She was gripping the pocket of his suit jacket as if she were afraid he might leave her. Nikki took her hand and led her to the piano bench in the corner where they sat down. Normally, she would have comforted the girl by telling her that her mother was now in the hands of the Lord, but from what she knew of the woman, she didn't believe it likely that was the case and she wasn't about to fill the child's head with falsehoods.

She took Jennifer's hand in hers. "Why don't you tell me something your mama did that you never want to forget?"

Jennifer's face crinkled up and tears pooled in her eyes.

"Her smile. She had the most beautiful smile. I never want to forget that."

"That's a nice thing to remember, darling. Maybe you can make a little book and write down all the wonderful memories you have of her. You can even ask your daddy to help you."

Jennifer wiped a tear from her cheek with the back of her hand and nodded, then put her arms around Nikki and buried her face in her jacket. Nikki patted the child gently on the back and then broke her promise to herself.

EVERY PEW IN THE SANCTUARY was filled and a few people were standing in the back. They had opened the doors to let in some air, but with the sadness on everyone's face, the atmosphere was oppressive. Georgie sat wondering if Ron had read the card she had inserted in the flowers she sent and signed *From the Haydocks*. She had never been good at Bible studies, and the only thing she could think of to put on the card were the words that she knew had comforted her mother after her father died: "The Lord is my refuge and my fortress, my God, in whom I trust."

The organist started playing *Shall We Gather at the River*, signaling that the service was about to begin. Suddenly the pastor appeared from the side door next to the altar. He reached the pulpit and asked everyone to rise as Ron and Jennifer entered and filed into the front pew.

A soprano voice accompanied by the organ broke into a lilting hymn, and the congregation joined in. *There's a light in the valley, there's a light in the valley, there's a light in the valley for me...*

When the hymn finished, the pastor began to speak. "We're gathered here to remember Mary, the wife of Ronald Elliott. We haven't seen much of her in the past five years, and we've missed her. It would have been nice if she had been closer to us, but I'm not going to speak of that time. There is a memory I do want to honor, though. It's of a sweet little nineteen-year-old girl who stepped up to this very altar to marry one of our sons. For several years, she faithfully came with Ron's aunt, Lucy Elliott, to participate in Bible studies. Also, both Mary and Ron cheerfully and generously chaperoned several of our teen outings..."

Remembering what her mother had said about the fuss the elders had made, more than anything, Georgie wanted to assure Ron that Mary had asked for forgiveness for her sins as she fell to her death. Then she'd have every right to be buried as a Christian. Didn't Jesus forgive the penitent thief who was dying on the cross next to him? It had been years since she had heard her father read that section from the Bible as they sat in the living room on Good Friday, but today the words that Jesus spoke to the thief when he asked to be forgiven came flowing back to her: "Amen, I say to you, today you will be with me in paradise."

The service ended with the organ playing a solemn hymn as the casket was rolled down the aisle with Ron and Jennifer following behind. Georgie peeked furtively at first, but once she could see that Ron's eyes were cast down, she couldn't keep her eyes off him and the little girl.

The child looked just like Georgie remembered Mary looking during their school days. Georgie's eyes fell on Ron again and she had to look away. Never had she wanted anything so much as to rush to his side and hold him. Yet she could do nothing other than take comfort in the fact that Ron and she hadn't done anything that would now be filling them with guilt.

They waited until everyone had filed out before her mother attempted the walk. The funeral procession had left for the cemetery on the hill behind the church, but quite a few people were milling around outside in the parking lot. Georgie felt everyone's eyes on her and their family as they made their way to the car.

Her mother elbowed her and whispered, "Mind your manners, girl, and smile at everyone as if nothing's wrong."

On the drive back to the apartment, her mother's words echoed in her brain, and all she could think of was that life was an endless string of hollow smiles hiding oceans of heartbreak.

CHAPTER TWENTY-THREE

WEDNESDAY MORNING GAIL pulled out of Abbott's fruit stand with another four bushels of peaches and headed to her mother's. She stopped for a light and took the moment to rub her forehead. She had taken two aspirins before she left home, but the medicine still hadn't kicked in.

On Tuesday, after they were done canning, her mother had again refused to talk about Chimney Rock, and at one point she had even locked herself in her bedroom. Gail had pleaded with her for a half hour to get her to come back in the kitchen, but her mother kept telling her she would only come out if she promised never to talk about Chimney Rock again. Gail couldn't do it. They were well past the pretending stage and she was determined never to play that game again.

It hadn't been until the garage door squealed open, announcing her father's arrival, that her mother came out, timing her exit from her bedroom to coincide exactly with his entrance into the kitchen. It had been chilling for Gail to watch her act as if nothing were wrong the entire rest of the evening. A strange sensation had washed over her as she sat at the dinner table. She finally realized that she was no longer encased in the special secret world her mother lived in, a world in which she always felt loved.

Darn! How long had the light been green? She glanced in the rearview mirror. Thankfully, no one was behind her. She put her foot on the gas and proceeded down Route 9. Last night, she'd fallen asleep the minute her head hit the pillow, but woke around midnight and spent the rest of the night fighting with herself. Why was she so determined to undo the fabric of lies the family had been hiding behind? Shouldn't she leave well enough alone? She had a wonderful husband, parents who loved her, the twins.

Then there was her mother's weak heart and fragile nerves. It had been years since she had taken to her bed, but Gail still remembered the dismal months when her mother had lain in the darkened room. Her dad was getting too old to handle that sort of thing and would have to let his store go if it happened again. The more she thought about it, the more she worried that her mother's behavior was a clear signal they could be careening toward that kind of conclusion if she wasn't careful.

What on earth was her mother so afraid of? It had something to do with Chimney Rock. She was certain of it. She'd long since gone beyond the suspecting stage. Now she was convinced it was the key to all the secrecy shrouding the family's past. She'd never been so close to asking for answers. If she let this opportunity pass, she was sure she would never have the courage to bring it up again and her parents would take their secrets to their graves.

She had to try a different tactic. Instead of confronting her mother, she'd let her know just how disturbing the flashbacks she'd been having were. That might be the only thing that could reach her, and she had to do this well before her father came home.

Their third day of canning went as usual, except never once did her mother make eye contact with her. As the afternoon wore on, Gail kept looking up at the clock and rushing her work so they'd have the last of the jars packed and boiling in plenty of time to talk. But it seemed to her that her mother was doing everything she could to slow the process down. When her mother accidentally spilled the syrup mixture all over the counter, they had to prepare more and bring it to a boil before they could fill the jars.

When they finished putting the last jar into the canner, her mother started for her room. Gail gently took hold of her mother's bony arm, led her to the table and sat her down.

"Come on, Mom. We've got to talk."

Startled at the sound of the garage door going up, Gail glanced at the clock. It was only five. Why would her father be coming home so early? Her eyes shot over to her mother, and seeing how calm she was, she was sure she had asked her father to come home from the store early and had purposely stalled the processing of the peaches.

Well, that being as it may, Gail was still going to proceed with her plan.

Her father entered the kitchen.

"I know you girls are getting tired, so I came home early to take you to dinner at the barbeque joint down the road."

He went over to the counter, picked up his paper and mail and went into the den in the next room.

"I'll read the paper while you girls get ready."

Gail waited until she could see her father comfortably seated in his rocker in the den, then she put her mother's hand in hers and spoke in a low tone.

"I really need to talk to you, Mom. I'm not feeling well. These flashbacks I've been having have made me pass out too many times now, and I'm afraid I might get seriously injured the next time. I could have really gotten hurt when it happened to me in Chimney Rock."

At the mention of Chimney Rock, Pearl yanked her hand away and jumped up.

"I don't want to talk about it! I can't!" She clutched her head and wailed, "Leave me alone!"

Her father slowly put his paper down and rose from his rocker. Gail looked up at him as he entered the kitchen. There was no dismay on his face, just a defeated expression. He went over to his wife and gently put an arm around her and sat her back down.

"Pearl, it's time," he said.

"No, Ray! We can't!"

Her father's voice was low and soothing as he patted her head. "Everything's going to be just fine, Pearl. We can all get through this. You girls just sit there and I'll be right back." He turned and started toward their bedroom.

Gail looked at the pitiful hunched over figure of her mother.

"Stop, Daddy! It's okay. I don't need to know anything."

Her father turned and looked at her, then shook his head.

"No. It's time, girl," he said, and shuffled down the hall.

Gail took her mother's hand again. The coldness of it, and the blank stare on her face frightened her.

"I love you, Mummy. Like Daddy says, we can all get through this."

Her father came back carrying what looked like a newspaper clipping. He crossed the room and with a shaky hand offered it to her. Then he went and stood behind her mother's chair, gently caressing her shoulders with his heavily veined hands. Gail glanced at the clipping. A large photograph of a little girl smiled at her. Gail's eyes shot back at her father.

"Read it," he said.

She studied the headline: "Four-Year-Old Missing in Chimney Rock." She wrinkled her forehead and again looked up at him.

Her father slowly shook his head and spoke as if he were talking to himself. "I knew it was wrong when we did it, and I've never been able to forgive myself."

Gail was incredulous. "Is this me?"

Her father barely nodded. "Yes."

She picked up the clipping and read it through, then put it down again.

"Daddy, I don't understand. How can this be me?"

"It is, honey."

She looked over at her mother who was staring blankly ahead and rocking back and forth in a trancelike state, mumbling scriptures.

Then Pharaoh's daughter went down to the Nile to bathe, and her attendants were walking along the riverbank. She saw the basket among the reeds and sent her female slave to get it. She opened it and saw the baby.

Ray bent down and whispered in his wife's ear.

"That's okay, Pearl. Everything's going to be all right. You just settle down now."

"Good, God, Daddy! How did this happen?"

Her father sank onto a chair, and with his hands in his lap and his shoulders slumped, looked over at Gail. There was such sadness etched on his face that she would have cried if she let herself.

"We had a little girl. Her name was Gail. She was frail as a baby... always getting colds, sore throats. I thought if we moved to California or some place out west she would do better. So we left Alabama and went. But our little girl died anyway. Your mother fell apart. She was already forty-one when Gail was born so there wasn't going to be any more children. She stopped eating, sleeping... all she did was read the Bible. She got so thin I thought she was going to die, so I packed everything I could fit in our station wagon and came to Spartanburg where someone said the railroad was hiring.

"The first weekend we were here, I thought I'd take her somewhere nice for a couple days, and Chimney Rock seemed like as good a place as any. I can remember it like it was yesterday. We got a motel room, but she didn't sleep all night and insisted we go back to Spartanburg in the morning. We stopped at a little restaurant on the river next to a bridge to get some breakfast, but they weren't open yet. I remember thinking your mother might like to look at the river while we waited, so I coaxed her to walk down to the bank with me.

"We were standing there when I saw something floating down the river. It looked like a doll. When it was just about to go past us, something made me plunge into the water after it... and it was you. The current was so strong that it was a struggle to get back on shore. You weren't breathing and you were cut... bleeding... limp like a little rag doll. I blew into your mouth and put you over my knee and pressed on your back, and all of a sudden you were coughing. Your mother fell to her knees and kept thanking God for sending Gail back to her."

He wept quietly, then got hold of himself again.

"You were like a precious little doll. I held you in my arms and asked you your name and you just stared back at me. I remember wondering then if the bump on your head had made you forget who you were. God forgive me, but when I realized you had to be the same age as our Gail... and with the way your mother was carrying on... I bundled you up and took the both of you home."

Gail's mouth hung agape.

"Daddy, I can't believe this."

"It's true. Every ugly fact."

Then his sister asked Pharaoh's daughter, 'Shall I go and get one of the Hebrew women to nurse the baby for you?'

Ray took both of Pearl's hands in his.

"Honey, please. Don't get yourself all worked up."

Gail reached over and placed a hand over theirs.

"Don't worry, Mama. Just like Daddy says, everything's going to be all right." She looked up at her father. "We better get her in bed."

Ray helped Pearl to her feet and Gail lovingly took off her mother's apron. Together, they helped her to the bedroom. They sat her on the bed and Gail undressed her while Ray took off her shoes, a routine that the two were familiar with. Neither of them spoke as they listened to Pearl's recital of the names of people in the Bible who were raised from the dead.

Jesus raised the son of the widow of Nain from the dead; the daughter of Jairus, Lazarus...

Once they got her tucked in, they each bent down and kissed her, then the two went back in the kitchen and sat down next to each other.

Gail fingered the newspaper clipping and thought out loud.

"So, you were in a new town where nobody knew you, and you just said I was Gail. Why not? You had the birth certificate."

"That's about it."

"Who are the people I belonged to?"

"The Haydocks. They owned a store in Chimney Rock and lived over it."

"I know it."

She was starting to put all the flashbacks together and they were forming a picture.

"Did they have any other children?"

"Yes. Two older girls."

"That's good. At least they didn't lose everything they had."

Her father wrung his hands. "Oh, God."

Gail reached over and gently patted her father's hand. After a while she asked, "Was one of the girls named Georgie?"

"The papers never said. But I read where the father died last winter."

Gail took a deep breath and moaned as she exhaled.

"Oh, Daddy... what a mess."

"Gail, it wasn't as if we had planned anything. You just fell in our lap. It was all so easy." He kept rubbing his hands. "It was that one split second when I should have rushed you to the hospital and notified the authorities. But instead, I stole you for my wife. It's strange how two God-fearing people who never did a thing wrong in their lives, could, out of the blue, with no fore-thought whatsoever, commit such a horrible sin."

"Dad, don't do this to yourself."

"I have to. We did this to you, too, and I want you to know, so some day you can forgive us. The minute we got you in our car and started back to Spartanburg, your mother came alive again. You vomited almost everything we fed you for a couple of days, but little by little you got better. I held my breath waiting for your memory to come back, but it never did.

"After you began to get well, I started reading in all the pa-pers about how they were looking for you. But when I told your mother we had to take you back, she got on her hands and knees and begged and cried at my feet. She had convinced herself that it was God's intervention. A miracle. That she had prayed to Him to send back her Gail, and that's why He made sure we were there at the very moment you went by. She actually be-lieved it when she said 'Why else would He have delivered a girl the very same age as our Gail unless He wanted us to have her?' Anyway, the days went by and then the weeks and then the years."

He took Gail's hand.

"However you want to handle this, honey, is fine with me. I may be seventy-five, but if they put me in jail, I've got it coming. It's just your mother..."

"Dad, don't talk like that. Nobody's going to put you in jail. Let's just keep things the way they are."

He dropped his head in his hand and swallowed a sob.

"It won't be for long, darling. Your mother's heart is..." His voice cracked. "...and I'll ..."

"Daddy, please don't!"

Gail put her hands over her face and wept.

He put his arm around her and gently squeezed.

"Then I want you to go to those people and tell them how sorry I was for what we did. I hope they find it in their hearts to forgive us."

Gail took a napkin out of the holder on the table and blew her nose, then slowly got to her feet, weariness in her every movement.

"Those peaches have been boiling for over an hour. I better turn them off."

She went over and snapped off the burners and joined her father who was now standing at the table gazing at the army of jars. He put his arm around her waist, and she around his shoulder. As her thoughts settled on the sad conclusion of the afternoon, she knew this would be the last summer for the Spartanburg peaches, and never again would this kitchen witness she and her mother happily canning the "best tasting fruit on the planet."

CHAPTER TWENTY-FOUR

ALI HAD ALWAYS CONSIDERED herself a bit player in the Haydock family saga. That was why she liked being the one tasked with copying all the deeds at the Rutherford County Courthouse. Somehow, it made her feel like she mattered. The whole project was an exercise in futility, but it distracted her mother from mourning her father, and that made it important, an essential assignment. And the fact that her mother was now anxious to get more deeds, told Ali that she might be starting to get over the shock and sadness of Georgie's confession.

When Ali ran downstairs to the store to remind Georgie that she was going to Rutherfordton to scan some more deeds, she found her busy pricing some toy cars.

"Remember, you've got to get lunch for the boys," Ali said. "And fix a tray for Mom. You can have the boys take it in. I told them they can go to Joey's house after lunch, and I'll pick them up on my way home."

Georgie put the tagging gun down.

"Sis, do me a favor. Do you remember the guy whose picture we found at the cliff house when we were kids? He was leaning on an axe in front of the staircase."

"Yeah. I remember. The dashing devil with the mustache."

"I ran across the picture in my keepsake box the other day and... I don't know... I kinda wondered what his name was. If you could find this out for me, I'd appreciate it. I wouldn't mind

209

knowing where he was from, either."

"Oh, that'll be on the deed."

Well, that's a new one, thought Ali, as her Ford Fusion sailed east down Highway 64 toward Rutherfordton... my big sister actually asking *me* to do something for *her.* The winding road ran for twenty miles, sloping away from the mountains and digging its claws into the foothills. Every time she caught a glimpse of the Broad River that ran alongside the road, the thought of her baby sister rotting beneath it surfaced.

She turned off 64 just inside the Rutherfordton city limits and then onto the west end of Main Street. She continued up the rolling, heavily treed street sprinkled with charming older homes until she reached the quaint downtown. She swung into the parking lot next to the courthouse, found a space and reached for Cal's briefcase.

Her mother had come across two more families in some early 1800 deeds and she wanted her to research them: the Twittys and the Millers. In those days, the deeds used the metes and bounds method that listed the neighbors on all sides of the property; and that was how her mother had been coming up with leads.

She crossed the street to the courthouse, and as usual, the Civil War sentry was still on his tall stone pillar guarding the front of the building. Along the stone benches outside, smokers slouched, burning up time and their lungs while they waited their turn to see a judge. Ali noted how bored all of them seemed and suspected it was because they'd probably been through the legal system so many times they were accustomed to the hurry-up-and-wait routine.

Climbing the fourteen granite steps to the entrance where the guards would be waiting to scan her briefcase and purse, she got the same feeling that always came over her every time she entered the building that was a vortex for all kinds of hopes and disappointments. It guarded precious legal documents and meted out far-reaching consequences. It generated certificates of birth and death, marriage licenses and divorce decrees, and housed the huge musty books she would go through in search of her mother's dream.

She went into the deeds room, opened her briefcase on a table and got out a pad and pen. Good. The list of deeds for "M" and "T" would be in the same book of grantees prior to 1917. She wrestled it from its rack and grunted as she managed to get its edge onto the counter and then slide it up onto it. She opened it to "Miller" and could see there were several pages with line after line of purchases by people with that name. She checked her notes. Her mother had given her "James and David Miller."

She copied down the deed book and page numbers of the several dozen properties they had purchased, and then flipped over to the "Ts," looking for "Allen Twitty." She copied down the information for his purchases, as well. These three men were obviously land speculators. A farmer or settler wasn't going to buy that many parcels from the state in the early 1800s.

From reading bits of deeds, she'd gathered that after the Revolutionary War, when General Rutherford drove the Cherokee into Tennessee, large tracts of the gorge were bought from the state by land speculators from this very town. It amazed her that this city, which today had just over four thousand residents, was considered a booming metropolis when Asheville, the big city on the west side of the gorge, was still nothing more than a settlement.

By now, she was familiar enough with most of the huge tomes, that she could identify the handwriting of a lot of the scribes who wrote the deeds. She would flip to the page and establish if the property was in Chimney Rock Township. If it was, she would see if it was on the waters of the Broad River. And if that were the case, she would tap the button on the scanner that resembled a ruler, wait for the green light and then carefully roll it across the deed. It would be her mother's job to give it a closer examination.

It took her till four o'clock to review and then scan all the deeds. She was starting to put her things back in the briefcase when she remembered Georgie's request. Her feet were sore from standing on the hard floor for five hours and she wanted to go home, but she wasn't going to pass up this opportunity to prove to Georgie that she knew what she was doing.

Okay, she'd have to start by going through a more recent set of grantee books to find the record of the two parcels her parents had purchased. She looked up "Haydock" and found the downtown property they got from their Aunt Myrtle, and then what had to be the rental on Southside Drive from a Myron Perkins in 1989.

She jotted down the book and page number for that one and then found the book. She copied the typewritten deed even though she knew it was too recent to be the one she was looking for. Then she went back to the grantee book and looked up Myron Perkins and discovered a listing of a deed issued to him in 1949 from a Jeremiah Cooper.

Again, she jotted down the book and page number, went over to the stacks, got out the book and found the deed, but it was still too recent for Perkins to be the man Georgie evidently had a secret crush on. Her back was starting to ache from all the lifting, and a glance at her watch told her it was getting close to five when they'd be locking the room. But she had a strong hunch Jeremiah was the man in the photograph.

She hurriedly looked him up in the grantee book and murmured "bingo" when she saw that a Jeremiah Cooper had bought a piece of property in 1891 from none other than James M. Flack! Jeremiah *had* to be the guy who built the house and staircase. She rushed over to the racks and got excited as she examined the deed that was over a hundred years old and written in an elaborate longhand.

Before she scanned it, she wanted to make sure this was the right one. She read that Jeremiah was from Charleston County, South Carolina. Yes, the seller was James M. Flack and the property was one acre on the waters of the Broad River in Chimney Rock Township. She started to run her scanner over it when something caught her eye. Suddenly, the hair on the back of her neck stood straight up. There it was, as clear as day, "...30° west 38 poles to a stone in a drain near the wolf den on the cliff..."

She couldn't believe her eyes! She read it again to make sure. Her hands shook so much when she ran the scanner over the deed's two pages that she had to do it a second time. Her head swam with excitement. Her mother had been looking for this wolf den since she was in her teens. She couldn't wait to get back to her car to phone Georgie.

"You won't believe this, girl," she squealed. "I found the wolf den on the cliff!"

"You're kidding."

"*Noooo.* And do you believe it. It's where our cliff house is!"

"We've climbed and dug all over those rocks. There's nothing there."

"I know that; but think of it, Georgie, this is going to thrill Mom to pieces."

"Yeah. And she's going to have us digging up there for the rest of the summer. Remember when she found the turkey footprint carved in the rock up on Round Top?"

"I know, but think how much fun this could be for her and the boys... and Georgie... she's gonna want you to help."

They were silent for a few moments, then Georgie asked, "When are you gonna tell her?"

Ali let out a girlish squeal. "You know what I could do?"

"What?"

"Just take everything back like usual and let her discover it herself!"

They both giggled.

"What if she doesn't find it?"

"Don't worry. If she doesn't, I'll figure out some way to lead her to it."

They were silent again as the two sat with their thoughts.

"You know, Georgie, it's strange the way everything is happening this summer. It's really making me worry about Cal."

"Oh, no, you don't! Get those thoughts out of your head and concentrate on that diet I wrote up for you. That handsome hunk of a man of yours is gonna be here in three weeks and he's gonna want to get his hands on you. You just think about having another honeymoon. By then, Mom should be able to handle the boys for a couple of nights."

Ali was hoping her mother and Georgie would be back on friendly terms by then, but she didn't dare say it out loud.

213

"I know you're right, Georgie, but there's been so many weird things happening. Like you remembering this Jeremiah dude just when Mom was sending me back for more deeds. And that nutty woman stalking us this summer."

Ali didn't think she needed to bring up Shelby's drowning or Mary's horrible death, since those two nightmares were already floating on the surface of everyone's thoughts. Georgie said she had to get the trash out on the street for the next day's pickup, so Ali said she'd see her in the morning, and started back home.

By the time she got the boys back to the house, she was almost too tired to deal with her mother, but she went into her bedroom and handed her the scanner. As she turned to go back to the kitchen, the idea hit her.

"Mom, do me a favor tomorrow and print out the last deed I scanned. It was something Georgie wanted."

"And what was that?"

"When we were kids, we found a photo of a man in the rental house and she wanted me to find his name for her."

"Well, did you?"

"Of course," she said proudly. "I had to dig down four owners deep, but I got it."

Ali left the room thinking she was too tired to cook and ordered a pizza from the Riverwatch. She let the boys play with their electronic games while she made a quick salad sprinkled with tuna fish for her mother and her, then set the table before taking off to pick up the pizza across the street. As she walked down the front steps, she could see Georgie had already gotten the barrels full of merchandise in from the street, put out the trash, and gone home.

The pizza was ready, and as she stood on the other side of the street waiting to cross, she thought she heard Mike yelling something to her from the living room window. A pickup stopped to let her pass and she looked up, but Mike was gone, so she started up the stairs to the kitchen. Suddenly the door flew open with Mike jumping up and down screaming.

"We're gonna be rich, Mama! We're gonna be rich!"

Dinah stood behind him frantically signaling for Ali to hurry.

214

"Get in here! I found the wolf den on the cliff! And dang if it wasn't under my very nose all along," she exclaimed as she shoved the door closed behind Ali.

"Gee, where is it, Mom?"

"Right there at our rental on Southside. I found it in that deed you scanned for your sister." She put her arms around Mike, rocked him from side to side and looked up at Ali.

"I want you to call Debbie and get her in here tomorrow 'cause we're all goin' up there to look for that gold."

"Mom, you don't want to be doin' that. There's gotta be over fifty steps to that cabin. The boys and I can do it for you."

"Oh, don't you worry none. I can make it up there." Her eyes narrowed as she thought. "Ali, call that sister of yours and tell her we're all comin' up there early tomorrow morning and she's to stay and help instead of coming to the store." Dinah clapped her hands and threw her head back. "Lordy, Lordy!" She suddenly stopped as if she were having an afterthought. As she spoke, she shook her finger. "And when I get that gold, the first thing I'm gonna do is to give that girl her money back."

Ali put a hand on her mother's shoulder.

"Mom, remember, if it wasn't for Georgie asking for that deed, you'd never have found it."

Dinah flicked Ali's hand off, then clapped her hands and rubbed them vigorously.

"Let's hurry up and sit down and eat, everyone, 'cause I gotta call those two sisters of mine!"

Ali sat across from her mother while they ate, and imagined that the exhilarating passion emanating from her was a reflection of what her great-great-grandfather, the illustrious J.M. Flack, was like. There'd always been an edginess to her mother that she kept hidden away until something triggered it, and then it sprang out like a jack-in-the-box. Ali had seen it appear dozens of times and knew it was what her father had loved about her. The woman sitting in a wrinkled housecoat with mussed hair was simply a costumed character. Hiding underneath was her father's youthful playmate who'd run all over the mountains with him like a gazelle as they looked for hidden gold.

A ripple of melancholia ran through Ali as she realized that it wouldn't be long before her mother would have to accept that there was no gold, and this thread that was woven through the story of her life was about to ravel out. Oh, but at least her boys were getting a glimpse of her mother as she used to be, even though fleeting. That, if nothing else, made it worth the disappointing conclusion that was coming.

THE NEXT MORNING, Georgie, hearing Ali's car pull into the lot, ran down the stairs as Ali was helping her mother from the front seat.

"Don't just stand there," Dinah was hollering to the boys. "Get out those shovels and picks!"

The boys ran to the back of the car.

"Mama, open the trunk!" shouted Isaac. "We've got to go get the gold!"

Georgie looked at Ali, who was giggling, and rolled her eyes.

The boys grabbed a shovel and pick and ran with them up the stairs. Georgie got out another shovel and followed behind Ali, who was walking her mother to the staircase. Georgie tapped Ali on the back, handed her the shovel and told her to go on up with the boys.

"Yeah. You go on and keep an eye on those boys," said Dinah. "I'll be comin' right along."

Dinah slowly managed the first flight with her cane, then out of breath, rested on a landing for a few minutes before turning and looking up behind her. She started to get up again when Georgie took her wrist and looked at the second hand on her watch while she counted the heartbeats.

"Let's give it a few more minutes," Georgie said.

Isaac and Mike came clambering down the stairs.

"We're gonna help you up, Grandma!"

When Dinah looked up at Georgie, she nodded for her to go.

It took forever to reach the next landing, and at one point Mike almost went over the side.

"Grandma, when are we gonna go around the world?" asked Mike.

"The world? Boy, right now, we got to concentrate on getting me up those stairs."

"Okay, you boys, go on up," said Georgie. "Your grandma's got to rest again."

They were now inside the musty, dark part of the staircase that was enclosed. Georgie got her mother settled on a built-in bench in the corner and took her pulse.

"You're doing fine, Mom. Let's give it a five minute rest before we get movin' again."

Georgie wanted to hug her mother so badly, but she had to hold herself back. For the first time, for as far back as she could remember, she was finally totally confident her mother loved her. The fact that she was allowing her to be this close after what she had done, proved it. Georgie suddenly felt plain next to her mother's vivaciousness, and she could see why her father had loved her so. Her mother was spoiled and capricious and often maddening, but she had such oomph and gusto that she was like a light you never wanted to see dimmed.

After a few minutes, Georgie reached out her hand and smiled to herself when her mother took it and let her put her arm around her waist to help her up the rest of the stairs. Once on the porch, Georgie sat her down again.

"We're ready, Grandma!" shouted Mike who was holding a shovel upright at the doorway to the cabin.

"Boys, you come over here and sit by me," Dinah said.

Mike and Isaac neared.

"We've got to do this in an organized fashion," Dinah instructed.

"Can I keep one of the gold coins?" asked Mike.

Isaac nudged him so hard that Mike lost his footing.

"Shut up and let's hear her plans," he demanded.

Georgie was standing inside the cabin behind the wall. Ali was next to her in the doorway watching the boys as they listened to their grandmother. When Dinah told them she was going to be the one to carry all the gold down to the car, Georgie put her forehead against the wall and started to chuckle. Ali reached over and pinched her.

The boys finally coaxed their grandmother to get up, and the whole procession moved to the back door, which led out onto a huge stone ledge. A rectangular rock no more than three feet wide and six feet long was an actual bridge from the ledge to a massive stone that was part of the cliff, which cantilevered over the edge of the mountain. Georgie was quick to bring out a chair for her mother. She placed it on the ledge next to the house where Dinah could comfortably direct the operation.

All morning the boys dug and crawled around underneath the enormous rock, bringing small relics they found to Dinah. At first, it unnerved Georgie to see them scampering back and forth over the narrow rock bridge, since there was a twelve foot drop on one side of it and a good fifty foot drop on the other. There was a considerable amount of excitement when the boys found a round disk, which once cleaned, turned out to be nothing more than a button.

"Grandma! There's a tin can way back under here!" yelled Isaac who had disappeared into the cavern.

"Well, bring it here, boy!"

"I can't, Grandma. It's stuck."

"Georgie, you get in there right away and get it out."

"Oh, Mom. It's probably just some garbage someone threw away."

"Now you get in there, girl, and get it right out."

Isaac came from under the rock, and Georgie got down on her hands and knees and looked in. There was only one way she was going to be able to reach way in, so she slid onto her stomach and kept wiggling as far as she could, twice hitting the rock with her head and the ground with her cheek. When she couldn't go another inch, she reached way in and felt around until she touched what seemed like a small bucket.

She felt around in the dark until she found a small flat stone and started digging out the pail. Finally she had enough exposed to get a good grip, and she pulled it out. But as she tried to wiggle herself backwards, she realized, that when she was digging, she had twisted her body in such a way as to get herself wedged between the ground and the rock.

She could barely turn her head as she yelled for the boys to pull her out. She waited a moment, then felt two clammy little hands around one ankle and then the other. They pulled, but she didn't budge.

"Do it again! And really pull hard this time!"

She felt the clammy hands gripping her ankles again and then the sensation of being dragged out and almost swung out over the edge of the rock bridge. Her right leg and hip were hanging over but she had somehow managed to get a grip on the rock.

She heard the boys scamper toward her.

"Don't anybody touch me!" she screamed. "You two get back on that ledge!"

She felt her weight shifting toward the abyss and instinctively gave it everything she had and rolled onto her side and then onto her back on the narrow rock. She lay there for a moment looking up at the sky, then slowly sat up and hugged her knees. Mike came up to her and bent down to her eye level.

"You don't look so good, Aunt Georgie."

*"Reeeeally? ...*I wonder why."

Her mother had covered her face with her hands, and Georgie could tell she was laughing by the way her shoulders shook. Georgie reached back behind her and picked up the pail. She studied it and shook her head.

"Mom, this is nothing but an old pail we used to dig with back here when we were kids."

Mike snatched it from her hands and ran it over to Dinah who started examining it.

"Dang! You're right. We still sell these in the store."

"Aw, Grandma, does this mean there isn't any gold in there?" groaned Mike.

Ali, who had been in the kitchen making lunch and had come out onto the ledge just as Georgie was hoisting herself back onto the rock bridge, stood with a hand over her mouth. Georgie could imagine what a filthy mess she was and couldn't blame her sister for laughing.

Ali had brought out a damp cloth to wipe off the boys, but she gave it to Isaac and motioned for him to take it to Georgie.

Georgie started to wipe off her face, but the way Ali rocked back and forth like she used to do as a kid when she had something on her mind, gave Georgie an inkling she wanted to say something important.

"What is it, Ali?" Georgie asked.

"Well, I was just thinking. If Grandpa was supposed to have hidden that gold during the Great Depression in the 30s, he wouldn't have come up here to hide it on property he sold to Jeremiah Cooper way back in 1891, now would he?"

Georgie thought about that for a moment and suddenly threw the washcloth at Ali and screamed.

"You stinker! You knew that all along, didn't you?"

Diana's mouth fell open. "Ali! How could you let us go on this wild goose chase? I almost killed myself climbing up those stairs."

"Ooh!" screamed Georgie. *"You* almost killed *yourself!"*

Ali started to laugh and then the boys, and finally Georgie. Then Dinah slapped her legs and joined in.

"Gee, Grandma, does this mean we're not gonna be rich?" asked Mike.

Dinah grabbed Mike and squeezed. "We're gonna be rich... but not that kind of rich...'cause your daddy's comin' home and that'll be plenty enough for us to be grateful for."

"Okay, boys," announced Ali. "I want you to strip down to your underwear before you come in, and go straight into the bathroom and wash up."

Georgie got up and brushed herself off, then found a clean section on her tee shirt and wiped her face with it.

"Come on, Mom. Let's go in. I've got to take a shower, wash my hair and get some antiseptic on these knees."

"Wait, Georgie. I want to talk to you first."

Georgie looked her in the eyes and stopped breathing.

Her mother spoke in a voice saturated with sadness.

"I've had time to think everything over. Our little Shelby falling in that river was a terrible accident. That's all it was. God does that sometimes to test us... and I guess I failed. I've been thinkin' on all this, and I was wrong to keep puttin' you and Ali down the way I did. I reckon I just couldn't help myself. You see, it was my way of keeping Shelby alive. My way of kinda bringing her into the conversation so she wouldn't be forgotten. I can see now the way I was doin' it was just plain hurtful.

"Every time I picture you at six insisting you didn't know what happened to your sister, I realize you must have been scared stiff to lie so convincingly that no one had the least suspicion you had anything to do with it. Besides, the kitchen door being unlocked proved to all of us that someone had entered the house from the street and stole our little girl away.

"Georgie, I know you wouldn't have kept your secret all these years unless you truly believed we wouldn't love you if we found out. I'm sorry that the way I acted made you believe such a horrible thing. Maybe it was because the whole nightmare was beyond me. Even now, I can't help wondering why her body never showed up. That winter when they let all the water out of the dam and drained the lake and didn't find anything, we were convinced she hadn't drowned."

Georgie wanted to discourage her mother from questioning Shelby's drowning.

"The river was running so fast she could have been swept over the dam and gotten snagged in a million places all along the Broad River."

"I guess."

Georgie put her hand on the knob and started to open the door with her back to her mother.

"You're tired, Mom. I want you to get some rest." She bit her lip and hesitated for a moment. "If you want, you can stay up here with me for the rest of the afternoon and maybe take a nap."

"I'd like that."

Georgie started in the door and paused again, her back still to her mother.

"I didn't mean any of those things I said to you, Mom."

"I know you didn't, baby."

CHAPTER TWENTY-FIVE

E VER SINCE THE 1890s when Jerome B. Freeman, the Chimney Rock Park's first promoter, made headlines for the monolith by hauling a mule to the top of the chimney, right up to the 1950s when they started the Chimney Rock Hill-climb, Chimney Rock Park's publicity stunts had captured the attention of thousands all over the Southeast. The motor-race, running 2.7 miles uphill with 18 turns, became part of North Carolina auto-racing legend, attracting everything from Bobsy-Porsches to Mini Coopers, and from Volvo sedans to cars custom built to tackle the mountain.

The town of Chimney Rock had always been inexorably linked to the park, and the park was growing. Since the State of North Carolina bought the park in 2007, it had invested over eighty-two million dollars purchasing land on both sides of the gorge surrounding the town and enlarging the park's area from its initial 1,000 acres to well past 5,200.

On this day, Mary Jaeger Gale, the general manager of the firm that managed the park, was in her office waiting for a visit from Ron Elliott. Mary's history in many ways reflected the effect the park had on those who came in contact with it. She came to the village of Chimney Rock as the bride of shop owner Steve Gale. Prepared to teach English in a local school, she was asked to handle the park's public relations that summer while school was out, and now, thirty-two years later, she was still there.

These days, she was finding it especially thrilling to be on the threshold of an era that would see the town of Chimney Rock and its sister to the east, Lake Lure, at the heart of what the state envisioned as one of the country's major outdoor recreation destinations. Every time she went to Raleigh, the state capitol, she witnessed almost every one of the state's divisions methodically, deliberately, crafting a 100-year vision for the park as well as a 25-year master plan.

She could see all the pieces coming together as the state's various agencies discovered what a special place the gorge was. Nowhere else had they seen such a unique area with so many different features packed into such a confined space. Her only regret was that she'd never live long enough to see it fulfilled, and all she could think of was that the best was yet to come.

When Ron called and asked for an appointment to see her, she knew he would be asking for a job as their naturalist. Angie Stuart, who currently held that position, had come into her office a few days earlier and told her she was taking another job in Idaho. At the same time, she'd dropped a hint that Ron might consider taking her place.

The thought of having a nationally recognized botanist of his caliber on their staff was almost too good to be true, but Mary couldn't see this sole parent of an eleven-year-old traipsing all over the state managing land trusts. Nor could she picture him hiring a housekeeper to look after the little girl who had clung to him so desperately at her mother's funeral at the Chimney Rock Baptist Church.

Even though Ron had moved on from the park, he had never left it entirely, because that was the way it was. Once someone became involved with the place, it became a part of them. And since it was almost a rite of passage for everyone living in the town to have worked there at one time or another, the park was ingrained into the very fiber of the community.

Mary had already prepared an employment contract and hoped to get it inked that very day.

FOR RON ELLIOTT, there was more to the park than its colorful history, and he wanted to get in his two cents. He was sitting on his bed putting on his shoes when Jennifer walked in.

"Are you going to drop me off at Terri's?" she asked.

He put his other foot in a shoe and started tying the laces.

"Yep."

She came over and plopped down next to him.

"Daddy, are you sure you want to stop managing those big lands and go back to your old job at the park?"

"Yep."

"You don't have to do that, Dad. I can take care of myself all week and you can come home on the weekends."

"Sure. I can see the county folks now, waiting to greet me on Friday night so they can whisk me away for endangering the welfare of a child."

"Nobody's got to know you're not here."

"Why didn't I think of that? We can put a scarecrow on the living room couch and if anyone comes looking for me, you can just tell 'em I'm taking a nap."

He put his arm around her shoulder. "Honey, there is no place on earth I'd rather work right now than at Chimney Rock State Park."

"Are you sure, Daddy?"

"Yep. But let's not get the horse before the cart. I'm not hired yet."

"Oh, they'll hire you, all right. They love you up there."

"And do you know what's the first thing I'm gonna do?" He stood up and went over to the dresser and combed his hair. "I'm gonna make you my unofficial assistant."

"Come on, Dad, what kind of assistant is *unofficial?*"

"The kind who gets off the school bus at the park gate and waits for her dad to come pick her up."

"Would this unofficial assistant be paid anything?"

"Paid? I'm marking it all down in my little black book and when I'm old and feeble I'm gonna get you to pay me back for the education you'll be getting."

"Oh, Dad. You're hopeless."

Ron dropped Jennifer off at her friend's and then drove to

Chimney Rock. When he got to the park, he pulled into the lot next to the house the management company used as an office. He spotted Mary Gale's little Mustang convertible and smiled to himself. Ever since the park held the hill climbs, everyone knew she had a thing for cars. He took the front steps in twos, went in and said hello to all the staff who were hanging around the reception room, primarily to greet him.

Mary's voice floated from her office. "If that's Ron, send him right in."

"Go on in, Ron. She's waitin' on ya," someone finally said.

He went to the doorway and shyly looked in. Mary rose from a desk stacked with files and told him to come in and sit down. She wanted to give him a big hug, but was afraid the both of them would burst into tears. She settled for her usual friendly, yet professional, comportment.

He wasn't seated twenty minutes before the particulars of the contract were agreed upon. He was being brought on as the park's naturalist and would also operate specialized group tours and natural history-related programs. It was agreed he would be allowed "leave without pay" from time to time so he could perform contracted botanical services for national forests, including rare and sensitive plant surveys. He'd start a week before Angie left, so the transition would be seamless.

Ron was satisfied with the deal he had gotten, but needed to secure one more concession.

"My little Jennifer... well, as you can imagine, is gonna have a hard time for a while." He rubbed his jaw. "I'd kinda like to have her come up to the greenhouse after school so she won't have to go to an empty house. For a while, anyway."

"That would be fine with us, Ron. In fact, Marsha picks up the mail every day around four. You can have Jennifer get off the bus at the post office and Marsha can bring her up. We just need to know when the bus is going to get there. And you know Carrie will take good care of her if Marsha's late for any reason. Heck, if Jennifer wants, she can help us fold and stuff envelopes here in the office when we're in a crunch. She can even go out with our trail guides and learn the ropes if she's interested. After all, that's what we do here—train the land stewards of the future."

Ron dropped his head to his hand, overcome with emotion. She gave him a moment to get himself under control, then got up and stood next to him, putting her hand on his shoulder.

"Don't worry. We'll take good care of her, Ron. We're all family here, and that's what family does."

HOPE IS A BENCH in the shade in the middle of a long, tiresome walk in the sun, and today, Dinah felt optimistic as she went with her two daughters to the Rutherford County Sheriff's Office. The timing was right. There was too much gossip going around Chimney Rock, she had told the girls, and she felt it wise to go and get Shelby's case closed once and for all. At least as closed as it was ever going to be. That wasn't her real motive, though. It had been several weeks, and still the woman hadn't returned, so she was hoping a little publicity might flush her out.

The sheriff's department was located directly across from the county courthouse in a utilitarian looking brick building. They went to the window in the small entrance portico and asked for the detective. Dinah was annoyed that the one who had handled the case for almost twenty-five years had recently retired, and they would now be dealing with someone entirely new: Jamie Keever.

The door opened and the imposing figure of Chief Detective Keever loomed over them. He led them down the hall to his office, a twelve foot by twelve foot space packed with banker boxes full of files. They were stacked on the floor and on file cabinets, and even against the wall on his desk. This bear of a man easily dislodged four boxes from a chair so all three women could be seated.

Dinah had already talked to him on the phone, and he was aware of why they were there. He held a pen in his hand, poised over a yellow legal pad, as he prepared to take Georgie's statement.

Georgie's unemotional revelation of the events of all those years back echoed eerily in Dinah's brain as the words spilled out and were transferred to the detective's pad. Her thoughts drifted to the darling little girl who had captured her heart like none other. Why was that? She loved Georgie and Ali, of course, but Shelby was different. Maybe it was because she knew Shelby would be her last, and she wanted to savor every moment of her childhood. She had been too busy to enjoy Georgie and Ali as infants.

She was startled when Ali took her arm. "Mom, we can go now."

The three of them rose and solemnly followed the detective who led them to the door. No one said anything on the ride back to Chimney Rock. The two sisters sat cloaked in the finality of Georgie's words, with Dinah thinking about what the detective had said: the case would be kept open until there was evidence of Shelby's demise.

Detective Keever made a copy of Georgie's statement and took it into the Sheriff's office.

After the sheriff read it and asked him a few questions, Keever said, "What are you going to do?"

"This was a pretty high-profile case in its day," said the sheriff. "There's still a lot of folks around who will remember it." He picked up his phone and started to dial. "We better call Channel 13's satellite station at the college, and then give it to the papers."

Georgie tossed her slippers and pajamas into the open carton on the bed and gave the cabin a final check, then she picked up the carton, locked the door and started down the staircase.

As she got into her car and headed for the bridge, she couldn't help thinking that when she moved in four months ago, she never dreamed her life could change so drastically. Halfway across the bridge, she stopped and zoomed down the window. It was hard to believe, but the paralyzing anxiety she'd always felt when she heard the water crashing on rocks was gone. Her mother's words had erased it. *Our little Shelby falling in that river was a terrible accident. That's all it was. God does that sometimes to test us...* Georgie knew those simple straightforward words would comfort her the rest of her life.

She pulled into a parking space in front of her mother's store. Her mother knew she'd be leaving early in the morning, but she still couldn't go without a final goodbye. As she was getting out, she hollered a hello to Debbie who was dragging a barrel of walking canes out onto their sidewalk. In fact, the whole street was swarming with shopkeepers setting up their outside displays. She presumed they all knew she was going back to Boone today by the way all their waves seemed to be saying goodbye as she looked around and caught their eye.

She laughed to herself. Whether she liked it or not, she was now as much a part of the town's history as her mother or any of the Flacks. She had sensed that the story of her confession had leaked several weeks ago when she noticed incremental changes in the way everyone treated her. At first it was shy, sympathetic smiles, but when the story hit the papers after their visit to the Rutherford County Sheriff's Office, the empathy reached a crescendo.

She knew there were folks who would always harbor some resentment for her keeping her secret for so long, but that didn't seem to matter to anyone in town right now. Now was the time to call upon the mantra that had kept the town alive for over two hundred years and had always prevailed when one of their own was threatened: *We're all in it together.*

"Is my mom down yet?" Georgie hollered over to Debbie.

"She's in the back." Debbie waited until she got closer, and then whispered, "Watch out. She's in a bit of a huff over all the things you moved around."

"Thanks for the tip. When I see her, I'll ask her how she likes all the changes Ali made."

Debbie laughed.

"Debbie, don't forget to call me if that woman shows up again. Get her name and phone number. Whatever you can."

When Dinah, who was sitting at her desk in the back of the store, saw Georgie, she opened her arms and the two women hugged.

"I got a call from Ali last night," Georgie said. "It looks like she's all settled in their apartment and the boys like their school, but mostly they're on pins and needles about Cal coming home tomorrow."

"Are you planning to come to his homecoming party next week?" Dinah asked.

"Of course. I thought I could swing down and pick you up and we could go to Charlotte together."

That settled, Georgie left, and as she drove along the swaying curves on the way to Boone, she felt a sudden contentment. She had picked this particular day to leave because her regular four o'clock appointment with Dr. Harold was scheduled for that afternoon. She would put on a nice dress for the occasion, for this session would be special. She was finally going to reveal all the secrets he had patiently waited five years to hear. She was pleased with herself and a little melancholy at the same time, because not only would this session be unique, it would also be her last.

CHAPTER TWENTY-SIX

IT WASN'T CHRISTMAS YET and already four inches of packed snow lay on the ground in Boone. Bruce Springstein was belting out a song about a pink Cadillac from a CD as Georgie bounced around the downstairs, dusting furniture. Comfortable in a pair of sweat pants, a baggy sweater and thick fuzzy socks, she was finishing up the last of her housekeeping chores.

The buzzer went off on the dryer in the hall upstairs, so she grabbed up the sweater and pair of shoes she had placed on the bottom step and ran with them up the stairs. She was almost finished folding the clothes when the phone rang. She picked it up and went over to the window and watched the snowflakes float by as she listened to her sister.

"We're all going to be at Mom's till the day before New Year's. We're leaving right after the kids get out of school for the holidays. Can you come for Christmas?"

"Are you kidding? After all those weeks I took off and because I don't have any kids, they're expecting me to work the holidays."

"Aw, come on, Sis. The boys really missed you at Thanksgiving."

"I've got duty on Christmas and New Year's, but I suppose I can swing coming up for the days in between."

"Great. The boys will be thrilled. You should have heard them telling some of Cal's friends about pulling you out of that cave. Believe me, the story gets better every time they tell it."

Silence fell between them for a moment.

"It was a weird summer, wasn't it?" Ali said.

"It was weird all right."

"Have you and that doctor gotten back together?"

"No. He's moved on to a widow he met at the country club."

Georgie wanted to ask Ali if she had heard anything about Ron, but couldn't make the words come out of her mouth. It would kill her to find out he was going with someone, yet she knew it was inevitable. The conversation ended with her yanking out her iPad and noting that she'd be in Chimney Rock for five days between the two holidays.

Two weeks later, Georgie pulled into Lake Lure in what looked like the dead of night, but it actually wasn't even past ten. She swung around the curve into Chimney Rock, and the sight of all the stores wearing their Christmas finery made her smile. Strings of small white LED lights raced along all the roof eaves and balconies and ran around all the doors and windows. There wasn't a nook or cranny that didn't have an elf or some holiday icon tucked in it. Any shrub that could pass for a Christmas tree was draped with lights, and every lamppost sported a lit star. Snow was the only thing missing to make the place look like a Christmas card.

She was suddenly pleased with herself for putting off her gift shopping. Now she could take the boys around to the stores and let them have whatever they wanted. She'd take Ali over to Bubba's and let her pick out something for herself and Cal. Wrapped in her trunk was her mother's new blood pressure monitor that would send out an alert if the cuff wasn't wrapped properly. More importantly, it could be plugged into her mother's computer so her readings could be tracked over time and emailed to her.

With Ali's promise to have the gas heater turned on at the cliff house, Georgie expected the place to be warm when she got there, but she was anxious to see everyone and too wound up to go to sleep, so she decided to stop by her mother's. This would be the first family Christmas celebration she would be attending since she ran away, and the Christmas spirit was bubbling inside her like never before. She turned onto Terrace Drive, pulled in behind Ali's car and got out. She still had the key to the back gate, and as she unlocked the door, she had to force out the memory of the night she stood there with Ron.

Light from the kitchen cast a sepia glow on the deck, and she caught sight of a kaleidoscope of color that had to be coming from a Christmas tree inside. Her tap on the kitchen window brought the boys running in their pajamas. Mike flung the door open, jumped into her arms and wrapped his legs around her. She fell back against the door frame laughing. Ali and Cal spilled out from the living room and everyone hugged.

Georgie was surprised at how well her mother was doing as she swiftly entered the kitchen; and when she gave her a hug, Georgie noticed how much she had slimmed down. The lilt of a Christmas carol from a holiday special floated out from the TV in the living room as her mother quickly dished up a bowl of chili and placed it on the table.

"Here, sit down and eat," she ordered. "It's about time you got here. I've been waitin' on you all night."

"I told you not to."

"I knew you'd stop by." She tapped Isaac on the back. "That's it, boys. Time to go to bed... and that means me, too."

With that, everyone cleared out except Ali who pulled out a chair and sat down.

Georgie knew her sister well enough to figure she had something to tell her.

"Okay, spill it. What's on your mind?"

"It's about tomorrow."

"What about tomorrow?" said Georgie as she reached for a piece of bread.

"The dinner."

"What dinner?"

"The one Mom's invited Ron and his little girl to."

Georgie put down the bread, pushed her bowl away and buried her face in her hands. "I don't believe this is happening."

"It's happening all right. Tomorrow at five-thirty."

THE NEXT DAY, THE PIES were baked by eleven, the turkey went into the oven at noon and Georgie was on the street with the boys by one. There was something about an invigorating day in the mountains that people found irresistible. With schools closed for the holidays, the street was packed with families who had joined the stream of humanity flowing through the town. The sound of feet shuffling on the wooden sidewalks blended with the Christmas music wafting from out of nowhere as the crowds ambled in and out of the stores and restaurants.

Ali had told the boys they could only get school clothes, so Georgie let them pick out a couple of rugby shirts at Bubba's, then each of them got a bag of candy, along with a Nehi. They played checkers until Mike lost for the second time and wanted to leave. He ran out of the store and stopped at the Riverwalk entrance.

"Let's go down there, Aunt Georgie!"

"No, Mike!" shouted Isaac. "Remember what Mom said? Aunt Georgie doesn't like it down there."

Mike slapped his hand over his mouth. "Oops! I forgot this is where you drowned your sister."

Isaac shoved Mike against the railing. "You idiot!"

Georgie grabbed the railing and started down.

"It's okay, Isaac. I can handle it."

Georgie had wanted something to keep her mind off the dinner they were having that night, but she hadn't bargained for this. Descending the winding staircase was surprisingly easy, but she hesitated at the bridge.

"Is this where it happened, Aunt Georgie?" Mike blurted out.

Isaac grabbed his arm and yanked him almost to the ground. "Mike! You're an even bigger idiot than I thought."

Georgie went over to the narrow wooden bridge and started to cross, but stopped at the huge rock at its base. Ahead she could see the one that Shelby had pulled her onto. She pointed to it and looked at Mike.

"We fell off that one over there."

Isaac punched Mike in the arm. "Now are you satisfied? Let's go back." He took Georgie's hand. "Come on, Aunt Georgie. It's time to go home."

Mike folded his arms, scowled and stomped toward the steps.

"I was just trying to do what Mom said and distract her from thinking about eating with that guy who dumped her."

Georgie and Isaac caught up to Mike and walked along with him.

"That's okay, fella," said Georgie, patting him on the back. "You get an "A plus" in distracting."

"I do?"

"Uh-huh. You sure do."

RON SAT ON A STOOL in the kitchen, polishing his shoes.

"You sure are sprucing up for this dinner, Dad."

He looked up at Jennifer. "I wonder if I've got any socks to go with these?"

"Let's go in your room and see."

Ron followed her in, and she quickly found the same pair of black dress socks he wore to the funeral that she had hidden in the back of his drawer.

She went over to the closet, flipped through the shirts and took out a light blue oxford.

"Here. Wear this one. It'll go with your eyes." She pulled a tie off the rack. "This will look good with it."

"I think a tie is a little much, don't you? We're only goin' to Chimney Rock, not the Taj Mahal."

Jennifer folded her arms and planted her feet firmly apart.

"We're going to eat dinner with the woman who wrote that letter Mommy hid from you, aren't we?"

"Yep."

"Is it true she drowned her sister?"

"How do you know all this stuff?"

"As your assistant, I happen to be privy to all the gossip that hits that mountain." She looked at him and raised an eyebrow. "And what I don't find out at the park, I learn at the post office, where by the way, everything floats in *much sooner* and in *much more detail.*"

"That's good to know. The next time I'm in the mood to

chew the fat I'll stop in."

"Anyway, Dad, it was in all the papers. I can read, you know."

Ron picked out a pair of slacks and laid them on the bed. "I'm gonna take a shower. Have you figured out what you're going to wear yet?"

"I was thinking of going Goth."

"Good." He stiffened his arms and legs and stomped toward her. "I can go as Lurch."

She ignored his playfulness and leaned back against the dresser.

"Carrie feels sorry for her."

"Who?"

"Georgie Haydock. Carrie said she knew she had been hiding a secret all the time they were in school together. She's sort of like a tragic figure."

Ron shook his head and sighed. "The gossip never stops around here."

"Well, like you always say, Dad. 'We're one big happy family.'"

"Let's try to keep the emphasis on 'happy.'"

"Dad, would you have left Mom for her if you had seen that letter?"

Ron sank down onto the bed and gathered her in his arms.

"Honey, I want you to remember something. When she wrote me that letter, your mother had already left me. Remember?"

"I know that, Daddy. And I know a lot more than you think I do. I was just curious is all. Would you have?"

"I don't know, honey. I really don't."

"I've thought about it. And I think it would have worked out if you did. She said nice things about Mama in that letter. Kinda like she was planning on being friends with her. You know, Dad, that's all Mama really needed. Some nice friends."

Ron squeezed Jennifer and thought about Georgie's letter. He knew every word by heart.

"It was a nice letter, honey. I found the words about your

mom consoling."

She strolled over to the dresser and ran a finger around Mary's picture.

"Why didn't you go see her after I found it?"

"Oh, I don't know. I was still getting over what happened to your mom, and..." He scratched his head and then ran his hand through his hair. "You know, the more I think about it, the more I think this dinner isn't such a good idea. Maybe I should just call them up and tell them we can't make it."

She started toward the door. *"Oh, no, you don't, Dad.* We're going. I wouldn't miss this for the world," she said and strolled out of the room.

CHAPTER TWENTY-SEVEN

C AL WOLF-WHISTLED AS GEORGIE walked in the kitchen. "My! Don't *we* look good."

"Well, if you can't dress up a little at Christmas..." said Georgie.

He threw up his hands. "Hey... I'm not complaining."

Dinah came rushing in the room and stopped short when she saw Georgie. She eyed her up and down.

"Don't you have any lipstick?"

Cal, who had just gotten a beer out of the fridge, grinned as he gave Georgie a wink before disappearing into the living room.

Georgie ignored her mother's question and studied the kitchen table that had been extended to seat eight.

"I think we need some candles."

"Whatever," Dinah said.

Georgie looked into her mother's eyes.

"Mom, I beg you. Please don't embarrass me and Ron in front of the kids tonight."

"I promise I won't," said Dinah as she affectionately patted Georgie's head. "Let's just have an old-fashioned mountain Christmas." Her mother was quiet for a moment, then added, "Why don't you go and sit in the living room, nice and pretty like. They'll be here any minute."

"I will, Mom, but first I want to straighten up the table a little." She went over and opened a cupboard and took out two Depression glass candle holders.

"Do we have any candles?"

"No. You'll have to run downstairs and get some."

Georgie started down the stairs to the store, and as she turned at the landing, heard a knock on the kitchen door. She leaned against the wall out of sight and listened to her mother warmly greet Ron and Jennifer. She closed her eyes and wished time would stand still. To feel his presence near her for all eternity.

She heard her name mentioned and her ears perked up. Her mother was evidently talking to the little girl.

"Georgie and the entire family are looking forward to meeting you... we've all heard such wonderful things about you..."

Oh, Mom! Please don't mention anything about her losing her mother! Georgie took a deep breath and sighed with relief when her mother stopped gushing and took them into the living room where Ali could monitor her remarks.

She found the candles and ran back upstairs. She put them into the holders and listened to the cacophony streaming from the living room. The boys were fighting over who was going to show Jennifer the latest apps on their iPad, adult conversation rose and fell, and the hum of the TV sounded in the background. Georgie placed the candles on the table and turned to see Ali standing in front of her.

Ali took her hand. "Come on, Sis. Let's get it over with."

Georgie sent her sister a wary look.

"It's gonna be all right," Ali assured her.

"Oh, Ali. I hate Mom for doing this... and I love her for it, too."

Georgie adjusted her ponytail, then smoothed her hands over the front of her pale pink cashmere sweater, then nervously fingered the single strand of pearls. She smiled at Ali, took a deep breath and walked into the living room. Ron rose to greet her, and the broad shoulders and gray blue eyes in the handsome face almost brought her to her knees.

Jennifer, who was sitting on the floor with the boys, turned and looked up at her. Georgie crossed the room and took Ron's offered hand. After she gave him a tentative hug, he leaned over and put his hands on Jennifer's shoulders.

"This is my daughter, Jennifer."

The girl rolled her eyes. *"Da...ad,* what did I tell you?"

"Sorry. I meant Jenni with an 'i'"

Jennifer looked up at Georgie and said hello, then glanced back at the boys who were watching her every move.

"Are you two going to guess what goes up and down but stays in the same place, or not."

"A jack-in-the-box!" shouted Isaac.

"No. Stairs. But that wasn't a bad answer," she said.

"Do you want to see our grandma's fossil collection?" asked Isaac. "We've got rocks our family's collected for over a hundred years."

"And we got a ruby as big as your eyeball that's worth a fortune," bragged Mike. "And we got a collection of snake skins, too," he threw in for good measure.

When Jennifer stood up, Georgie could see she was small-boned like her mother, and at eleven, barely as tall as Isaac who was ten. By the way she was dressed in a bright pink long sleeve sweatshirt dress and white tights, it was equally apparent she was a very 'girly' girl.

"Okay, show me," Jennifer said to Isaac, and the three of them ran out of the room.

From the conversation Dinah was having with Ron, Georgie gathered he had talked to her at some length when she invited him to dinner, and she wondered how much her mother had told him about her. She admired the way Ron seemed so comfortable with Ali and Cal as he leaned back in his chair, his long legs stretched out in front of him and crossed at the ankles.

Ali came in with beers for everyone. She had taken the turkey from the oven, and the aroma mingled with the scent of the apple and peach pies that had perfumed the air all day.

After a while, her mother excused herself to make the gravy, joining Ali in the kitchen where she was making the salad.

"Cal, are you coming?" Ali called from the kitchen.

"Where?" he asked.

She stuck her head in the room and gave him a look.

"Oh!" He'd finally caught on to the purpose of the mass exodus. "Sure, I'll be right there."

Georgie and Ron found themselves alone in the room. Someone had mercifully turned off the TV, and the room was silent except for the muted sound of Christmas music drifting from a speaker on someone's balcony down the street.

Georgie felt suddenly naked and raw as if all the natural rapport they'd had between them had never existed. When she thought of how he never responded to the letter she had poured her heart into, a wave of humiliation from the rejection rolled over her and she suddenly felt like she and the dinner were imposing on him. She had to get out of there.

"I better go in the kitchen and help."

"Please stay."

She sat there wanting him so badly it hurt, and fearing she'd die if she never saw him again.

He leaned forward in his chair with his forearms resting on his legs and spoke in his soft Western Carolina mountain drawl.

"You need to know that Mary hid your letter from me, and it wasn't until after her accident that I read it. Jennifer found it in a book."

Georgie put her hand over her mouth and let out an anguished cry. Then she tried to fight off her rising temper, but it got the best of her and she gave him a narrow-eyed glare.

"Even without getting a letter, you should have wanted to come and see me. Why didn't you?"

"I drove over to your house that night and parked across the street. I saw you take that doctor up to the cabin and figured that's who you chose."

"Oh, God," moaned Georgie.

"After I read your letter explaining things, I planned to look you up in Boone in the spring... but first I had to take care of my little girl."

Jennifer and the boys burst into the room.

"Come on, Dad. Dinner's ready!"

As his daughter took his hand and led him to the kitchen,

Georgie went around picking up the empty glasses, giving her time to pull herself together before joining them at the table. Dinah seated Ron and Georgie next to each other, and Jennifer across the table, between the two boys. They all held hands for the blessing, but after the "Amen," Georgie sensed Ron's grip lasting for an extra second or two. Did she imagine it? Perhaps, but his words, *I planned to look you up in Boone in the spring,* echoed in her brain.

"Mama," said Mike. "Jenni said that there's a tree that's named after her, and her name is in all the 'cyclopedias. Is that true?"

Everyone laughed.

"You'll have to ask Ron," Ali said.

Mike looked at him. "Well? Is it?"

Ron tapped his fork on his plate. "You bet: crataegus jennae." He winked. "It's got an 'ae' at the end, because it's named after a girl."

Jennifer sat up straighter with her head held high with pride as she slowly raised an eyebrow at Mike.

"See? Told you so."

He made a face. *"Contagious...* I wouldn't want to be called *contagious."*

Everyone laughed again.

Ron asked Cal about the flora in the Hindu Kush Mountains, wondering if they had hawthorns, and that got Cal talking about Afghanistan. Cal seemed pleased with an opportunity to remember that country for more than war. He described the spectacular scenery at the Khyber Pass and told Ron about the cedars, pines and rhododendrons on the northern slopes.

Georgie leaned on the table with arms crossed and took it all in. When Ron did the same, his arm touched hers and it made her heart skip. Once the meal was over, Georgie said it was only fair that she do the dishes since she didn't do any of the cooking. Then she shooed everyone out of the kitchen and picked up an apron.

Ron came in rolling up his sleeves.

"I didn't do any of the cooking either."

241

She found it hard to look him in the eyes as he took the apron from her and tenderly put the strap over her head. He almost touched her as he reached around and tied the apron strings behind her. She closed her eyes and inhaled his manly scent.

They worked in silence, side by side. He loaded the dishwasher while she put the food away. As they finished off the pots and pans together, the same titillating feeling she'd had when they were at the movie took hold. He was sending her a message that he loved her. She wanted to stop and put her arms around him, but she told herself, no. She would yield, but only after he came for her.

Mike yanked on her apron and startled her. "Aunt Georgie, Jenni is bossin' us around again."

Georgie looked over at the living room and could see Isaac and Jennifer sitting on the couch playing a game on the iPad, and she understood Mike felt left out.

"You know what, Kiddo?"

"What, Aunt Georgie?"

"We're gonna finish with these dishes, then I'm gonna put on some coffee, and then I'm gonna play one of those iPad games with you. How's that?"

Mike smirked slightly. "Uh... That's okay, Aunt Georgie. You don't play so good." He turned and ran back to Isaac and Jennifer.

"Well, thanks a lot," she chuckled as she measured coffee into the coffee maker. Finished, she leaned against the counter and held her breath waiting for Ron to say something. They stared at each other for a long moment and his soft blue eyes spoke to her of love. He neared, and just as he was about to brush a wisp of hair from her face, Jenni appeared from out of nowhere.

"You two don't have to whisper," she said.

Georgie gave her a questioningly look.

"I know everything. I read your letter." Jenni opened the fridge and gathered up three cans of soda. She looked up at Georgie again. "And not only that, I go to the post office every day. And believe me, if you want to know what's going on in this town, you go to the post office every day."

Jennifer raced back in the living room, leaving Georgie standing there with her lips parted.

Ron shook his head and grinned. "Well, you've passed the test. She evidently approves of you. When our neighbor's sister comes over on Saturday to help me with the housecleaning, she doesn't trust her alone with me for one minute."

Georgie laughed and went into the living room.

"Anyone for dessert?" she asked, then she noticed Jennifer lying face down on the floor and the boys grabbing her ankles.

"What on earth are you guys doing?"

"Oh, we're just showing her how we got you out of the cave, is all," said Mike.

Georgie looked over at Ali and then her mother, and the three of them laughed as they gathered once more in the kitchen. Once the pies were dished out, the kids asked if they could eat in the living room. Ali said it would be okay as long as they didn't make a mess.

Georgie wanted to pinch herself. Assembled there in that worn little kitchen that was such a part of her life were the two men she and Ali had yearned for and were afraid they would lose all that crazy, weird summer. Ali hadn't said anything, but Georgie suspected her sister was pregnant again. Georgie's eyes kept floating over to Ron's hand as he fingered his cup, and she yearned for his touch, and to have his baby inside her.

Ron sat back and rested his arm on the back rim of her chair as if by some unspoken consent she now belonged to him. The gesture didn't go unnoticed by her mother whose eyebrow shot up. A surge of happiness rushed over Georgie as she realized she would finally be getting what she wanted more than anything else in the world. She studied her mother and her happiness dimmed a little when she realized the same thing couldn't be said about her. She'd never get what she wanted more than anything: Shelby.

Her mood lightened again as Cal and Ali told them about the house they were having built outside Charlotte. Cal had started working for his brother in the wholesale meat business their father had started, and Georgie suspected the family had come up with a big chunk of the cost of the structure as a sort of signing bonus.

A sudden ruckus broke out in the living room. Then Mike came running in.

"She's bossin' me around again."

"Okay, we'll let you play," boomed Isaac's voice.

Ron rose. "I think it's time for us to be going." He winked at Dinah. "I think we better quit while we're ahead." He went over to the entrance of the living room.

"Saddle up, partner. We're pullin' out."

"*Awww,* Dad. It's still early," begged Jenni.

"Come on, sweetheart. Let's go."

With everyone clustered at the kitchen door, Ali handed Ron a cardboard box with a pie and a large Tupperware container she'd prepared with turkey and all the trimmings.

"So what are you doing with Jennifer during the vacation?" asked Dinah.

"She's been working in the park with me."

"Why don't you let her spend the day in town with us tomorrow?"

"Yeah, we can go bike riding and I'll show you my fort," said Isaac.

Jennifer looked up at her father. "Can I, Dad?"

"Sure. I'll drop you off on my way in." He looked at Ali, "Is eight too early for you folks?"

"Perfect," said Ali. "The boys will be up."

DINAH STACKED THE DESSERT DISHES and took them over to the sink while Georgie collected the plates from the living room and Ali and Cal got the boys ready for bed.

"Did he say anything?" she asked when Georgie came back in the kitchen.

"Actually, he did, Mother."

"Well?"

She bit her lower lip and Dinah could see tears pooling.

"He said he was planning on looking me up in the spring."

Dinah came over and put her arms around her. "That's only proper, baby. After all, his wife's only been gone four months."

Georgie put her arms around her mother and buried her face in her neck.

"I love him, Mom. I love him so much, if I lose him again, I'll die." She pulled away and wiped her eyes. "But what if Jennifer doesn't like me?"

Mike and Isaac suddenly appeared in their pajamas with Ali and Cal behind them.

"You don't have to worry about that, Aunt Georgie. She said she liked you because you're unfamous," said Isaac.

Georgie's eyebrows furrowed. "Unfamous? Uh, do you mean 'infamous?'"

"That's it! Infamous!"

After everyone got kissed goodnight, Ali and her family went to bed, and Georgie took off for the cliff house, with her mother assuring her everything was going to be all right.

Dinah put a clean dishtowel over the apple pie on the counter. First, she checked to make sure she'd locked the kitchen door that led to the deck, then went over to the one that opened to the street. As she turned the dead bolt, the sound of the click tore at her heart as she remembered the two people missing from her Christmas table.

BEFORE SHE RETURNED TO BOONE for New Year's, Georgie was hell-bent on getting the back room of the store arranged and all the stock priced and out on the counters. Her mother had promised Debbie time off to spend with her sister in Gaffney, so it was going to be just the three of them for the next few days.

Georgie was finishing unpacking a carton of lunchboxes when she heard her mother and Ali chatting with someone at the front of the store. She'd just opened another box when Ron loomed in the doorway.

"I told your Mom I came to take you to lunch."

She smoothed down her hair with her hands. "I've been working back here all morning, maybe I should..."

"You look fine. Let's go."

They said goodbye to Dinah and Ali, and he started to lead her to his car.

"We can just walk over to Medina's," Georgie said.

He opened the passenger door.

"Get in."

She knew his stubborn streak well enough not to argue.

He backed out of his parking space and drove east until he hit Southside, then turned and drove over the bridge and to the cliff house. He turned off the ignition and looked at her.

"You've got some crackers or somethin' up there don't you?"

Georgie felt herself trembling as she got out of the car. She was almost fleeing from him as she raced up the stairs, unlocked the door and rushed in. She was feverishly straightening her bed when he came up behind her and spun her around so she was facing him.

"Ron, aren't you worried this is too soon... after Mary's..."

He put his hands on her hips and drew her close enough for her to feel the heat from his body. He brushed his lips across her face and kissed her ear.

"Ron, what if Jenni doesn't like me?"

He started unbuttoning her sweater and then pulled it open.

"She already does."

"Does what?"

"Likes you," he said as he peeled her sweater off and tossed it on the bed.

"Oh, Ron. My mother thinks we're going to lunch."

"Believe me," he said as he ran his lips across her forehead. "Those two knew I wasn't taking you to lunch."

She kept repeating she loved him as she gave herself to him for all the times he had made her wait. She gave herself for the thirteen years without him. But mostly, she gave herself for the wanting of a baby of her own.

It was dark outside when she woke in his arms, and they were one as they showered and dressed each other. He told her she was more beautiful as a woman than she had been as a girl, and she told him he was always beautiful.

Then he said for her to pack her things.

"What do you mean?"

"You're coming to my house tonight."

"But what about Jenni?"

"We talked everything over last night, and she wants you to come. The little darling wouldn't let us leave this morning until she had the house all straightened." He put his arms around Georgie and gave her a tender kiss. "You're going to have to be patient with her, Calico. Because of the way Mary was, Jennifer's a lot older than her years. I'm hoping that with you and me she can finally let herself be a kid again."

Her mother's apartment was mayhem as they opened the kitchen door. Michael was chasing Jenni down the hall, and she escaped into the bathroom and slammed the door in his face. Isaac popped his head out from the living room and hollered at Mike, who abruptly turned and ran after him.

"We didn't wait dinner for you two," said Dinah.

She stood in front of them, unfazed by the racket and the fact that they had been gone for the whole afternoon. She opened the oven and took out two plates filled with turkey and all the trimmings and put them on the table.

Jenni hollered hello as she ran past the kitchen and into the living room. Ron laughed and said something about being yesterday's news as he sat down and dug in. Cal came out of the guest bedroom with his cheeks rosy and his dark hair mussed as if he had just awoke. He came over to Georgie in his stocking feet and gave her a bear hug.

"Thanks for hanging on to that bike for me, Sis. I had a great ride today."

"Wasn't it too cold?"

"Not really. It must have gotten up to sixty... maybe sixty-five by mid-afternoon."

Dinah was already offering Ron seconds by the time Georgie sat down to eat. Ali came out of the bedroom and was now leaning against the counter with her arms folded, watching them as if she were a school lunchroom monitor. Georgie was grateful no one remarked about their long lunch.

A spine-tingling scream came from the living room. Everyone raced in. Jenni stood by the window crying and holding her hand. Georgie quickly examined it.

"What happened?" she asked Isaac.

"The window slammed on her hand."

"What were you doing with the window open?" Ali demanded.

"We were gonna climb out onto the balcony and Mike slammed it shut."

Ron started to scoop Jenni up in his arms, but Georgie whisked her away and into the kitchen where she sat her down. She swiftly got a large pan, filled it with ice and water and gently put in Jenni's hand as everyone huddled around and watched. Then she pulled up a chair next to her.

"Can you move your fingers?"

"Uh-huh."

"Good. Can you make a fist?"

"Yes, but it hurts."

Georgie carefully felt all the bones in her hand.

"I don't think anything's broken, but let's get the swelling down."

A look of relief crossed Ron's face and he sat down again. Dinah quickly put a piece of apple pie in front of him and told him to eat.

"Yes, Ma'am."

"You don't have to ma'am me, son. I've known you since your ma died and you came to live across the street with Lucy. I want you to call me Mom." She bent down and looked Jenni in the eye. "And seein' as you don't have a granny and every little girl needs one, *you* can call me Grandma."

The boys were clinging to Jenni's chair when Cal told them to go and pick up their things. After a while, the swelling started to go down and Georgie wrapped Jenni's hand in an elastic bandage. As Ron and Jenni got ready to leave, Ali and Dinah huddled together as if they were waiting for something to happen.

Jenni took up her tote with her good hand and announced to the boys, "Your Aunt Georgie's comin' home with *us.*"

Mike gave her a narrow-eyed look, while Ali and Dinah

broke out in hugs.

Once they reached Ron's car in the alley, Georgie offered the front seat to Jenni.

"No," she said. "Kids are supposed to sit in the back."

Ron started down Terrace Drive, and after he swung onto Main Street, he reached down and grasped Georgie's hand.

As the car made its way up Route 9, Jenni's voice resonated matter-of-factly from out of the darkness.

"I want us to be a regular family."

"Yes, of course." Georgie said as she squeezed Ron's hand.

"My Dad needs that."

"Yes, he does."

"Actually, I could use a little of that myself," said Jenni.

With that pronouncement, no one said anything for the rest of the ride as they all mulled over the dramatic changes that the past two days had wrought.

That night, after Jenni was tucked in, Ron and Georgie lay in each other's arms.

"Ron, you know that regular family stuff Jenni was talking about?"

He nuzzled her. "Uh-huh."

"I could use a little of that, too."

"MOM, ARE YOU GONNA be all right here alone on New Year's Eve tomorrow night?" asked Georgie as she finished stacking an armful of boxes next to her mother who was perched on her stool at the front counter.

"I can't understand why in tarnation you've got to go to Boone tonight," Dinah fumed.

"I've already explained that," Georgie began patiently. "I've got to work all day tomorrow and then again on New Year's Day. These people need their meds and I'm the one who's supposed to give them to 'em."

"When is Ron getting here?"

"Any minute now. I've got their things in my car already."

"If Jenni doesn't want to go, you know you can leave her here with me."

"Are you kidding? She can't *wait* to see my house. And it's good that we spend our first New Year's Eve together."

"When are you coming back?"

"Sunday night. Jenni's got to be in school on Monday and Ron back at work. I'm going to that interview at Pardee Hospital in Hendersonville on Tuesday. But whether I get a job or not, I'm giving my notice."

"This is happening so fast, honey. Are you sure?"

"Mom, I've never been so sure of anything in my whole life."

They both looked up as Ali trooped in from the back room.

"We're all packed and ready to go as soon as Cal and the boys get back from locking up the bike," Ali said. She went over and hugged Dinah. "Gee, Mom. I hate seeing you here all alone for New Year's."

"Don't worry about me. Debbie will be back tomorrow and I'll be just fine."

"Mom, I don't want you sitting here thinking about Shelby anymore. It's been too long and we've got so much to be grateful for," said Ali.

Dinah patted her hand, then gazed into the distance. Ali was right about her having a lot to be grateful for. Dinah thanked God for blessing Georgie and Ron, then she thanked Him for bringing Cal back to Ali and the boys.

But Ali didn't understand about Shelby. How could she know this yearning was incurable? How could she know that every time someone walked in the store, a haunting tide of hope rose and then ebbed to the sad wasteland of disappointment? She had long stopped searching the faces of school girls on playgrounds or playing on streets as her car passed by, for Shelby would now be twenty-nine. But this child was not to be abandoned by her mother. If it took the rest of her life, she would never stop looking for her.

The store was locked up and as they left its lonely silence behind and started up the stairs, Dinah decided she wasn't going to let her pain taint Ali's and Georgie's lives any longer, and she made up her mind never to mention Shelby again. Instead, she would secretly cherish her in her heart until her last breath.

CHAPTER TWENTY-EIGHT

E ASTER—TWO MONTHS since her mom had died. Gail was now in the heartbreaking process of dismantling the cherished home where she'd been raised. The revelations of the past had taken their toll on Pearl, and Gail and Roger had spent the most of February at Spartanburg's Mary Black Memorial Hospital watching her fade away. When her father died three weeks later, Gail almost had to be carried to the funeral.

She hadn't stepped foot in the house since four weeks ago when she came to pick up a suit for her father to be buried in, but it was now time to go about the sad business of clearing away the remnants of these gentle souls' existence on this earth.

She went into the bathroom with a box and collected all the prescription drugs, then went over to the tall chest of drawers in the bedroom where her mother sometimes kept medicine. Lying on top was an ominous looking large manila envelope with her name on it. She recognized her father's handwriting and, in her heart, knew what it held. That knowledge made her legs grow weak. She sank onto the bed and her hands trembled as she slowly opened it.

The newspaper clippings from the Asheville *Citizen-Times,* that her father subscribed to, had been carefully cut out. A business-size envelope lay on top of the clippings and had "Dinah Haydock" neatly printed on it. She turned it over. It was sealed. The thought that it contained her father's confession sent shivers

251

down her spine, but she dared not break the covenant of not opening someone else's mail.

The most recent clipping, dated the previous September, was on top. The headline read: *Mystery of Missing Four-Year-Old Solved.* Georgia Haydock was reported to have fallen in the river at age six with her four-year-old sister who had presumably drowned. Georgia had gone with her mother, Dinah Haydock, and her sister, Alabama, to the Rutherford County Sheriff's office to report the drowning that had taken place twenty-five years earlier. The sheriff was quoted as saying the case was still open.

This had to be the same Georgie who had held on to her so tight. How unfair, she thought, that the little girl who had tried so hard to save her, had carried the guilt for her drowning all these years. It had only taken a split second for her to fall into the river, yet it had set off a chain of lies and deceit that had permanently impacted two families for twenty-five years. So sad. It made her wonder just how many crimes had been cleverly covered up with a blanket of lies over the years... crimes that no one even knew had been committed.

She looked through to the earliest clippings. "The mother was so distraught, a doctor was called." She tried to remember a mother, and it hurt when she kept drawing a blank. The only concrete memory was of Georgie gripping her hand and the two of them falling into the river. Yet, when she had gone into their store with the boys, all her senses told her she was connected to it in some way.

Gail tried to resume her packing, but couldn't get the vision of the distraught mother out of her head. A sudden yearning to know this woman took hold. She could hear her father's sad voice. *When your mother and I are gone, I want you to go see them and tell them how sorry I was for what we did.* Thinking about it now, she realized he was giving her permission to return to her family. She went over and picked up the sealed envelope again, then tapped it on her hand and thought.

"It's a good thing Easter came 'round, Georgie, or we'd never have gotten together," said Ali as the two straightened a case in the store.

"Sis," said Georgie, "Let's move that one in the back corner so it's at an angle."

"You want to wait till Cal and Ron get here?"

"No. We can manage it once we empty it."

As the two systematically unpacked the case, Ali chatted away. "I wish you and Ron hadn't just gone to a justice of the peace and gotten married the way you did."

"Ali, it wasn't as if this was our first marriage. I wasn't about to march down the aisle in a white gown. Mom and Jenni were there and they thought it was plenty nice enough."

"Well, the way we're scattered all over now, it's a good thing Easter gave us an excuse to come see y'all, or we wouldn't have seen you till summer."

Georgie hollered over to her mother who, as usual, was sitting on her stool at the front door.

"I bet Cal and Ron are almost done giving everyone rides on the bike. Do you want me to go upstairs and cut up the ham so we can all have sandwiches before Ali leaves?"

"Hold your horses. We got plenty of time."

Ali chuckled. "How's Mom been?"

"Pretty good, now that those damn lots are sold. It's just that sometimes I catch her in one of her trances."

"Do you think she's thinking about Shelby?"

Georgie nodded. "And Dad. She won't admit it, and swears up and down that she doesn't pine for them anymore, but I know she's just putting up a front. Guess she's got one of those wounds that just won't heal. That's all there is to it."

Georgie studied her sister for a moment. "Okay, Ali. What's on your mind?"

"How about you? Is your wound healed?"

"I'm getting there. Every once in a while that old guilty feeling comes over me, but I remind myself of what Mom said: *Shelby falling in that river was a terrible accident. That's all it was. God does that sometimes to test us.*"

AS THE TWO WOMEN STRUGGLED with the case, Dinah

reached under the counter to straighten some bracelets, wondering where all the customers were. When she heard the door open, she told herself, *It's about time!* While she fiddled with the bracelets, out of the corner of her eye she watched for the person to come near enough so she could offer to help, but no one came.

She finally finished straightening the jewelry and looked up at the door where a motionless figure stood. Her eyes fixed on the woman, but all she saw was a little four-year-old with golden hair and sweet dimpled cheeks. A killing feeling of loss and wanting wrenched her whole being as tears stream down her face.

GEORGIE AND ALI STOPPED pushing the case when they heard Dinah's cry. Their eyes shot to the front of the store. A woman was standing there, a woman who looked enough like Georgie to be her twin. The hair stood up on the back of Georgie's neck and she started toward the door, holding on to the edges of the counters to help keep her balance as she went. Barely breathing, she didn't take her eyes off the woman. Also transfixed, Ali put her hand on Georgie's shoulder and trailed behind her.

The woman spoke to their mother as the two girls neared.

"Are you Dinah Haydock?"

Dinah rocked back and forth crying "Oh, God, yes."

"I think I'm your missing daughter."

Dinah flung open her arms. "Thank you, Lord. Thank you for bringing my baby back home."

Georgie stepped toward the two who now had their arms wrapped around each other, but Ali held her back.

"Give them a minute," she whispered.

The girls listened to their mother's plaintive sobs. "I knew you were alive. I knew it and never stopped looking for you."

Georgie turned and faced her sister, tears streaming down her face. "I didn't do it, Ali." She collapsed into her sister's arms and sobbed uncontrollably. "I never drowned her, Ali. I never drowned her."

EPILOGUE

"CONTAGIOUS JENNI, ARE YOU READY?" Ron yelled down the hall.

"Oh, Daddy, this book of yours has gone to your head. You're just too full of yourself."

Jenni came out of her room wearing a delicately flowered dress. At sixteen, with her porcelain complexion circled by a bevy of glossy black curls, she was the image of her mother.

"You look beautiful, honey. Just like your mom," said Ron.

"Georgie said my mother looked like Elizabeth Taylor when she was a kid. Is that true?"

"No. She was prettier."

"Oh, Dad."

They stopped at Ronnie's bedroom door. Georgie was running a comb through the six-year-old's blond hair.

"Come on, you two. Let's get over to Grandma's. I'm hungry," bellowed Ron.

Georgie smiled. "You guys get started. I'll be right out."

The three of them trooped down the hall with Jenni holding her brother's hand.

Georgie checked herself in the mirror and pinched her cheeks. At thirty-seven it wouldn't hurt to refresh the bloom on them a little. Ron's book on hawthorns had finally been published, and the park was having a launching party in his honor the following day, but this afternoon, the whole family would be assembled at her mother's for a cookout to celebrate the occasion.

When she got outside, the kids were already in the car. She took a deep breath of the aromatic late spring air, and got in.

"Where's your dad?" she asked Jenni.

"He went to check on the possum."

Georgie watched Ron come out of the barn with their three dogs dancing around him. She was suddenly filled with so much love for this man who took such good care of all God's creatures that tears welled in her eyes.

He slid onto the front seat and patted her leg. He had made love to her in the shower an hour earlier, and she was still glowing from it.

"Georgie?" A small voice piped from the back seat.

"What, Ronnie?"

Her son calling her by her first name made her smile. From his infancy he'd heard Jenni calling her that, and now the two of them used her name and "mom" interchangeably, depending on the mood of the moment. Today, Ronnie was evidently in a "Georgie" mood.

"Do I have to play with Sarah?"

"It would be nice if you did," said Georgie.

"Aw... she cries a lot. Can't I just play with the boys?"

"Don't worry, Ronnie," she heard Jenni whisper. "I'll play with her."

By the time they reached Terrace Drive, four cars were already lined up along the alley. As they got out, the fence door swung open and one of Gail's twins yelled out, "They're here!"

Georgie called over to Ron. "Don't forget the books!"

He smiled and popped open the trunk.

Cal already had the grill going and was frying up onions and peppers to go with the sausages. Aunt Jackie and Uncle Pete were laughing with Roger, and LuVerne was busy setting out food, but not too busy to slap Mike's hand when he reached for a brownie.

There were hugs and kisses all around, then Ron took his place at a table and got busy putting personal messages for everyone in his books before signing them. Jenni sat next to him, proudly pointing out her namesake to Isaac.

Georgie took the glass of wine her Aunt Jackie poured for her, then she went over, leaned against a post and absorbed the joyful scene. She couldn't help thinking that no one would suspect that four of the women in this happy family portrait were hiding carefully camouflaged scars.

Georgie had been a certified wound nurse for twelve years now and considered herself an expert on not only the nature of wounds, but also the effect they had on those who got them. Her mother and her two sisters and she had all been gravely wounded, and there was no question that it had made an impression on their character and left its mark; yet, they had all come to terms with life's capriciousness.

Her mother's wound was the deepest and had festered the longest, and Georgie wasn't at all convinced she would ever heal entirely from the years of heartbreak. She watched her mother laugh as she bounced Ali's little Sarah on her lap. Georgie wanted to say: Smile, Mom. Soak up all the happiness you can. Let it wash over you and soothe the scars on your heart.

Georgie's eyes rested on Ali who she considered the least damaged of the four of them, for Ali had the sweet, kind nature that doesn't dwell on tragedy and therefore heals quickly. Gail's wound had also healed quickly, but left her permanently disadvantaged. She would never know the man who was her father, or remember the smell of his leather jacket as he rode her on his bike through the gorge; she would never experience the dozens of hare-brained searches for gold up and down those rugged mountains; she would never know what it was like to grow up running with glee through this little village at the foot of a famous rock. Georgie felt some solace, however, that Gail would at least eventually hear all the town's history and the wonderful stories of the Flacks, for part of her mother would always live in the past.

Then she thought of herself. The years of trying to survive with a gaping wound were gone. She couldn't even remember it clearly anymore, as if it were a rippling reflection in a pool. She looked around the room at all the people she loved. Her eyes fell on her husband's beloved daughter who had needed a mother and chosen her, and then on little Ronnie, the baby she had always yearned for. She looked at the man she loved who had wanted to help her heal, yet patiently waited for her to cure herself. She thanked God for that fateful day when she couldn't stand to see her mother and Ali tormented any longer and finally found the courage to confess her secret. That generous, brave decision had set into motion the series of life-changing incidents that transpired like a falling row of dominos.

Georgie was suddenly awakened from her reverie by Ali waving to her from across the deck. She made her way over.

"What?"

"Oh, it's Debbie. Her sister locked herself out of her house and she's got to go over there with a key. I need to help Cal with the steaks. Can you handle the store until she gets back?"

"Tell her I'll be right down."

She went over and whispered in Ron's ear that she had to cover the store for twenty minutes, and then ran down the stairs. Debbie was grateful and promised to hurry back. Georgie got up on her mother's stool and looked out the door that was propped open to let in the fresh spring air. Her eyes wandered up to the flag on the Chimney and she smiled to herself. No matter how hard she tried to recall the regret she'd always felt when she saw that flag, she could no longer conjure up the feeling.

Her concentration was suddenly broken by the figure of an elderly man coming through the doorway. He used a cane and kept stabbing at the floor with it like he was trying to kill something. It took him a while, but he finally lumbered his weighty body over to her counter. When she smiled at him and said hello, he gave her an almost imperceptible nod before looking her up and down.

He picked up a rubber snake from the barrel, examined it and then tossed it back in. "You know. I've been coming to this here town every spring for over forty years now, and I always stop in this here store. And I'll be hogtied if you ain't sellin' the same ole snakes you've been sellin' the whole time. Who on earth buys these things?"

"People."

He drummed his gnarled fingers on the counter and looked around as if he were exasperated. "Where's the lady who always sits there? I look forward to passin' the time of day with her when I stop by."

"That's my mother. She's upstairs."

He squinted and his eyes glanced around Georgie's face as if he were trying to figure out who she was. They suddenly lit up. He grinned broadly and his leathery face became a wrinkled mass with two pale green eyes barely visible behind bushy white brows.

"I know who you are," he said triumphantly. "In fact, I've known you since you were in diapers. You're your ma's oldest. Aren't you?"

Georgie smiled and nodded.

"I remember when you used to bounce around in a little chair and eat Cheerios your mom put in your tray." He pointed to a place beside her. "Right there."

Georgie smiled contentedly. She and Ali were almost as familiar to people as that monolith. This had to be the millionth time someone had recalled knowing her as a kid.

"You and that sister of yours used to race all over this store, and you almost knocked me over one time. Well, that was a long time ago, and I can see you don't do that kinda thing anymore."

She laughed.

"So you're still here, huh?"

Georgie gazed out the door again at the flag flapping in the breeze on the chimney and then nodded.

"Yep. I'm still here," she said smiling to herself. "And there's no other place on earth I'd rather be."

ACKNOWLEDGMENTS

When I began writing *Dancing on Rocks*, the fourth novel in my Blue Ridge Series of "stand-alone" books, I tried to look up the history of Chimney Rock where the novel takes place. When I discovered there wasn't any history other than that of the park, I started on a one-year journey that took me to the archives of the Rutherford County Courthouse; the Ramsey Library Special Collections at the University of North Carolina, Asheville; the Belk Library at Appalachian State University in Boone; and the Davis and Wilson Special Collections libraries at the University of North Carolina, Chapel Hill.

At the same time, I contacted Jackie Price, whom I met when a group of nurses, who had read *Render Unto the Valley*, invited me to speak at a lunch at The Esmeralda Inn. Jackie had told me that she and her sister, LuVerne, were both Haydocks and born and raised in Chimney Rock. As it turned out, they were descended from James M. Flack, the town's early developer. From this starting point, the town's history began to evolve. While LuVerne Haydock, who kindly volunteered to assist me on the quest for Chimney Rock's history, went around to libraries and searched on the internet for leads, I scanned more than two hundred and fifty early deeds in the county courthouse, put them on my computer and summarized them. However, I didn't know where any of them actually were. Meanwhile, LuVerne, was searching for old maps that might give us a clue.

By this time, I had so much invested in the project, that I figured, if I drew surveys of all of the deeds, I might be able to put the pieces together. I bought a protractor and got an exercise from Google that taught me how to use it. Once I had all the surveys drawn, and LuVerne had located some old maps, I was able to put together a map showing the earliest owners of land in Chimney Rock. By studying these owners, along with the information gathered by LuVerne, we were able to develop a history of the village from its earliest beginnings, which I could thread through my novel.

It was a lot of work for the snippets of history that got woven into the plot, but it was especially important to me that all the history mentioned in *Dancing on Rocks* be accurate, because the Village of Chimney Rock is one of the main characters in the novel. These efforts also gave me a deep appreciation for all the historians who had provided backgrounds for my earlier novels.

The other main characters in the book were inspired by the folks who populate the Village, its stores, and the Chimney Rock State Park. I am especially grateful to naturalist Ronald Lance, who was the inspiration for Ron Elliot in the novel, and whose character and history helped imbue this story with the essence of the generations of dedicated botanists and naturalists whose devotion has made Chimney Rock Park the icon that it is today.

I am grateful to my three editors, Sandy Horton, Leanna Sain and Annie Pott who made my book better. Deborah Long Hampton of the John F. Blair Publishing firm did another wonderful job designing the cover. Again, Carolyn Sakowski of John F. Blair has generously supported my efforts to bring this book to publication. Danny Holland, Alice Garrard, Margie Warwick, April Young, of the Mountains Branch Library, Barbara Meliski, Phyllis Sipple, Clint Calhoun, Chuck Horton and John Wilkerson all deserve my heartfelt thanks for their help and camaraderie during this project.

Ron Morgan, the Lake Lure Fire Chief and Emergency Management Director, Detective Jamie Keever of the Rutherford County Sheriff's Office, and Ronnie Wood of the Chimney Rock Volunteer Fire Department, most generously assisted me with my research into their investigative and search and rescue procedures. Katie Doherty, G.I.S. Coordinator for the Rutherford County Tax Department and Faye Huskey, Director of the Department of Deeds, were most helpful in assisting my search through the county records.

Lastly, I want to thank beloved teacher and writer Fred Chappell, the well-respected reviewer, Rob Neufeld, and writers Tommy Hays, Mark deCastrique and Vicki Lane for their kind and generous commentaries about this story of a small mountain village.

BLUE RIDGE SERIES of Stand-Alone Books

Render Unto the Valley. Karen Godwell isn't as much ashamed of her mountain heritage as of what she once had to do to preserve it. She reinvents herself at college and doesn't look back till her clan's historic farm is threatened. She returns only to come face to face with who she was and what she did. Cousin Bruce sees life through the family's colorful two-hundred-year past; Tom Gibbons, a local conservationist, keeps one eye on the mountains and the other on Karen. Her nine-year-old daughter is on the mission her dying father sent her on.

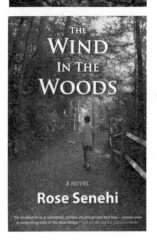

In the Shadows of Chimney Rock. A touching tale of Family and Place. A Southern heiress reaches out to her mountain roots for solace after suffering a life-shattering blow, only to be drawn into a fight to save the beauty of the mountain her father loved. Hayden Taylor starts to heal in the womb of the gorge as she struggles to redeem her father's legacy, never suspecting the man who killed him is stalking her.

The Wind in the Woods. A romantic thriller that reveals a man's devotion to North Carolina's Green River Valley and the camp he built to share its wonders; his daughter's determination to hike the Blue Ridge—unaware that a serial killer is stalking her; and nine-year-old Alvin Magee's heart-warming discovery of freedom and responsibility in a place apart from his adult world.

Other Novels by Rose Senehi

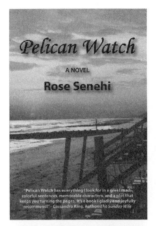

Pelican Watch. Laced with the flavor of South Carolina's low country, this love story is told against a backdrop of murder and suspense. Nicky Sullivan always nurses injured animals, but this time she's going to heal herself. She flees to a SC barrier island and discovers a kindred spirit in Mac Moultrie, a salty retired fisherman. From the moment she meets Trippett Alston, she's smitten, but the dark forces swirling around the island threaten to keep them apart.

Windfall. Meet Lisa Barron, a savvy marketing executive with a kid and a crazy career in the mall business. Everyone knows she's driven, but not the dark secret she's hiding. She's keeping one step ahead of the FBI and a gang of twisted peace activists who screwed up her life in the sixties, while trying not to fall in love with one of the driven men who make these massive projects rise from the ground. What will she do if her past catches up with her? Grab her daughter and run, or face disgrace and a possible murder charge?

Shadows in the Grass. Striving desperately to hold onto the farm for her son, a widow comes into conflict with the handsome composer who builds a mansion on the hill overlooking her nursery, never suspecting that the man who moves into the rundown farm behind her has anything to do with the missing children.

ABOUT THE AUTHOR

Dancing on Rocks is Rose Senehi's seventh novel and the fourth "stand alone" book in her Blue Ridge Series. *Render Unto the Valley,* her third novel in the series, was the winner of the 2012 IPPY Gold Medal for Fiction-Southeast.

"When I started developing a plot for my fourth novel in 2005, I needed to find a small town in the mountains where my heroine's father lived, so I took off from Pawleys Island, where I was actively engaged in real estate, and started my search in North Carolina. When I came upon the village of Chimney Rock I was so struck by its rustic charm that I decided to buy, as a vacation place, one of the cottages nestled in the mountainside behind the little downtown.

"That story turned out to be *In the Shadows of Chimney Rock* and the first novel of what would be my Blue Ridge Series. And when it kept breaking my heart every time I left Chimney Rock to go back to the beach, my vacation place slowly evolved into my permanent residence. However, South Carolina's Low Country will always have a special place in my heart.

"Researching the history of the Hickory Nut Gorge and weaving stories around it, has been a wonderful experience. These four novels are part family saga, part mystery and part love story. Throughout them, I have strived to paint a portrait of the mountain culture I have fallen in love with and portray historical events as accurately as possible. I do hope you enjoy them."

P.S. I especially enjoy leading discussion groups with book clubs.

Visit Rose Senehi
www.rosesenehi.com
www.hickorynut-gorge.com
or email at:
rsenehi@earthlink.net